Se[illegible] Like Love

Chrissie Harrison

Valericain Press

Valericain Press Limited
Richmond, London, UK
www.valericainpress.co.uk

Seams Like Love – 1st edition.

Paperback ISBN : 978-1-0682559-1-5
eBook ISBN : 978-1-0682559-2-2

A catalogue copy of this book is available from the British Library.

A share of royalties from every sale is donated to Her Game Too, which is a voluntary and unfunded campaign that works to tackle sexism in sport and empower women and girls to be involved.
www.hergametoo.co.uk

To Sophie, Lilly & Melie

1st Over

Welcome to the Garden of Eden.'

She poked his pot belly. 'That joke is so threadbare it's untrue.'

'Indulge the old man, eh, daughter of mine?' Ray cocked a bushy eyebrow, not taking his attention off the road.

Eden eye-rolled. '*I* will. Not sure about anyone else. But *please* tell me you don't call it that in public.'

'Couldn't bear the shame, eh? The whole "doting father" thing?'

'I'm twenty-seven. Yes, in your eyes I'm still eight, and I'll always be your little girl, but just don't become one of those embarrassing dads. Okay?'

'You mean I should stop walking along the boundary rope, declaring to all and sundry that I nurture this pitch, night and day, all for my baby?' Ray glanced across and winked.

'I would disown you faster than—'

'Your mother did?' he suggested.

Eden's stomach always knotted when this topic was mentioned. At least they'd settled into gallows humour about it.

Time will do that.

It's been a long five years.

The car slid through the Aurora Stadium's entrance.

'I could handle the piss-taking,' she said. 'Part of the job, right? Sharing a pavilion with twenty other girls. But if a visiting team overheard, assumed you curated the pitch for one of the Scorpions' bowlers—'

'Their *best* one,' he interjected.

She glanced at the strapping on her left pinkie finger. *Moot. Especially now.*

'—and complained to the stewards that home advantage was way more unfair than necessary—'

'Thanks to nepotism,' he added.

She frowned. 'Is it nepotism? Or merely favouritism?'

'It's definitely an ism, daughter of mine.'

'And you can cut the "daughter of mine" mollycoddling too, *father of mine.* It's bad enough that you're giving me a lift.'

'You could have said no,' Ray pointed out, waving to a fellow staff member as they passed.

'I'm saving the planet,' Eden replied.

'You said you were here for extra practice. Saving the planet probably comes second to that.'

'I'm a cricketer, not fucking Bono.'

'You want to walk the rest of the way?'

'For *swearing*?' she asked in disbelief.

'For exercise.'

She pointed through the windscreen. 'It's a hundred yards. Hardly a chore.'

'Still, want me to drop you here in case you're spotted being given a ride by Daddy?'

She whacked him on the thigh.

He tutted. 'Shame you didn't break a finger on *this* hand.'

'Fuck off.'

They pulled into the parking area. Across the gravel, someone was getting out of their car. Eden turned away, her jaw working.

Ray sighed. 'How long are you going to be like this?'

'As long as I want. That okay with you?'

I don't want. I hate this. But who's going to wave a magic wand and make everything right? Shit happens. This is a cruel game—love, as well as cricket.

'It's bad enough that Matt has been dragging his bottom lip around for weeks.'

'Well, now you have two lip-draggers in your garden. Sorry. We'll try not to drool on the grass.'

'You could always get back together,' Ray suggested.

She shot him a smirk. 'Ah. Relationship advice from you. Perfect.'

'You're not too old for a clip round the ear.'

'And you're not too old to find the second Mrs Palmer.'

'Ah. Relationship advice from you. Perfect.' He pulled on the handbrake.

Much as Eden joked, it was oddly heartwarming getting a lift to work with Dad. Yes, she'd rather be travelling with a housemate—even better, a boyfriend—but that was a knee-jerk thought. When you've lost something precious, the holes in your life seem to be everywhere.

Ray pointed at the passenger door. 'You want footman service, or what?'

She poked her tongue out, then checked the area. Matt was nowhere to be seen.

She tugged the handle. 'What do you want for your birthday?'

'My daughter happy.'

'The impossible I can do today. Miracles take a little longer. A bottle of whisky, okay?'

'Says the girl telling me I drink too much.'

'Okay, a bottle of elderflower cordial.' She leant across and pecked his cheek.

'And I wonder where your mother got her attitude from...'

'Not sure it works in reverse, *father of mine*.'

He jabbed a finger. 'Go on, hop it.'

'Gladly.' She jumped out, then pulled her kit bag from the back seat.

'Go well,' he called over his shoulder.

'Not funny.' She slammed the door and set off towards the stadium entrance.

Dad wasn't trying to be funny, only to show, as ever, undying love and support. He knew that she couldn't "go well" for two reasons. Firstly, this was only a training day, and secondly, she wouldn't be fit enough to play the first match of the season—which wasn't until next week—anyway.

She sighed heavily, hefting the deadweight bag higher on her shoulders.

It was pointless to keep scanning the way ahead, hoping not to bump into Matt, yet it was instinctive. Things had been the same for weeks and would continue to be. What was the alternative? She couldn't leave the club—she'd moved here specifically to be near Dad. It was cruel to expect, even suggest, that Matt get a job elsewhere. They'd have to coexist, be civil.

I can do that. He can too—he's a nice guy.

She entered the stadium building. Debs, the club secretary, raised a hand in greeting.

'Morning,' Eden called.

'New kit's here.'

'Great, thanks. I'll collect after training. How's Griff?'

'Don't ask.'

Eden sauntered over, letting the bag slide from her back. 'What's he chewed now? Table leg? Family heirloom? Something in your *special bedside drawer*?' She grinned mischievously.

'Remind me why we pay you, Eden Palmer?'

'Because I'm a very sought-after pace bowler.' She looked away. 'Or was,' she mumbled.

'Still are,' Debs replied. 'But fewer insinuations would be appreciated.'

'Done. So, house training's not going well?'

Debs grimaced. 'I'm too impatient for this. Should have bought an older dog.' She leant in. 'Don't want him, do you?'

'Is it me, or was there a slogan like, "A dog is for life, not just for Christmas"?'

'Can't it be for a different person's life?' Debs asked hopefully.

'Well, not mine. I'd have a pup, definitely a cat, but not with this schedule. Or someone else to pick up the slack.'

Debs nodded knowingly. 'Ah. "Someone else".'

Eden didn't rise to that. Her breakup with Matt was common knowledge. Hard to keep it secret when they both worked at the ground and had gone from loved up to barely speaking. It had been a wet winter in the South East, but frost had broken out in this corner of Maidstone.

The door clanged.

'Ede!'

She'd recognise that voice anywhere—Phoebe, her team bestie.

'Laters,' she said to Debs, hoisting up the bag.

Phoebe hustled over and the duo walked to the changing rooms.

With every step, Eden's pulse quickened. This felt bigger than any game day. There were always nerves, but with 122 career matches under her belt, playing was natural. Having to make nice with her longtime best friend was discombobulating and hateful. Having to be welcoming, chummy and collaborative with someone who'd ruined her winter was a huge ask. And this was only Day 1.

It's going to be a long season.

She painted on a smile and entered the changing room.

Brooke was in the far corner, pulling on her training kit. Even this unremarkable act wrenched at Eden's soul. It had been ten years since they'd worn the same strip, been on the same side of the scoresheet. Now, it was heartwarming to be reunited again. Awkward as hell to be forced into close proximity after everything that had happened. Disheartening that they'd be competing for places in the match day squads.

Whoever said cricket is a cruel game was the wisest person on Earth.

Eden moved through the hugs, high-fives and laughter, crossing the room to her nemesis. Brooke's body language wasn't downbeat. Wise—it would be unseemly, unprofessional, for them to live under a thundercloud for the next six months.

You can do it. Be the bigger person. Or at least not a grouchy cow.

She pulled Brooke into an embrace that was like hugging a beautiful thistle.

'Welcome to the Scorpions, Tweedie.'

'Thanks, Ede. It's good to be here. Odd, but good.'

Winter had been kind to her new teammate. Lots of Australian sun. Lots of cricket. Much as Eden had avoided the stats pages, she knew Brooke had performed brilliantly, underscoring why the

Scorpions had given her a contract. Eden had barely been able to train.

Brooke probably knew that too. Yet had she been in touch, offered support? No. She hadn't even pinged an excited message to say she'd signed with the team weeks ago.

In truth, things had been cool between them for over a year. For two seasons in a row, their friendship had taken a back seat to their rivalry.

Would Brooke's presence on the squad make things worse or better?

2nd Over

Matt had seen Ray's car arrive, but wasn't going to say anything. Father and daughter travelling to the stadium together was hardly news. Better to ignore the topic, hope the pain and disappointment would ease as the weeks rolled on, as the season got into full swing, as the workload increased.

As maybe he found someone else to snuggle up with at night.

In the groundsman's hut, he pulled on his work gear and brewed a strong cuppa.

Ray came in. 'Morning.'

'Morning.'

This was how it had been for the last few months, a workmanlike atmosphere. The reason was blindingly obvious, but the cure was less clear—if it even existed. The easy option, the coward's way out, was to leave the club, find a position elsewhere. Yet that would imply he'd done wrong.

Besides, opportunity might be knocking here, and he didn't want one relationship breakdown to affect his career too. Sure,

Eden might have let the split cause ripples in her work life, but that was her problem. Matt's biggest issue was having to work for her father, the Head Groundsman. Well, not work for. The work was easy, rewarding. The personal side, less so.

Almost every day, Matt thought he saw a look that suggested Ray was awaiting an apology, an admission of culpability for Eden's mental and physical challenges during the closed season.

You can wait forever, Ray Palmer. It's your daughter who needs to sort her head out.

Sometimes, Matt considered apologising merely to clear the air—an insincere confession—but any inadequacy on his part wasn't what triggered Eden's downward spiral. It was something out of his control. He'd done everything in his power to be there for Eden. It simply hadn't been enough.

However much he'd loved her, some things couldn't be fixed, undone, erased. Perhaps only time would help. And that was what he hung onto—time might make it easier for Matt and Eden to coexist at the club. After all, things could be worse. They might actively hate each other. But he could never hate her, either as a person or for what had happened. He merely wanted her to heal, regain her mojo, and soar to the heights she was capable of reaching.

He wanted her to play well, even joyfully, in the Garden of Eden.

Ray's nickname for the Aurora Stadium pitch was lame but endearing. The man's love for his daughter warmed Matt's heart. She had a person who cared for her, who offered a shoulder to cry on, a hug of encouragement, an understanding.

Perhaps, one day, Matt would ask Ray whether he'd been on a hiding to nothing. Was Eden fundamentally a tricky person to handle, to date, to be with? He doubted it. Their sixteen months together had been wonderful.

'Oy oy,' Ben announced cheerfully, breaking Matt's introspection.

With the playing season imminent, the ground staff's numbers were swelled, as usual, by temporary staff. Ben brought a youthful enthusiasm to the group. Matt was still getting to know the guy—he'd only been on the roster for a week—but sensed a welcome injection of levity into the recent stale atmosphere.

'Alright, Ben,' Ray said.

'"Eggs", please, boss. If that's alright.'

'Whatever works, Ben... I mean Eggs.' He pointed out the door. 'Get the covers off, there's a lad. Girls'll be wanting to use the practice pitch.'

'Sure. Matty?'

Matt raised his coffee mug. 'Be out in a mo.'

The lad adjusted his baseball cap and trotted out the door.

'"Eggs",' Ray scoffed good-naturedly.

Matt flashed an amused look. 'Nicknames are part and parcel here, right?'

'I suppose.'

Footsteps heralded the arrival of Alan, the senior of the team. This was his last season, having been at the ground for four decades. He once said that the first time he'd mown this grass, it was black and white, not green.

Alan's upcoming departure was one of the reasons Matt was determined to stay on. He'd done well, made a good impression on Ray—until recently—and was confident of taking Alan's Assistant Groundsman role. At age 28, that would be a coup.

After a brief three-way chat about the day's tasks, Matt headed onto the pitch. The players were emerging from the changing area, with support staff carrying equipment. Involuntarily, he slowed as Eden jogged across to the bowling strip, chatting with fellow seam bowlers Gemma and Rose. She didn't spot him, although there was no point in hiding. They'd been orbiting each other for weeks, even exchanging a few shallow pleasantries, but the atmosphere remained thick.

If clearing the air with Ray was necessary, and a good idea, that went double—no, a hundredfold—with Eden. Yet, what could he say? Besides, she had another fish to fry.

Brooke Harris was the other person in the pan.

He knew the story. He'd lived it for weeks. And, while he didn't agree with Eden's assertion that everything was Brooke's fault, he still felt sorry for his ex-girlfriend, who now had to share the stadium with *two* people she had a beef with. Whilst recovering from the mental travails, the jab-jab-hook that professional sport can inflict.

Could she get back to being as fit, talented, confident, and utterly wonderful as when the season started a year ago last April?

'Oi, Matty,' Eggs called. 'Who's that?'

Matt jogged over, tutting. Eggs didn't seem to be aware that it was rude to point.

'Brooke Harris. Right arm medium.'

'Right arm what?'

Matt eye-rolled. In the past week, it had become blindingly obvious that Eggs hadn't joined the team because he liked cricket... or knew much about it. *Other* aspects were higher on his priority list.

'Medium pace bowler. New recruit from the Central Stars.'

'Right, yeah.' Eggs eyeballed each girl in turn. 'What about her? Chatting with the bloke in the hat.'

Matt watched the familiar figure, glanced at Eggs, then looked at Brooke. If the lad was sizing up someone to hit on, he clearly didn't have a 'type'. Brooke's slimmer, more petite figure contrasted with the dark-haired Eden's frame. A taller, curvier frame that Matt knew every inch of.

He sighed. 'That player is Eden Palmer. She's a bowler too. The *bloke* is the bowling coach, Jonno.'

'Okay, sure.' The lad nodded, trying to appear sage. 'Lot of the coaches are blokes, aren't they?'

'Yes. And the ground staff. And fitness team. And backroom staff. But that'll change, over time.'

'Yeah. More women around makes sense. I'm all for it, me. Ray should get a couple in with us. That... Eden, for starters.' He winked.

Matt laid a heavy palm on Eggs' shoulder. 'I think she's happy where she is. You know, being an elite athlete and everything. Anyway, word of warning. Give her space, okay? She's had a rough time recently.'

'How come?'

'Long story.'

Eggs shrugged. 'Long season, innit though?'

Matt sighed. 'Okay. At the end of every season there's a... Cup Final. Last time, the Scorpions lost. They were beaten by the Central Stars and, this is the short version, Eden thinks it's all her fault. Which may or may not be true, depending on your perspective.'

The lad's brow knitted tightly. Matt heard cogs whirring. 'Central Stars? You said that's where the blonde one came from.'

'Exactly. So Eden's not thrilled with having to share a changing room with Brooke.'

Eggs grinned. 'I'd defo share a changing room with her. Shower too.'

'Good luck with that.'

Eggs nudged him. 'Isn't about luck, mate.'

Matt grabbed his arm. 'Go easy, okay? Here's a free tip. Dating a cricketer isn't an easy ride. It can be a pressure-cooker lifestyle.'

Eggs grimaced. 'Whoa. War story, is it?'

Matt closed his eyes. Best to be open about things. The lad was bound to find out eventually. 'Eden and I… broke up… last year. She hit rock bottom. Broke her finger too, so she's not playing yet.'

Eggs pointed. 'Looks like it.'

Matt watched Eden start her run-up, accelerate, and bowl. The ball rapped into the middle stump on the set of rubber wickets.

'She can bowl, but not bat. And if you can't bat, you can't play. Okay? Enough questions. Oh, and by the way, Ray is Eden's dad, so that's another reason to go easy around her.'

'Oh. Got it. But he's a sweet guy, right? Not a "Stay away from my daughter" type?'

The words speared into Matt's chest. Ray *was* a sweet guy, a great boss and mentor. He'd have been justified in kicking Matt all the way to Lord's and back for what had happened.

He hadn't, thanks to their relationship, and—Matt liked to think—that Ray empathised with his situation. Christmas hadn't been all tinsel and baubles in the Palmer household either. Perhaps Dad had had enough of Eden's extended stroppy spell? Emotions would surely have been running high.

'Ray's great,' he replied noncommittally. 'But Eden's still hurting.' He met Eggs' eye. 'So don't walk on her wicket.'

3rd Over

Eden let herself into the suburban semi, kicked off her trainers and dumped the kit bag in a corner of the living room. In the kitchen, she pulled a homemade smoothie from the fridge and leant on the counter.

During practice, she'd focussed on her game, because it's always healthier to move towards something good and satisfying, something she was in control of—her fitness and technique. Whatever happened on a personal level, the most important thing for her and the team was to play well.

There had been a few dark nights of the soul during the winter, times when she was close to jacking it all in and focussing on her accountancy career, but that had passed. One bad game would not kill her career. It was allowed to knock her down, but she would get up. Today, she was kneeling. Soon, she'd be standing. Then running.

She sank onto the sofa and switched on the TV for company. The house had felt very empty these past weeks since Millie had gone to live with her girlfriend. In other circumstances, Eden would have invited Matt to move in—their relationship seemed ready for cohabitation—but the breakup had kiboshed that.

What now? She could cover the mortgage, no problem, but it was unfamiliar not to have a housemate. Invariably, it had been a teammate. Eden adored the camaraderie and banter.

She picked at a cushion feather.

I'm not much company, anyway. Hard to bite my tongue about what happened. Can't bitch to any of the girls. No need—they were at the game.

And whenever she reflected on that One Day Cup Final defeat, the darkness descended, the feeling of not being good enough. The knowledge that pressure situations made her crack. The sense that Brooke was, and always would be, better. With ball *and* bat. With men too. And online.

She swallowed down the bitter taste. Jealousy was wrong and unhelpful, not least because, deep down, she wanted Brooke to succeed. To get the England call-up she deserved. To find love, as Eden had found it with Matt. Found it and lost it.

Now, more than ever, it was important for Brooke to do well—especially for the Scorpions. She'd been brought in to bolster the squad, to help the team go one better than last season. Eden wanted every one of her teammates to shine. Thinking otherwise was unconscionable.

There was just one problem. If Brooke hit top form, Eden would never get picked. She'd spend a year on the bench. And that felt like salt being rubbed into the wound.

Was it okay to hope for Brooke to do well... but not *too* well?

Or am I being a horrible person?

This debate will run and run...

After breakfast the following morning, Eden decided to take her mind off the issue by studying for her next accountancy module.

With a cup of coffee, she curled up on the sofa with some reading material.

An hour later, she gave up. Her heart wasn't in it. Self-motivation wasn't normally an issue, but The Brooke Problem wouldn't go away. She was proud of her study progress over the winter. Ordinarily, she'd have been abroad, playing, but the broken finger had prevented the opportunity of foreign climes and good paydays. She could have wallowed in self-pity for four months, but used the time productively. It was a great distraction from autumn's horrors and the fallout.

She switched on the TV while she pondered how to use the day. The local news was headlined by the report of a massive sinkhole opening up on a residential street across town. Hardly the pick-me-up Eden needed.

Something pricked at her memory, so she checked the calendar and Instagram, and quickly a plan was set. She gathered a few things together and headed out.

The first task was Dad's birthday present. She considered buying him a set of weights, yet another crime novel, or a new socket set for the garage—he was restoring an old Beetle. If the split with Matt had felt like the end of the world, she only had to remember how Dad crashed following his own breakup. The man had put on five stone—most of which remained. Eden nagged him to eat better and visit the pub a little less, but clearly the Palmers had a predisposition for letting heartache roll on too long.

Instead, she chose a pricey bottle of whisky, a tongue-in-cheek Best Dad Ever mug, and a new tablet to replace his ageing model with the cracked screen.

Afterwards, she indulged in some retail therapy—two tops and a pair of jeans, had a delicious lunch at a favourite eatery, then headed out of Maidstone to a nearby town.

The cricket club was a familiar haunt—Eden's playing career had its origins here with the Under-11s. Happy times. Now, she returned as the wise head, a coach for the girls' Under-15s. Not enough places in the UK boasted a thriving girls' and women's cricket community, but this corner of the country was doing well. There were rising stars, including Eden's mentee, Lily.

Eden had spent the last three years earning her coaching badges. It was a subconscious way of showing Mum that she could succeed in the sport—beyond winning matches and then retiring in her mid-30s. It would never be as well-received as a stellar accounting career, but Eden hadn't quit cricket five years ago and wasn't about to bail now. The coaching was also a way of paying things forward, encouraging the new generation—and was incredibly rewarding. Just a shame that Mum lived halfway round the world and couldn't see how her daughter had tried to do the right thing.

Today, Eden was merely there to watch the season's first practice session. She pulled on a sweatshirt against the chill, grey April day, and went to the nets. A dozen players were batting and bowling. Nearby stood a few parents and two other coaches. Eden did the rounds, catching up with them and giving an update on her strapped pinkie finger.

Nobody here knew chapter and verse on the events since September—she didn't need any more pity—but everyone sensed that Eden's winter was one to forget. Today, certainly, as she watched Lily bowling ball after ball, it felt like life was on the up. At the Scorpions, she had the chance to start anew, prove that injuries are temporary inconveniences which can happen to any player at any time.

Things *had* to get better.

A few minutes later, Lily finished her practice spell and jogged over, panting. Eden took her in a hug.

'Your slow ball is really coming along, Lily.'

'I learned from the best.' The girl slugged from her water bottle.

'Well, I don't know who that is, but I'm pretty sure it's not your coach.' She winked.

'You *are* the best, Eden. And, like, anyway, even if you weren't, you did tell me that improving my death bowling is the biggest thing I could do.'

Eden patted Lily's shoulder. 'The biggest thing you could do is give me your Billie Eilish ticket.'

Lily's eyes flared. 'Now you're the *worst* ever. That was my birthday present from Mum and Dad! Anyway, there's like six of us going.'

Eden nodded, beaming. 'Ah, I'm too square to be seen with a bunch of hip teens.'

'You're never square, coach. You're great.' She looked away, waving to someone. 'Okay, gotta go. Have to pick up baby brother from football.'

'Have fun.'

Lily grinned. 'At the concert? I *will*.'

'Laters.'

'Laters.'

The girl jogged towards her waiting mum. Halfway there, she slowed to speak to a boy who'd intercepted her path. The boy fumbled paper and pen from a pocket, accidentally dropped the pen on the grass, retrieved it, and proffered both to Lily.

Eden's heart melted.

Oh my God.

The youngsters conversed—the lad visibly nervous about his heroine worship—then they parted with a smile and a wave, and Lily cast a wide-eyed glance over her shoulder.

Eden gave a double thumbs-up.

Promise me one thing, Lily. When you find an amazing boy, don't screw it up. Oh, and the same goes for best friends too. Just try to be the best you can be.

She walked back to the car, wondering if any Scorpions had a spare concert ticket.

4th Over

Matt pottered around the kitchen, tidying. It wasn't very bachelor to be house proud, but old habits had died when Eden came along.

Buying the house should have made him grow up anyway. To some extent, he had—helped by a lecture or two from Mum. Of course, he'd do anything for her, especially then, three years ago, when she was still in the pit of grief. Dad had always kept his affairs in order, but Matt's inheritance was merely a wafer-thin silver lining on a dark cloud.

Mum was unashamedly proud that her son used the money wisely, and was pursuing the career Dad would have approved of. "My son, the groundsman" didn't have the cachet of "My son, the lawyer" or "My son, the surgeon", but Mum never cared what her friends thought.

The mortgage was easily manageable, and the savings account was healthy, but Matt didn't live extravagantly or frivolously. He'd rather have Dad back and be in a worse living situation—renting or sharing. Sometimes the price you pay for money is loss.

He set the dishwasher running, grabbed his stuff and headed to the stadium.

Milky sunshine bathed the practice ground. Today was an intra-team friendly, a full squad warmup ahead of the season's first game at the weekend. Twenty-five players flitted around the small pavilion building, beside which stood a disused scoreboard. Among them were Eden and Brooke.

Ray and Eggs were rolling the wicket. Alan and the five other staff were attending to the main stadium pitch, which lay beyond the access tunnel under the East stand. Matt toured the boundary, coffee flask in hand, checking that the rope had been laid in a smooth arc.

Soon, he passed players in groups and pairs, working on their warmup routines, chatting and joking. All acknowledged him—they always did. The venue was one big happy family. Everyone played a part in operating the vast Scorpions machine.

He'd never been overawed, even from his first day. The players were ordinary people. Eden too. Whilst it wasn't a 9-to-5 job, he'd slipped easily into being part of her lifestyle. True, her weeks away in the Southern Hemisphere were pretty lonely, but she—like he—was following her dream.

If he did harbour any imposter syndrome, it was that someone so beautiful, talented and smart would date him. Yet none of those things had caused the breakup, and you can't legislate for external influences.

He watched Eden's demeanour around the group. Monday's tension had eased. Surely she'd become resigned to sharing the space with Brooke. Hopefully, their friendship would slowly mend.

Who would have The Conversation first—he and Ray, he and Eden, or Eden and Brooke? And would any or all of the outcomes be rainbows and unicorns? Things couldn't carry on like this.

Close by, a few players were kicking a football around. Matt slowed to a halt, watching the joy and pratfalls. As the ball was punted around the loose circle of seven players, it sailed over Brooke's head, bounced high, then rolled towards Matt. On a whim, he tapped it up with his toe, caught it on his knee, then let it down, hopping it from foot to foot. His pulse thudded, brow knit in concentration.

A few yards ahead, Brooke came to a halt. He lifted his eyes to her, finding a surprised expression, then flicked the ball up in an arc. She caught it on her left boot, played keepy-uppy for a few seconds, then lobbed it back. He took it on his chest, let it slide down, then did bounce-left-bounce-right while she gazed on, pulling at her blonde ponytail.

That playful gesture broke his focus, and the ball escaped his control, so he kicked it back, and she caught it.

'Looks like you're wasted mowing lawns.'

He didn't point out that groundskeeping was much more than mowing—because an impish grin betrayed that she'd said it in jest.

'Maybe *you're* wasted playing cricket.'

She feigned lobbing the ball at his head.

'What I meant was, good skills,' he added.

'Harry!' a player called.

Brooke swivelled, tossed the ball up, then punted it back to Rojo.

Matt drained the takeaway cup he was still holding. His attention was caught by the shallow bump in the small of Brooke's back, something concealed under her shirt.

He dismissed the curiosity because she was looking him up and down, worrying her lip.

'So... hey,' she said.

'Hey. How's things?'

'Settling in. You?'

He shrugged. 'Same old.'

'Really?' She moved closer.

'Seasons come, seasons go.'

'Hmm.' She glanced around. 'I'm... sorry that you and Eden broke up.'

His chest tightened. 'And I'm sorry you and Eden kind of broke up too.'

She offered a sober smile. 'We both want to win. Nothing wrong in that.'

'Still, brave of you to come here, having cost them the Cup.'

She shook her head. 'It's not personal. And it's only one season, one comp. If I'm charging hard this year, they'll thank me for it.'

That was true, but he only saw the emotional fallout. If Eden had space, she was more likely to get over it, to let the tension dissipate. Ideally, Brooke wouldn't be here. Whilst she hadn't *deliberately* caused the mess, through Eden's eyes it had been a personal vendetta, especially as it had caused her to come off the rails.

Yet Matt didn't *directly* have a beef with her. They'd spoken at the odd game last year and got on well. However, things had changed.

He fiddled with the cup's ridged contours. 'Why did you come here? Of all the teams?'

Brooke's pretty jaw hardened. 'I was asked, okay? It's a chance to play for a coach like Susie. Sometimes you need to have thick skin and do what you think is right.'

'I... suppose.'

'I'm not here to stir, Matt. Quite the opposite.' She stepped into a confidential space.

'You're here to play. I get it.'

'And *you're* still here.'

'What was the alternative?'

She shrugged. 'Not suggesting there is one. I mean... is it hard with Eden around? Will you still sit on the sidelines and cheer her on?'

'Of course. I don't suddenly *hate* her. What happened, happened. I can't undo it. Nobody can. Wishing her to play badly, to spoil her career, is cruel. I don't want her to be unhappy. I've seen that up close, and it was *horrible*. Hard to deal with.'

Brooke's face fell, her chin tilting down. 'Yeah,' she murmured. 'Sorry. I think I was part of that. In some way.'

'No comment.'

She looked up, eyes flaring. 'Ah. I'm the big bad wolf who split you up? Does this mean you and I are *not* okay?'

'We're not anything at the moment, are we?'

'Still, it would be nice to know if I need to tiptoe around you.' She raised a hand. 'I mean, I *will,* if needed. I'm not here to make friends. I didn't join the Scorpions for the barbies and karaoke. I came to win trophies.'

He scoffed. 'You were doing well enough already.'

She eased back. 'Ah. So we *aren't* okay.'

'Look, this isn't about you and me. I just mow the grass around here... apparently.'

She winced. 'Sorry.'

'No harm done. If anyone's going to be tiptoeing, it's me. I'm already doing it with Eden, so what's one more? Plenty of other people here who'll speak to me.'

'I'll speak to you, Matt. I'll speak to Eden too. That's for certain. Pretty embarrassing if we're in the middle together and I run her out because I refuse to even say Yes, No, or Wait.'

He chuckled. 'Yeah. That would make things even worse. Affect the team too.' He surveyed the players, who were gathering up the equipment. 'But *is* there an atmos in the dressing room? The girl who stole the Scorpions' win?'

Brooke laughed, musical, girlish. 'It took my whole *team* to do that. And we draw a line, Matt. Players switch clubs. I didn't come here to be a thorn in their side, certainly not Eden's.' She inspected his eyes. 'And I hope not in yours, either. Need the ground staff on my side, right?'

He smiled. 'Of course. But I don't think Ray will rename this "The Garden of Brooke"!'

She glanced at where Eden's father was chatting with the match referee. 'No. Doesn't have the same ring to it. Do I have to win Dad over too? Am I the enemy with him?'

Matt grimaced. 'No more than I am.'

She frowned, perfect eyebrows knitting. 'He blames you?'

'Ray just wants her happy in love and at work, and she's been neither.'

'We all want that.'

He gestured around. 'Hopefully, you'll be happy at work here.'

'I will. They're an amazing bunch. But it'd be even better if I found love too.' The tip of her tongue ran across her upper lip.

His neck hairs prickled. 'I suppose.'

'New town. Lot of new people to meet. And this is a nice place to start.'

'Day for it,' he said, easing the subject away from an avenue he felt she was heading for.

She smiled uneasily. 'Yeah. Team friendly. Scorpion versus Scorpion. Very on-brand, huh?'

'Still... Go well. Both of you.'

'Thanks. We'll try.'

'Ten minutes,' Susie called from the pavilion steps.

Brooke grimaced. 'Better not piss off the coach. See you around.' She trotted off to join her cohort.

Matt waved a hand in farewell, then moved away quickly, not wanting to get distracted by Brooke's retreating backside.

5th Over

Eden pulled on her playing kit and headed onto the pitch. Her stomach churned. Matt and Brooke had been talking. Plain as day. Public enemies one and two.

What the hell do they think they're—

'Long On, please, Edie,' called skipper Danica.

Focus. What am I going to do—ban them from talking? It's a free country.

She took up the fielding position and put her game face on.

The squad had been divided in two, and, by a stroke of luck, Brooke was on the opposing side. Eden would be asked to bowl—she was signed off by the physio.

One positive aspect of her injury was that it had been her left hand, meaning her bowling was largely unaffected. She still couldn't bat, but that didn't matter today because the rules were bent for the friendly matches. Freya, for instance, was batting at number 3 and 7. Last year, Bryony had scored 100, then been subbed off to give someone else a go. That would never happen in a competitive match.

The burning question in Eden's mind was whether she'd get a chance to bowl at Brooke. How sweet would it be to take her wicket? Yes, the match meant nothing, and it would barely dent the pain, but it would be a *start*. It might accelerate the healing, make Eden feel like she *was* good enough, *could* compete with her friend when the chips were down.

It was petty to think like that, but she justified it easily. It's not wrong—hell, it's her *job*—to get batters out.

Don't make it personal. This is work.

She stroked her left pinkie. Amazing how one little broken bone could damage a friendship, kill a relationship, and cause a person to reevaluate their career.

Finger's healing. It's almost mended. I just need to do the same up here.

Late afternoon, she was back in the pavilion, packing up. It hadn't been a cathartic game—only one over bowled against Brooke, no wickets... but also no bouncers delivered. A horrible, worse Eden would have tried to cut the girl in two with every delivery.

She had taken three wickets—a very decent return. One caught, one LBW, and one absolute pearler which nicked Abi's off stump. Eden felt more human, more at peace, more at home, than she had since October. And the season hadn't even begun.

Nevertheless, the innings break had spiked her hormones, nibbled at her gut. Matt and a new lad—apparently bearing the ridiculous name Eggs—had rolled and re-marked the wicket. Whatever Matt had done over the winter, he hadn't let himself go. Of course, she could have been imagining it, the merest hint of guilt making her wonder why she'd dumped such a buff guy.

She'd shaken it off—what's done is done. Yet why was she annoyed that he and Brooke were chatting? Perhaps seeing them together exceeded the critical mass of resentment that she was able to cope with.

After farewells with the team, Eden headed to the car park.

'Edie!'

She slowed.

Phoebe trotted up. 'On fire today.'

'Thanks, babe.'

'Want to come for a drink? We're overdue.'

She snorted. 'Yeah, about six months.'

Phoebe rubbed Eden's shoulder. 'You had an excuse.'

'I would have been no fun at all.'

'It was horrible what happened, and I'd never want that for you, but I was there, waiting.'

'I know,' she replied sadly, feeling as though she'd cried on the wrong shoulder.

Phoebe had known her for much longer than Matt had. She also possessed more insight and shared experience. Had she expected too much from him? Miracles, for instance? Still, he'd fallen short, gone AWOL at precisely the wrong time, not read the room. He didn't seem to be reading the room today either.

'So, drink?'

Eden checked her watch. It was a covering gesture. She wouldn't be any fun tonight. 'Mind if we don't? Soon, though, yeah?'

Phoebe pulled her into a hug. 'Whenever you're ready, hon.'

Eden arrived home to find a cardboard box in the hallway.

Dad. The only other person with a key.

She hefted the box onto the dining table, went to the kitchen, made a decaf coffee, and sloughed onto the sofa.

What's in the box, father dearest?

During the closed season, when the groundskeeping workload was lighter, he'd finally begun the emotional and physical post-divorce clear out. He was moving home—the marital household held too many memories and was too big for one guy. They'd been hoping for two kids and bought a nice, detached place, but with only one youngster—long since departed, and the matriarch gone, Ray was rattling around. Would he find someone else?

In February, having patched things up after the festive falling out, she and Dad spent a day in the loft, deciding what to keep, what to chuck, and what to hand down. Seemingly, her own attic had its first guest.

If it's that old picture of Brooke and I graduating from Loughborough in accidentally matching skirts, your timing will be impeccable, Dad.

And if the photo *was* in the box? What to do? Keep it? Burn it? Put it on the mantelpiece to either taunt or inspire her?

Seized by curiosity, she hustled to the table, ripped off the poorly applied packing tape, and opened the flaps. She sank into the chair and took the items out, one by one. The photo wasn't there, and she was a little disappointed. Most of the belongings were old photos, holiday trinkets, and schoolbooks.

She thumbed through her final yearbook, recalling faces, high jinks, and the time she took 6 for 22 against the men's team. The report card generated a blizzard of emotion, so she took the paperwork to the sofa, curled up and read it a second time.

"Eden will be a high-flyer."

"Eden's study ethic will stand her in good stead."

"A naturally gifted bowler, and a great team player. However, she needs to do better at controlling her emotions on the pitch. Eden will do well if she can take her career one game at a time."

"Eden's inherent fitness and discipline are strong assets, but she must remember that the mental side of cricket can be the real test. If England come calling, which is not unrealistic given her potential, she will have to work hard to perform under pressure."

She scoffed, letting the paper flutter to the carpet. Since when did lecturers and coaches have such foresight? Had they time-travelled? Perhaps this report, rather than the photo, should be framed on the wall or stuck to the fridge door.

Would it have helped? Impossible to know.

Seeing her frailties announced in black and white was awful. She felt seen, caught naked in a hotel corridor... which had once happened for real, as Josh White would confirm.

She lay on the sofa. This was a fork in the road.

Either the words from the past were an explanation, an excuse to be who she was, a Get Out Of Jail Free card, two fingers to anyone who reckoned she was overreacting about what had happened. Or... she could use it as electric shock treatment, immersion therapy, whatever equivalence fitted. An eighteen-year-old Eden Palmer had descended into tears in the pavilion after being hit for six 6s in one over, seeing it as a sure-fire message that she couldn't bowl for toffee.

Wrong. She'd had a bad day.

Last year, September 18th—she'd never forget the date—Brooke had hit her for three 4s and a 6. Off the final over. To win the One Day Cup.

Her *best friend* had calmly stood at the wicket, a number 11 batting to save the game for the Central Stars, and ripped out Eden's heart and soul. Eden had crumbled like rice paper and cost her team the trophy.

And Brooke hadn't even said sorry.

Not even when things got much, much worse.

In Eden's hour of need, where was her friend? In Australia, lighting up the BBL and shagging some surfer dude called Apollo. Meanwhile, Eden was alone in a house in Maidstone, on the verge of giving up cricket, the thing she loved most in the world.

Only one good thing had come out of that episode.

She *hadn't* given up.

6th Over

There was something special about the first game of the season. The beginning of a new adventure. For Ray and the gang, it was also a test of their winter maintenance work. For Matt, it always felt like the moment a plane's wheels lifted from the runway—that sense of "Here we go...".

Matt was at the stadium at seven o'clock, deliberately arriving earlier than usual, a subtle way of making a good impression on the boss.

He and Ray began by taking the covers off. This was Matt's favourite part of a match day—the first couple of hours. A sense of the venue waking from sleep. Staff arriving, then players. The concession stands being unlocked. A smell of bacon butties drifting around. Dew on the grass, evaporating in the sun.

The Garden of Eden coming to life.

Soon, *she* would appear, making his heart fill. Not today, though. Probably never again. Now, his heart would be heavy. The old season would still cast a shadow.

'You alright?' Ray asked.

Matt jolted. 'Sorry.'

'Focus, lad.'

"Lad". When did I stop being "Matt" or "son"? Easy. December 12th.

He hauled harder on the tarpaulin rope.

'I don't want to lose you, you know that?' Ray said.

Matt didn't know. He'd expected the opposite outcome. A sacking, even. At times, he feared being a distraction to Eden, affecting her game. He'd hate that, and Ray would be disappointed in them both.

'No, I—'

'Don't let it ruin you, lad. Don't let a breakup define your life. I've moved on.' Ray's bushy eyebrows lifted.

Matt took that with a pinch of salt. Ray had crashed hard when his wife left. He'd let himself go. Drank. Put on weight. Dabbled in gambling. Yet he never missed a day of work. He could put his heartache in a box and deal with it when time allowed.

Undeniably, Matt had done a better job of handling a crisis than Eden had—but her burden had been heavier to carry. He'd only lost a girlfriend. She'd suffered worse.

'I'm... working on it, thanks, Ray.'

The man slowed to a stop. 'It'll get easier. For you, faster than it will for her, I reckon. I know my Eden. She's... an emotional girl. Tough as nails. Stubborn too. But what happened was...' His head fell. 'That could break anyone.'

Matt ventured to pat Ray's shoulder. 'I know,' he said softly. 'I was there too.'

Ray looked up from under a hooded brow, his jaw clenched, and Matt thought a haranguing was coming. Instead, the man sighed heavily, then heaved the rope, and Matt set off alongside.

They finished all the covers, then retired to the hut for a much-needed coffee. As Ray brewed, he appeared to be pondering something. Matt left him alone and scrolled his phone.

Ray handed across the careworn Scorpions mug. They sat on two of the sturdier chairs. Matt felt a creeping dread.

There had been a moment—during The Hundred, when Eden had taken the final wicket with one ball to spare, winning the game—that he felt so in awe of her, adoring of her, he wanted to pull Ray aside and quietly ask for his blessing. "Just, you know, if I ever summoned up the courage to pop the question".

He hadn't. Mercifully, in hindsight. To sow the seed of hope in Ray, and then break up with his daughter? Things were hard enough anyway.

Now, a desire for action grabbed him again.

'Look, boss... Ray. We need to talk about the elephant in the room.'

The man sipped his brew. 'Hmm.'

Matt swallowed hard. 'Or not, if this isn't the right—'

Ray's gaze was direct. 'I won't *sack* you, lad... Matt. You're a good worker. Vital part of the team. Okay?'

All he could hear was that one emphasised word. Was there a subtext?

'Um... yeah. Thanks. Means a lot. All the same... I'll move on, if you think it's best. I get the feeling the club's not big enough for me and Eden. And there's no debate whose side you'd be on.' He flashed a sad smile.

Ray's expression was warmer. 'You're blowing this all up. Relationships end.'

'All the same, I...' He dried up, unable to vocalise things, as afraid of being laughed at as he was of accurately hitting the mark, discovering what he'd feared.

Surely Ray would hold a grudge? Undoubtedly Eden blamed Matt for the split, for being unable to lift her from the gloom and causing her to break her finger. Why not Dad, too?

Yet there hadn't been raised fists, even raised voices, between the men over the last six months. They had coexisted, orbited each other, but the easy camaraderie had vanished. If Matt had ever thought Ray looked upon him as a son, that was gone. The man was more focused on getting his daughter back to good mental health.

'Let me ask you something. Why didn't you leave last year?' Ray arrowed his mug. 'Surely you saw this coming?'

'I don't know what I thought, boss.'

'Then what's changed? I didn't boot you out, so why now? Other than you're too good to lose, especially because all that happened was you broke up with your girlfriend.'

'A very specific one, though.'

Ray laughed, welcome levity. 'Believe me, Matt, I've come close to putting my fist through at least one of her boyfriends, and not nearly that close with you.'

Matt winced. 'But it crossed your mind.'

The man sighed. 'Yeah, alright, it did. But I'm not as light on my feet as I was before Liz left, and I reckoned you'd clock me back, so...'

'I never would.'

Ray inspected his feet. 'I know, lad. I just... After what happened, there was two kinds of people. Those who made Eden sad, and those who made her... less sad. I thought, hoped, you'd be the second.'

He scoffed sadly. 'Me too.'

'And she was sad as hell when you split up, so I reckoned you were one of the bad ones. And I don't like people who make my daughter unhappy.'

'What father does?'

'Hmm. Anyway, what I was meaning is you didn't throw in the towel on day one. You gave it a chance. Sometimes, I wish she would learn that kind of resilience.'

'She has a lot more resilience than me, Ray.' Sadness broke over his soul. 'I'm not the one who had a death threat.'

Ray stared into his mug. 'No. No. But we didn't lose her. Only the spark of her, for a while. So I suppose we're blessed.'

'We are. And I think that spark will come back.'

'It's almost there. As soon as she's playing again, all that crap will be forgotten.'

'Hmm.' Matt wasn't convinced. Besides, forgetting wasn't the same as forgiving, and Eden wasn't the only one who had to work on that.

7th Over

In Eden's mind, there were three kinds of games.

When you're playing, there's nothing better. When you're not picked, it's an exercise in containing disappointment.

This was the third: you can't play due to injury, and all you want to do is wish the days away until you're fit... and then hope you get selected.

Unsurprisingly, Brooke was named in the squad. You don't bring in a premier bowler and bench her for the first game. No, you hand her Eden's place... or that's how Eden saw it, despite knowing it was a truckload of sour grapes.

In the changing room, as the players milled around, pulling on their training kit, Brooke seemed distracted. Why wasn't she on cloud nine? Surely it couldn't be due to the thick air between them—Brooke was always much better at separating her work and personal lives.

Still, the unfamiliar distance meant Eden barely knew what her bestie had been doing lately... and vice versa.

Brooke ambled over. 'What happened?' She gestured at Eden's finger.

Now therein lies a tale. And it all started with you.

'Accident at home,' she replied obliquely.

'Bummer.'

'No shit.'

'When are you back?'

'A week, maybe two,' she said, cold and matter-of-fact.

Brooke smiled faintly. 'Your action looks really strong.'

'Thanks. Yours too.'

Brooke's attention wandered as gym coach Jason walked past. When she refocused, Eden raised an eyebrow.

'What?' Brooke hissed.

'I didn't say anything.'

'Yeah. You definitely didn't say how buff some of the staff were.'

Eden passed up the solid gold opportunity to reiterate that they'd barely passed a word since September. Nor did she remark that sharking at any bloke with a pulse was very on-brand for Brooke. Perhaps the conversations with Matt were nothing more than Tweedie's usual flirty, short-term attitude to relationships. If so, Eden had nothing to worry about.

'Jason's seeing someone. And *probably* not a good idea to date a guy at the club. We've had ... issues.'

Brooke looked Eden up and down. 'Exhibit A.'

Eden's hackles rose. 'I mean *coaching* staff. Matt doesn't count.'

'Right. Whatever.'

The awkward silence was broken by Brooke's mobile ringing. She tugged it from her pocket, wrinkled her nose at the caller's name, picked up, grimaced, then hustled away.

Eden was alone in the room.

I tried. And what did I get? A dig.

She took a deep breath.

Then try harder.

The door clanged. Susie, the coach, entered. 'Eden. Glad I caught you. Sorry it's late notice, but I need someone to do the cap presentation for Brooke. I know you two go back a long way. I think it would be fitting if you officially welcomed her as a Scorpion.'

Yeah, that's very on point. A sting in the tail.

'Of course, Suse,' she replied.

During the warmup stretches and resistance work, Brooke seemed distracted, pausing occasionally, staring into space. Eden wondered what was up. Brooke already had the challenge of integrating into a new club, establishing trusted bonds and learning the pitch.

As the cap presentation approached, Eden's pulse quickened. Yes, she was absolutely the right person for the job, but God, the irony! Welcoming an estranged colleague who'd likely be first pick over Eden *every* game? Just when she'd thought the winter's emotional and mental challenges were easing...

Grow the fuck up, Edie. Game face. Professional front. Or you'll get benched for a bad attitude, not a snapped phalanx.

Gripping the cap tightly, she joined the pre-match huddle. After words from Susie, then captain Danica, Eden stepped into the middle of the circle. The hastily penned bullet-point list shook in her hands.

She blew out a breath. Public speaking was never her forte, and this was worse.

'Harry. It's been too long since we played together, and it's a... pleasure... honour... to be the one to officially welcome you to the Scorpions and present your first cap.' She flashed a smile. 'The girl I met at Loughborough has become a brilliant cricketer, and I know you'll be a huge asset to this squad. We'll try not to steal your crumpets.'

The girls chuckled. Brooke was famous for enjoying a couple of toasted treats during the innings break.

'You always give a hundred and ten per cent in the field, and it looks like your footy skills are even better than they were at Uni, when you used to run rings round the boys.'

Brooke beamed.

'I'm sure you'll be very happy down here, and we'll have the best bowling unit in the country. But word to the wise, Rojo gets first pick of which end to bowl from.'

Rose laughed, nudging Brooke.

'So go well today, and every game, every day. You've been a good friend to me, and I can't believe we're on the same team.'

Then, quickly, before emotion could take hold, she stepped to Brooke, handed her the cap, and took the girl in an embrace that was as tense as it was warm. They posed for the official photo, exchanged an uneasy smile, then the group broke up.

Thank God that's over.

Half an hour later, the match started. Eden sat on the bench, bib on her back, and watched. As the minutes passed, the prickles evaporated, and she eased into the role of drinks carrier, helmet runner, and errand girl.

When Jade beckoned from Square Leg, Eden grabbed a water bottle and followed the boundary rope round to her position. Then, feeling unusually emboldened, she completed a circuit of the pitch, taking her past the groundsmen's area.

Matt and Dad were sitting on the hover cover, teas in hand. She considered blowing Dad a kiss, but Matt might think it was meant for him. Instead, she pulled at the hem of her bib, as if modelling it, an ironic show of being sidelined. Dad shook his head in despair. Matt grinned.

Seems like I can still make him smile.

Nearby, at Deep Backward Point, Brooke glanced across. Eden raised the water bottle. Brooke trotted over.

'Thanks, Ede,' Brooke said flatly.

Eden didn't rise to it. 'S'okay. How's the pitch?'

'Bit slow. Nice, though.'

'Fancy a couple?'

Brooke smiled obliquely. 'Always.'

Eden bit her lip. 'You...okay, Tweedie?'

She sighed heavily. 'Nothing that can be sorted.' She pointed. 'Anyway, I have a game to play.'

The "I" jabbed through Eden's heart. 'Yeah. Watch the bounce off that sprinkler cover. Nearly got one in the face last year.'

Brooke nodded curtly. 'Thanks.'

Eden scuttled away. Best not to upset the *new star player*.

Four hours later, she sat in the dressing room, swept up in the tide of the Scorpions' victory song, and the girls sang at the tops of their voices, banging bats against the hard floor. A life-affirming cacophony, a much-needed sense of belonging.

Brooke had had a good day—two wickets and two catches. She'd be a shoo-in next time. She should be high as a kite, yet something lurked behind her eyes. Was it merely her side of their cold front, or another issue? In days gone by, Eden would have been desperate to ask, to help. Did she need to, given that Brooke had another good friend here in Fiona? They'd played together a couple of seasons ago.

After the coach's debrief, the players headed pitchside for signatures and selfies with the fans. The first game of the season was always a big event. Better when the team had won.

As Eden joined the line of players at the advertising hoardings, her spirits leapt. Support, it seemed, was mutual. She shuffled along, signing bats and scoresheets, posing for selfies, exchanging words with familiar faces like Max, Lisa, and a few players' parents. A couple of yards behind, separated by Jade, came Brooke. Naturally, the squad newbie would be a key target for fans.

Soon, Eden reached Lily, and they exchanged a hug.

'Thanks for coming. I'm surprised. You look a little peaky,' she joked.

'I'm fine.' Lily's teen brows furrowed, then arched. 'Oh, ha ha.'

'It's not very public-spirited to go to a big indoor venue if you're sick. Are you sure you wouldn't rather—'

'You are the worst coach *ever*,' Lily snickered. 'You are *not* having my Billie Eilish ticket.'

'Don't care. Don't want to go anyway. I've heard she's rubbish on this tour.'

Lily poked out her tongue, then proffered the miniature bat towards Brooke, who signed with typical flourish.

'Sorry about Eden,' Brooke said. 'She's always been a nightmare. Be grateful you don't have to *play* with her.' She winked at Lily, who giggled.

'Thanks, Harry,' Eden grouched. As it stood, the prospect of actually *playing* together looked slim.

Brooke shrugged, then was marshalled along to a pair of excited youngsters who were leaning over the hoarding.

Lily shot Eden a question, so Eden mouthed, 'Don't ask.'

Lily zipped her lips, then focussed her attention on the next player.

Twenty minutes later, Eden was unlocking her car when she noticed Brooke slouched against the railing, engrossed in her phone. As she paused, Brooke looked up and a dismissive sneer passed across her face.

Eden chewed her lip, then tossed her bag in the back seat, locked the car, and rode into battle.

After a pause that *could* have been considered rude, Brooke tore her attention from her phone. 'What?'

'What did I do?' Eden asked.

Brooke's eye-roll said, "Where shall I start?"

'Forget it.' Eden turned away.

'Just... what was that, "You have been a good friend" supposed to mean?'

Her hackles rose. 'It means exactly that. Is there a *problem*?'

'Yeah. The "have been" part. It sounds *very* past tense.'

Eden laughed. 'Bollocks.'

'Then why not say I *am* a good friend? Huh? Why the... qualification?' Brooke's lip curled.

For fuck's sake.

'Okay, bad choice of words. Heat of the moment, nerves of being roped in at the last minute. Satisfied?'

The air crackled.

Brooke eyed her for an eternity, jaw working. Then the tension left her shoulders. 'Okay. Sorry.'

Eden let out an invisible sigh of relief. 'No. My bad. Anyway, good work today.'

Brooke's smile was faint. 'Cheers.' She pointed at her car. 'I should... Got a fire to put out.'

'Another one? That doesn't involve me dissing you in front of the girls?'

'No.' This smirk was forlorn. 'And, sorry. I'm feeling pissy about my rental. So...' she shrugged, 'Y'know.'

'No, actually. But what do I care, right? We only *have been* friends.'

Brooke's eyes flared. 'Are you *trying* to make this harder, Ede?'

'No way. The opposite. Long season ahead... newbie.' She forced a smile.

Brooke chuckled sadly. 'Looks like the universe, as well as you, doesn't want me here.'

That hurt—largely because it was true. 'Landlord problem?'

Brooke shook her head. 'Sinkhole problem.'

'Ah. Shit. Planet swallowed your stuff?'

'Not yet. But the street's unsafe. All residents out.' She laughed, hollow. 'Of all the houses to pick. And it's *so* close to this great coffee shop—'

'"Beans 'N Brews"?' Eden guessed.

'You're a fan?'

'Best latte in town. Best rocky road too. Not that I have it, of course, because I'm an athlete and my body is a temple.' She raised her left hand. 'Re-pointing almost complete.'

Brooke tittered. 'Yeah. Bummer.'

'Want a hotel recommendation?'

'Could be weeks. Rather have a landlord recommendation. Don't think any of the girls have a spot. Either that or I made a bad first impression.'

'You, Tweedie?' She gave a wry smile.

Brooke waved it away. 'Never mind. I'll ask Sandy. She's always organising places for overseas players. Needs to be soon, though. And if you know a Man and Van...'

'Not sure, but I'll ask around.'

'Thanks.'

She shrugged. 'What are ex-friends for?'

Brooke's lips pursed. 'Yeah.' A big sigh. 'Laters.'

'Laters.'

The girls parted, walking to their cars. Brooke's was brand new—must have been a well-paid playing contract. Probably better than Eden's wage. But then, cream always rises to the top.

Eden fished out her car keys. They dropped to the gravel.

Twenty yards away, Brooke slammed her boot shut.

Eden picked up her keys and toyed with them.

And she knew, at that exact second, she was standing at another fork.

8th Over

Matt halted at the car park entrance, trying to decipher the girls' body language. The atmosphere ebbed and flowed. When smiles appeared, hope filled his heart. If Eden could regain her natural good humour, it would be much easier to be around her—maybe even make up with her.

What he couldn't fathom was Brooke's introspection, especially after a good game. Was the spat with Eden weighing on her too? She seemed to have largely brushed it off—but then, she hadn't lost a match, been trolled and threatened, kicked out her boyfriend and then committed a ridiculous self-injury.

When the two parted, he headed for his car, which, unfortunately, was close to Brooke's smart new hatchback. She was leaning against the driver's door, feverishly typing on her phone.

The crunch of his feet on the gravel made her look up. 'Oh, hey.'

'Hey,' he replied. Stupid to ask if everything was alright, because clearly it wasn't.

'Sorry. Gimme a sec.'

'No, it's fine. I wasn't after a kickabout.'

She met his eye, a reflective smile breaking. 'Not sure I have the energy anyway.'

'Yeah. Get home, warm bath. That's my plan, anyway.'

'A Jacuzzi would *really* hit the spot.'

'Always.' He recalled a lazy weekend away with Eden. A lot of things had taken place in that spa bath... 'Feel settled in now? First game.'

Brooke chuckled sadly. 'Kind of.' She glanced at Eden's car. His ex was in the driver's seat, talking on the phone.

'She *will* get over this, won't she?' But were his current actions a help or a hindrance? He was consorting with "the enemy".

Sorry, Edie, I'm not tiptoeing around Brooke too. The spat between you two is not my fault.

'Bloody well hope so. I do *know* what happened. It was on the grapevine, even in Oz. If I ever find the guy...' Her nostrils flared.

He nodded hard. 'Me too.'

'Tag team, yeah? Punch his fucking lights out. How can anyone *do* that to a person?' She grimaced, as if swallowing down a bad taste.

'I don't envy either of you. It's an... iceberg, right, this sport?'

'Yeah. Good analogy. Sorry you were on the sharp end of it.' She shook herself. 'Anyway. Not the time. Stuff to sort out.'

'Sorry, yeah. You get home.'

She snorted. 'Home. Right.'

He frowned. 'Problem?'

'If I was a troglodyte, no. But for a cricketer, caves aren't really the thing.'

'Er...'

She fluttered a hand. 'Sorry. Private joke. Don't suppose you know anyone with a room to rent? At, like, a day's notice.'

'Why?' Then it hit him. 'Ah. I see the problem. No, I don't know anyone. Sorry.'

Except for me, of course. But there's no way I'm suggesting it. Friendly chat is fine, but if Eden discovered Brooke was staying in my spare room, she'd hit my nackers for 6.

'It's fine.'

'Bad landlord?'

'Sinkhole.'

He'd seen the news. 'Ah. Shit. Bad luck. The town welcoming you with open arms is one thing, but open craters is a bit much.'

She laughed. 'Perhaps it's payback.'

'You're saying Edie is a witch who can conjure earth movements, all because you smacked her for 17 off one over?'

'I mean, clearly she's pissed off, and we have a ton of stuff to work through, but she's not a witch. Or a bitch. We are—' Brooke briefly closed her eyes, '—*were* best mates, and I would be naïve as hell to think I could brush off a death threat like it was no big deal. We're in the same game, Matt. And I've had lows, as she'll tell you. I'm trying hard to give her space. Because she'll bounce back. She had a dip when her mum buggered off. Understandable. We had a lot of heart-to-hearts after that.' She beamed. 'And vodka.'

'Maybe you should suggest a drink. Revisit old times.'

'Not tonight. She's not in a good mood.'

'Isn't that the ideal time?'

'I suppose. But I have the small matter of finding somewhere to live. And a Man and Van. Don't know anyone, I suppose?'

Matt scratched his stubbled chin. 'Not sure, but I think Eggs said his mate has a van.'

'Eggs?'

'Yeah, the new kid. You've probably seen him. He's the one with drool on his chin at any given moment.'

She shuddered. 'Great. Can't *wait* to meet.'

'Aw, he's harmless. Anyway, notwithstanding the drool, want me to ask Eggs?'

Brooke chuckled. 'There is no way he's called Eggs.'

'And you're not called Tweedie. Right?'

'Fair point. But if he has a van, or access to a van, then yes, I'd appreciate a hand. Cross your palm with silver, or beer, or autographed glossies, whatever's your poison.'

'Beer for me. Probably glossies for Eggs... if you know what I mean.'

She winced. 'Thanks for the warning. But don't tell him I'm looking for a room, okay?'

'Your secret's safe with me. Although, if we're doing the removal, he'll find out anyway.'

'Apart from the fact that I won't need the room anymore, because I'll be moving into it.' Her brow lifted.

'True. But on the flip side, he'll know your address.'

'He'll also have met me, and realised I'm this kick-ass pro athlete who tears up friendships and romances for fun, and he'll run for the hills.'

He looked her up and down—the toned figure, neat waist, sparkling blue eyes, perfect earlobes. 'You're easy to hate. I can see that.'

She scratched her upper arm. He'd spotted the T1D sensor when she was in short sleeves earlier in the day. Things made sense—the belly pack was her insulin monitor. He couldn't imagine how hard it was to have a career like this. Brooke Harris was clearly built of strong stuff, yet with a dyed-in vulnerability that demanded discipline and empathy.

'And high maintenance,' she said.

'It'll be a brave person who offers *you* a room.'

A smirk played on her lips. 'I'm notorious.'

He leant in. 'So it's not *really* the sinkhole. You've just been evicted after one week.'

Brooke put a finger to her mouth. 'Shhh. The enemy is listening.'

He looked round. 'She's doing more than that.'

Oh shit. Am I in for the high jump?

9th Over

Eden got out of the car.

A year ago, she'd have been justified in being suspicious, jealous even, of another woman talking to Matt. Now, it was ridiculous. He was a free agent.

Besides, Tweedie can't really be after him. She has that Aussie guy, right?

So Eden wasn't pissed off. Far from it. Curious, maybe.

They're discussing me, pound to a penny. Little Miss Scratchy.

And they did have grounds for that opinion. But she had an excuse for being scratchy, wary, angry at the world. Last autumn, someone on Instagram had vilified her Finals Day bowling shitshow and vowed that if ever he met Eden, ideally in a secluded place, he'd ram a carving knife up her.

Not all ardent fans were in full possession of their marbles, perspective, or humanity.

But since then, nobody in Maidstone, or Kent, or even London, had so much as looked at her funny. Perhaps Scotty441 had been taken into custody for beating his wife, been stung by a Portuguese man o' war, or lost his wedding tackle in an unfortunate threshing incident.

We can but hope.

Nevertheless, Eden's recovery, her return to a civil life, to her normal mental and emotional even keel, had been glacial. With Brooke here, things could either go faster uphill or back downhill—and Eden was the one with work to do. In normal circumstances, she would be impossibly excited to play alongside Brooke. She would have been there, front and centre, on the girl's first training day, ready to welcome her with open arms. Only Eden's inability to see perspective, to move on, had prevented that.

Now, having spent weeks drifting, lost, desperate for someone to do or say *exactly the right thing* to make life better, she had a window into Brooke's current situation, which was comparatively easy to solve.

Matt had tried for weeks to drag Eden out of the mire, and failed. He'd chronically misjudged things, done more harm than good. And that had ended their relationship.

Often, she'd return to the same conclusion—one bad match had killed one great love. Yet, arguably, she was more invested in repairing something that had endured for years longer than she and Matt had . Few people knew Brooke better than Eden. They'd lived together, trained together, played together. Eden had been Brooke's safety net, a vital first line of support in the event of a diabetes crisis. Here, in a new city, in a new team, what friends did Brooke have? Few, if any. And who had the girl's back? Probably nobody.

Eden wouldn't let that happen. Some things transcend sport.

The plan was either very stupid or very brilliant, and she wasn't sure which. It had a good chance of backfiring. Matters *could* get worse. But, as her wise teammate Ellie Waites once said, failure is part of the game. *Any* ball might be a bad one, coming wrongly out of the hand, landing in the batter's slot and being unceremoniously despatched back over your head for 6.

Does it stop you from going back to your mark and doing it again? No.

It was time to bowl a good one. An absolute peach. Something to fox Brooke, but have her smiling, even patting her bat, in appreciation.

She walked up to Matt and Brooke, her stomach cartwheeling. They stopped speaking, as if rumbled, and the cartwheels turned into a gnawing, clenching anxiety.

Brooke must have seen the distress on her face. 'You okay, Ede?'

She moistened her dry throat. 'Yeah. Hey, Matt.'

'Hey.'

Well, this isn't at all awkward.

'Look... Tweedie... I thought...' She blew out a breath. 'I have a room. Crazy, worst idea ever, but...' She shrugged. 'Can't have a teammate commuting to the stadium from the *gutter*, can we?'

Brooke chewed her lip. 'Not sure. April showers, free clothes wash, right? And if it's a decent gutter spot, outside a swanky wine bar, maybe a Greggs across the way...'

Matt sputtered a laugh, then covered his mouth. That set Eden off, and quickly Brooke was smiling.

Eden put on a straight face—because this idea was as serious as it was wild. 'Have a think, okay? It'll only be for a few days, until you find a better offer, of which I'm sure there will be hundreds.'

'I have *one day* to get out. Not much thinking time. And I need a van.'

Matt coughed. 'With respect, Brooke, that's just *stuff*. *Stuff* is insured. And *stuff* isn't who Susie recruited.'

Eden eyed him.

Yeah, and stuff isn't what'll be staring at me in stony silence from across the living room tomorrow night. But as the old saying goes, "A friend in need is a pain in the arse".

Brooke observed her for an eternity. 'You're serious?'

'I mean, the small print *does* involve me being waited on hand and foot, and you have to use the public loos down the road. Plus, I want the rent in uncut diamonds, and no shagging Zeus, or whatever his name is, on the sofa. Especially while I'm watching Only Connect.'

Brooke smiled wickedly. 'Clean my pubes out of the shower trap?'

'Of course. Same as always.'

Matt's face was a picture. The convulsions in Eden's belly were now purely amusement.

Brooke fell sober. 'His name's Apollo. And we broke up. I can't do long distance. I mean, he was well-hung, but not thirteen thousand miles' worth.'

Matt blushed deeply.

Nothing to be jealous of, Matt. You were plenty fine.

'Sorry to hear that.' Which she was. Because it meant Brooke was unattached... and could make eyes at people here. Well, one specific person.

I suppose if she's living with me, I'll be able to keep watch on her. So perhaps there is an upside to this gamble.

Brooke shrugged. 'Easy come, easy go. Rather have a house than a boyfriend.'

'I can only do one out of two.'

Brooke winced expectantly. 'Move in tomorrow?'

'P.M? I have sponsor stuff A.M.'

'P.M. Send me the address?'

'Yeah. *Think* I still have your number.'

Eden found herself pulled into a hug. Was it merely gratitude, or Brooke trying to one-up Eden's move towards breaking the ice?

'You're a lifesaver,' Brooke said.

'I know.'

But please don't fall into a diabetic coma on my watch.

'And I suppose you own my arse now,' she whispered.

Eden's spine prickled. Brooke had a point... particularly if she considered her ex-friend—who possibly wasn't ex any longer—a scheming bitch.

'What is it with you and mentioning body parts in front of the Ground Staff?'

'I can hear every word,' Matt called.

Eden sniggered. 'He's a sensitive soul,' she murmured to Brooke.

'Still listening,' he said.

The girls broke their hug.

'What do you want as a moving-in present?' Brooke asked.

'Henry Cavill, greased up and ready to go.'

Brooke turned to Matt. 'Space for him in the van?'

'I think I retract my removal offer.'

'So you'd prefer me to fall into a big hole?'

He licked his lips. 'Why not? That's what Edie's been wishing for all winter.'

Eden nudged him. 'I told you that in confidence.'

Brooke merely turned for her car. 'Should have stayed with the Stars.'

'Hear, hear,' Matt and Eden called in unison.

Brooke waved. 'Laters.'

Eden met Matt's eye. 'What the fuck have I done?'

'Honestly? Either you'll wind up married by Christmas, or one of you will be on Crimewatch next week.'

'Who's your money on?'

'Oh, you, Edie. Always. *I'm* lucky not to be six feet under.'

She grimaced, feeling the nip of a dagger in her back. 'I was that bad, eh?'

'Not you. It. *That. Then.*' He explored her face. She'd forgotten how piercing his gaze was.

'Hmm.'

Brooke drove past. Eden offered a small wave.

What *had* she just done?

10th Over

Matt worried about asking Ray for the afternoon off, but he was on a mission of mercy, and nobody with a soul would deny such a request. Plus, the urgent removal was good for his daughter's longstanding friendship as well as her mental health.

Assuming Eden knew what the hell she was doing. Was it a case of "Keep your friends close and your enemies closer"? As Brooke qualified in both camps at present, Eden was onto a winner.

Eggs arrived at Matt's house in the van.

The vehicle had seen better days. In the Noughties. Matt didn't dare check the tyre tread depth. Or the MOT status. He hoped the seatbelts worked, or that Eggs drove like his grandma. Or both.

The van belonged to Eggs' mate Colin, who used to do "official" man and van stuff but now lived on a canal boat on the Medway. He'd been unable to part with the van, like some kind of heirloom, so rented it out for £50 a day.

They got to Brooke's rented place at two o'clock. Intact. Which was more than could be said for the tarmac fifty yards from the driveway.

Matt hopped out and negotiated passage with the police on duty, then Eggs parked the van as close to the house as permitted. Eggs strolled up to the front door like he owned the place. Matt gave chase. It was like taking a puppy for a walk. A horny puppy.

Brooke answered. 'Hi, Matt. Thanks a million for doing this. I owe you.'

'And me too,' Eggs said, peering as if she were a museum exhibit.

'Sure. And remind me, you're...?'

'Eggs.'

'I knew it was something.'

'He's definitely something,' Matt murmured.

Eggs swivelled. 'Eh?'

'Nothing.' Matt indicated the doorway. 'Shall we?'

'We *definitely* shall.'

'Sorry,' Matt mouthed at Brooke as they passed.

'It's fine,' she mouthed back.

Brooke had helpfully marshalled everything into the living room. It was a part-furnished place, but the removal load was a few suitcases and boxes, cricket and fitness gear, a running machine, a bike, and a bookshelf that clearly had provenance.

'Cuppa?' Eggs asked.

'Removal,' she stated.

'Right. Anything valuable?'

'Every single thing.' She caught Matt's eye.

Immediately, he was endeared to her.

'Okay,' Eggs said. 'We ain't insured.'

'I trust you implicitly... Eggs.' She put her hands on her hips. 'I mean, can we get that cleared up? Why Eggs?'

'Give you three guesses.' The lad's tongue circled his lips, hopefully in thought.

'Is it because you like eggs?'

'Nope. Two more guesses.'

She looked him up and down. 'You *hate* eggs, and it's ironic?'

'Uh-huh. Last guess.'

She threw her arms up. 'Your name is Eggsworth or something?'

Matt gave a faint tut. 'Close, but no edge to the keeper.'

'Parents called me Benedict. Arseholes,' Eggs scoffed.

'Ah. I see. Very good. *Ben.*'

He leant in. 'Thanks... Harry.'

Matt winced. Even he wasn't on familiar enough terms with Brooke to use her squad nickname. But then, he and Eggs weren't peas in a pod. Or even peas in the same allotment.

She tapped the running machine. 'This first, I think?'

After an hour of packing—interspersed with too much banter and a modest amount of surveying Brooke's physique—Eggs drove, creditably gingerly, to Eden's place. Brooke followed in her car.

'What d'you reckon?' Eggs asked Matt.

'About what? The Loch Ness Monster? AI? Love Island? All terrible ideas.'

'No, her.'

'Ah. Brooke. The client.'

Eggs scoffed. 'Client, my arse. Or *her* arse, in fact.' He waggled his eyebrows.

'She would chew you up and spit you out.'

'That'd be a start.'

'Leave her alone, mate. At least for a few weeks, okay? This is sensitive stuff here.'

'What, her moving in? Mission of mercy, you told Ray it was.'

'It is. It's also complicated. A *lot* about Eden is complicated.'

'Ah. Eden. Funny name. It's like that thing in the Bible.'

'Almost exactly,' Matt concurred, deadpan.

'Beautiful but dangerous, right?'

'That may be the most insightful thing you've said in ten days, mate.'

'Cheers. So is Brooke dangerous too, you reckon? Or just beautiful?'

Now there's a question. Doubtful that she's dangerous, except as a bowler... and a batter, when Eden's running in. Beautiful? Hmm.

'She's a pro cricketer,' Matt replied. 'And sometimes, that's a tough enough ask.'

Dating one could be even tougher, as he'd found out. Particularly when you didn't have the strength of character to handle the bad times. If you weren't a good enough boyfriend, friend, sounding board, counsel. If you fundamentally weren't up to the task. If, despite caring to your very bones about someone, you still fell short.

They pulled up outside Eden's house. Matt's chest felt heavy. He hadn't been here since the breakup. Going inside would be like crossing the police tape into a crime scene.

Eden had messaged to say she'd been held up in London due to an overrun on her engagement, but had left a key in a safe place, so he went to the side alley and located the security box. The code was familiar. He wondered if Eden had changed the PIN on her bank card. Of course he'd never find out, but at least she still felt comfortable letting him go inside her house. He wasn't the enemy. Perhaps, even in the darkest days, he'd never been.

He lifted out the key.

Oh hell.

This used to be his. It had the same heart-shaped keyring.

He leant against the wall.

On their 1-year relationship anniversary, they'd gone for a fancy dinner in town. Eden had insisted he meet her early for a drink, but gave an unfamiliar address. He arrived to find her standing outside a locksmith. She led him inside and they sat, holding hands, while the guy cut a copy of her front door key and she threaded it onto the keyring she'd bought earlier. Outside, she took him in her arms and said she couldn't think of a better symbol of her love.

His fingers closed around the key. A symbol of what might have been. In the months since that day, the world had moved on. Even at the club, Freya had got married, Ellie Waites was engaged, and Jade and Phoebe were moving in together.

He shook off the melancholy. Better to remember the good times, endless days of them. Still, he speculated whether the key would be bequeathed to the new housemate or be put back in its little box, away from Eden's thoughts. Out in the cold, a relic.

Brooke arrived, and they unloaded the van into the house. Matt didn't let Eggs go upstairs. When they were done, Brooke gave Eggs the £50, added a tenner, and suggested the lad buy himself a beer. With a belch of diesel smoke, Eggs left.

'Cuppa?' Matt asked.

Brooke smiled sadly. 'I suppose you know where everything is.'

'You will too, soon.'

'True.'

He busied himself in the kitchen, myriad emotions roiling in his head. Occasionally, he glanced into the living room, where Brooke was nosing around.

Forgoing the space beside her on the sofa, he handed over a mug, then took an armchair.

She sipped. 'Good tea.'

'Thanks. I remember Edie saying you never go more than a couple of hours without a brew.'

She laughed. 'Yeah. So now you'll understand why I can't last more than half a one-dayer in the field without needing a toilet break sub at least once.'

He winced good-naturedly. 'Thanks for that.'

'Sorry. Could have been worse. I could have told Eggs. He'd be picturing the details in a heartbeat.'

'I think he feels like a cock in a chicken coop. Idiot.'

'Then I can't wait for him to hit on one of the girls who doesn't... like cockerels, shall we say.'

He chuckled. 'Oh no, I'd *love* to see that!'

She set her mug on the coffee table, tucking a lock of blonde hair behind her double-pierced ear. 'Did you... give him the full SP on Ede?'

'I gave him the headlines. She's still recovering. In a lot of ways.'

'Actually, she's better than I expected.'

'Really?' he queried. 'She's worse than I hoped.'

Brooke met his eye. 'You forget, I've known her for a lot longer. She likes to... stew.'

'Seems so.' He exhaled hard. 'Then you should have expected a frosty reception, right?'

'Why do you think I didn't ring her up as soon as I got the contract, suggesting we room together?'

He gestured around. 'So why accept her offer now?'

'You mean, out of the frying pan and into the fire? Only one of us can afford to be stubborn, and she's nabbed that. I do want to fix this, Matt. Whether Ede wants to...' She shrugged.

'You'd rather live in silence than in a hole in the ground.'

'I hope not. But we have to share a ground, a changing room, a net, so why not a house? Maybe the old magic will come back.'

'I hope so.'

She angled her head. 'Thanks. That's... sweet.'

'I just want her to be happy again. Which will make Ray happy. And a happy boss is a better boss.' He didn't say, "And a boss who might promote me to Assistant", as that would sound self-serving.

Ultimately, he wanted things to be like they were before, even the early days when he and Eden were merely two people exchanging longing glances across the boundary rope, and she was a cricketer full of confidence, a girl who talked in glowing, happy terms about her best friend.

Brooke had fallen serious. 'It's only a game. But everyone wants to be on the winning side every time. Ede and I got... unlucky, that's all.'

'Yeah,' he sighed.

There was no mileage in pointing out the obvious—without the Cup Final battering, Eden wouldn't have been harangued online. Wouldn't have got the death threat. Wouldn't have plummeted into despair and a crisis of confidence. Wouldn't have been impossible to be around, berated him for a failure of empathy, told him to take a hike.

Brooke was the butterfly who had flapped her tail-end bat. And Matt's heart had been broken. Logically, he'd want her to suffer a *little* for that.

However, it was hard to wish ill on such a grounded, potentially likeable, and undeniably pretty woman.

11th Over

Eden let herself into the house. The move-in had clearly happened, as Brooke's car was on the road outside. Her chest tightened. She'd almost hoped that Brooke would decline the polite offer—holding out the olive branch would have been sufficient to temper Eden's guilt.

She didn't expect Matt to still be there. His presence felt like a trespass. Now there were *two* people in the living room who she never expected there again.

Eden found a smile. 'Sorry. What a bad host. Photographer was a diva.' She massaged her mouth. 'I may have actually broken some facial muscles.'

Posing for photographs was a necessary evil. Selfies with fans were fine, but formal stuff was yuck. She and Brooke were chalk and cheese. Brooke liked posting beach shots on Insta. Occasionally, over the long, dark winter nights, Eden had wondered whether, in a parallel universe, they would ever be friends.

Recently they had put their foot in that alternate reality.

'No problem. Matt and Eggs were great.' Brooke grimaced. 'Meaning all my stuff is intact and nobody tried to cop a feel.'

Eden glowered at Matt.

Two palms snapped up defensively. 'She means Eggs.'

Her hackles calmed.

Matt would never... would he? That would be the final straw. That would be radio silence, for both of them, forever.

Matt stood. 'Tea? Or is buggering off a better idea? Me, I mean.'

The tension left her. Whatever else had happened since the split, he hadn't become less giving, less adorable. The easy-going cheekiness was present and correct. All things that had attracted her to him.

She'd never asked a guy out for a drink, but Matt was buff, six feet tall with thick brown hair, broad shoulder, and those *eyes*. She hadn't even considered the potential issues of dating someone at the Aurora. She was too intent on kissing him. Which she had, on the first date.

She felt bad that the men had to coexist in a tricky atmosphere, but you can't run your love life by being scared of fallout. Relationships, like innings, end. But you go into bat hoping for a good knock, and those sixteen months with Matt were wonderful. *That* match—and Brooke—had caused the fallout, *not* the fact that she was dating Matt or that he worked for Dad.

'I think juice, actually, thanks. And maybe a bath. London is so...'

'Grubby?' Brooke suggested.

'Yeah. Like I have this... film over me.'

'That's just the stain of being in the public eye, Ede. Same old.'

Eden laughed—how the girl knew her.

Matt jammed his hands into his pockets. 'I'll shoot. Glad it all worked out. The move, I mean. Can't have our new Scorpion swallowed by an open sewer.'

Brooke stood. 'Thanks, Matt. I owe you one.'

Eden wondered if *she* would owe him one? One bottle of champagne, or one kick in the nuts?

'No problem,' he said, ambling to the door.

'Yeah, thanks.' Eden followed him into the hallway, glancing over her shoulder. 'But maybe keep the van on standby for a hasty bug-out.'

'Will do.' He fumbled in his pocket. 'Oh, this is yours.' He tendered the key from the security box. 'Or maybe Brooke's now.'

Her shoulders fell. The enamelled red heart keyring shone, taking her back to that night. The locksmiths, the bar, the restaurant. Returning here, watching as he slid the key into the front door lock for the first time. And then, to bed, where idle conversation and laughter ran into the small hours, pushing the chances of leisurely sex out the window.

And the following day, when there wasn't time for fun, because it was an early start for a game. A game in which her good spirits resulted in a four wicket haul.

She sighed. 'Thanks. Might take the heart off, though.'

'Depends whether you still love her, I suppose.' He smiled weakly.

'Can I get back to you on that?'

'Sure.' He opened the door. 'Good luck, Edie.'

'Thanks, Matt. I might need it.'

In the sitting room, Brooke was still on the sofa, tapping on her phone. The mugs had gone. Through the kitchen door, Eden spied them on the drainer.

Currying favour already...

'You don't have to sleep on the sofa. Or were you waiting for the tour?'

Brooke shrugged softly. 'Don't want to presume, that's all. This is a *big* deal.'

'What, me renting you a room, or doing it now?'

'We both know the answer to that.'

Eden flopped onto the chair, rubbing her neck.

Brooke shook her head. 'This was a bad decision.'

Eden frowned. 'Mine or yours?'

'You didn't have to offer, Ede. I'd find somewhere. Why put yourself through this?' Brooke's expression was unusually caring. 'Kill or cure?'

'Kill is *not* on the agenda, Tweed. If Susie senses something, both of us are for the high jump.'

'Cure, then?'

Eden let out a heavy breath. 'I don't know. It just felt... you needed a break. Hell of a metaphor, though. The ground trying to swallow you up. I'm not the only Scorpion who was pissed off at your heroic last stand.'

A twinkle appeared in Brooke's eye. 'You're saying it was a *group* hex?'

'Yeah. The week before you arrived, we all stood in a circle in the changing room, held hands, and conjured a tarmac-eating poltergeist.'

Brooke laughed. 'So they'll be annoyed you broke ranks and gave me a roof.'

'I might still poison your coffee. Or hide your insulin supply.'

'That'll be a short whodunnit.'

Eden smirked. 'I'll plead insanity.'

Brooke fell introspective. 'I know you were mad at me. Still are. But I was only trying to win the match. If the boot was on the other foot, you'd do the same.'

Eden's insides knotted. Truths can be horribly inconvenient. She waited for her friend to say, "Cricket's only a game" or something equally mollifying. But Brooke merely offered a hopeful, sage look.

'Yeah,' she conceded.

'I heard about the trolling. I wouldn't wish that on my worst enemy.'

'No. But you bloody well caused it. If you hadn't hit me round the park—'

Brooke leapt from the sofa. 'I'm not doing this.' She swept up her phone. 'I'll get a hotel. Nice try, Ede. Nice olive branch. But I'd rather live in the sinkhole than put up with this shit.'

'You never even said sorry.'

'It's not my fucking place to apologise for my *job*,' Brooke spat.

'Not even to *me*?'

'Really? You want me to come crawling on my knees?' She scoffed, heading for the doorway. 'You're some piece of work.'

'Goes double for you.'

'Fuck off, Eden.'

'You first.'

'Gladly.'

Eden pointed. 'Don't forget your bag. Or I'll be answering the door at one o'clock in the bloody morning because your reservoir ran out. Not for the first time.'

Brooke folded her arms. 'I'm sorry my illness is such a fucking inconvenience to *your* life.'

Eden's soul tore open. 'Oh God, Tweed, it isn't. *It isn't.*'

Brooke's jaw was firm. 'Everything about this is inconvenient, right? I'll go and make someone else's life a misery.' She turned toward the door.

Eden quivered. She'd used a fork in the road as an excuse to pull a knife, and had it raised high above her head, ready to permanently sever the friendship.

She grabbed Brooke's wrist. 'Don't go.'

The girl's expression was harsh. 'If I'm the one who caused this, how the hell am I supposed to fix it? You *had* someone for that, and you booted him out.'

'But he didn't *know* me. You do,' she beseeched.

Brooke shook her head. 'Not like *this*. Christ knows what Matt had to put up with.' She took Eden's hands, and her voice fell soft yet direct. 'It's just one game, Ede.'

A tear escaped her eye. 'You've no idea what it's like when someone wants you dead.'

'No. And I wish to hell it hadn't happened. What that git did was personal, the worst kind of personal. Me clattering a couple of fours because you had a bad over is *not* the same. I'm not your enemy.' She squeezed Eden's fingers supportively. 'It's been months, but clearly you're still not ready. When you are, we'll talk. But us being roomies is supposed to be a good thing, not a dagger-throwing competition.'

Eden swallowed hard. 'I want to get past it. I *hate* this. I've been waiting for someone to say the right thing.'

'You think that's *me*? I'm supposed to succeed where Matt, your dad, the psychologist, the team, and all the staff failed?'

'But you've known me the longest,' she protested.

'Not as long as Ray. Unless there's something *very* odd you never told me.' Brooke's smile was aimed at lightening the mood.

Eden managed a chuckle. 'No. But you know what it's like. The job.'

Brooke had had her fair share of trolling and low spells in the last decade, but was always better at moving on, putting a bad game, a horrible social media comment, a dip in form, behind her.

The girl's jaw hardened. 'Yeah. And I got past the... *other* thing. What *you* did.'

Eden's anger spiked. 'So this was about evening the score?'

Brooke scoffed. 'No. It was about the *Cup*. I said I moved on. I hated what *you* did the year before, but I can't judge anyone harshly for wanting to win. Otherwise, why play this game?'

True again. Tweedie said lots of meaningful stuff, but it wouldn't turn back the clock.

Eden nodded sadly. History was repeating itself. In desperation to win—the friendship this time, not a match—she was bowling a series of bad balls.

Yet, in the dark days, she hadn't given up on cricket. Now, she mustn't give up on the chance to pull a friendship out of the mire—as, arguably, she'd caused both messes on the same day. She needed to try less hard but think more. Things with Brooke wouldn't thaw overnight. It would take patience and effort, like regaining her batting action after breaking a finger.

Brooke clasped her shoulder. 'Look, it's your call. Your house. Inviting me here is what my best friend, the one I cherish, would do. But it's like a chicken being happy with a fox kipping over in the henhouse, right?'

'No. Only another, nicer chicken. Who lays better eggs.'

Brooke's brow lifted in amusement. 'Well, that's the only thing I plan to *lay* in your house.'

'Blimey. If you can actually lay eggs, I *definitely* don't know you anymore.'

'You mean eggs... or Eggs?'

Eden shuddered, sniggering. 'Maybe *that* was my evil revenge, paying the drooling groundsman to hit on you.'

'Did he never hit on *you*?'

'It's his first season.'

Brooke patted Eden's hand. 'Then the night is young.'

Eden glanced at the clock, a funky wall-mounted item Matt had brought her during a romantic weekend in Brighton. 'It is. And I'm starving. Stay for a bite?'

'A bite?'

Eden pinched her lip. 'And a while longer. Okay?'

'Sure? I mean, if you do want me to find another place, I'll risk getting all my stuff drooled on again during the move.'

'Would I do that to you?'

Brooke angled her head. 'I think the jury's still out.'

'Hmm.'

'Ceasefire, at least?'

Eden nodded. 'Yeah. Let's start there.'

12th Over

Matt found it hard living in a knowledge vacuum. He wanted to find out how Eden and Brooke were coping with cohabitation, but couldn't bring himself to text Eden, and it was too early in the friendship to message Brooke.

Still, there hadn't been anything on the local news, or the Aurora Stadium grapevine, about a grisly murder in the area, so he presumed things between the teammates were, if not better, certainly not markedly worse.

Today marked the second home match of the season. April's greyness had given way to early May sunshine, and the Scorpions' red shirts burned brighter on his retina, even at eight in the morning. He, Ray, Eggs and Alan were preparing the pitch.

The man-to-man chat with Ray had catalysed the boss to start delegating more to Matt. Was it wishful thinking that this was a foretaste of promotion?

Eggs sauntered over, carrying the white paint, ready to refresh the lines on the batting creases.

'Funny, innit?' Eggs said.

'What is?'

'"Crease". Sounds a bit like arse crack.'

'Absolutely,' Matt deadpanned. 'That's all I ever think.'

'No, but it's a mad game, innit? Not like footy. And it goes on for bloody hours.'

'Why didn't you get a job at a football stadium?'

'I fancied it here. Someone had a word, y'know?'

Matt scoffed. Things suddenly made sense. 'Okay.'

They finished their duties and went to join Ray.

'So did you come here for that Eden girl?' Eggs asked, failing to appear nonchalant.

'No. I came because it's a great place to work.' He glanced at Ray. 'And the boss is alright, in his way.'

Ray wrinkled his nose.

'You a cricket guy then, boss?' Eggs asked.

'I played a bit in my day. Local club, nothing fancy. But we're not here to watch, lad.'

'Oh, never said we were. Don't understand it all anyway. Too many rules.'

'Cricket?' Matt said. 'It's easy. Bowlers, batters, runs, wickets. That's it.'

'But all the tactics and people moving around after every bloody ball?'

Ray tutted. 'Honestly. It's a simple game.'

'Go on then, boss, explain it. Bet you can't, not before they do that coin-throwing bit.'

Matt held in a chuckle, toying with an offcut of sprinkler hose.

Ray drained his coffee cup, pinched his chin, and fixed Eggs in a gaze. 'You have two sides, one out in the field and one in. Each man that's in the side that's in goes out, and when he's out, he comes in and the next man goes in until he's out. When they're all out, the side that's out comes in and the side that's been in goes out and tries to get those coming in, out. Sometimes you get men still in and not out. When a man goes out to go in, the men who are out try to get him out, and when he is out he goes in and the next man in goes out and goes in. There are two men called umpires who stay out all the time and they decide when the men who are in are out. When both sides have been in and all the men have got out, and both sides have been out after all the men have been in, including those who are not out, that's the end of the game.'

Ray patted Eggs' shoulder. 'There you go.' He winked at Matt.

Eggs looked back and forth between the two of them, his mouth and eyes busy.

'Questions?' Matt said.

'Er... you said "man" a lot. What about the women's game? Is that different?'

Matt put on a straight face. 'Yeah. There is absolutely no danger of them getting smacked in the bollocks. Unlike you.' He batted Eggs in the groin with the hose.

'Boys, boys!' Ray scorned playfully.

'Sorry, boss.'

Eggs rubbed his damaged goods. 'But surely the girls can get a ball in the puppies?'

Matt's mouth fell open. 'Is that *really* your biggest takeaway?'

'I'm only thinking of poor Brooke getting a whack in the—'

Matt snapped up a hand. 'We get the picture. Not as crystal clear as you're straining to conjure, I'm sure.'

Eggs' brow furrowed. 'You reckon Brooke and Eden would ever have a fight? Like, a proper scrap?'

'Topless, in mud, I suppose?'

'Well, not pacifically, but—'

Matt looked at Ray. 'Remind me why you hired him?'

'My best mate's nephew.'

'Sounds like you need to find a different best mate.'

Ray swiped at him. 'Oi. You're not too old for me to clip your ear.'

Eggs laughed. Ray clipped his ear. Matt laughed...

...then fell serious. Brooke was jogging past. Her eye-roll was paired with an impish smile. He nodded in greeting. She finger-waved.

Eggs took this as a cue. 'Alright?'

'Yes, thanks.' She accelerated away.

Eggs made a throaty noise. Ray tutted paternally. Matt considered whacking Eggs in the nuts again.

'So... what is it between those two?' Eggs asked.

Ray stood, groaning deliberately. 'I'm going to take care of business.' He didn't want to hear this story for the millionth time, regurgitated and analysed. He'd lived the aftermath for eighteen months.

Matt wasn't thrilled about raking over the past either. Still, Eggs needed to know, partially to avoid putting his foot in it with either girl, whether or not he was hitting on them at the time.

Deep breath.

'So there's a thing in the game called a Mankad—' he began.

'I thought that was a thong.'

'That's a mankini, you numpty.'

'Oh right. Wondered what they'd be doing wearing those.'

'Can we focus?'

'Yeah, sorry.'

'The Mankad is a controversial topic. It's a kind of... sneaky way of taking someone's wicket. If you're interested, which I doubt, Google it.'

Matt rubbed his forehead. He'd always sat on the fence about the whole affair—not whether the move was in the spirit of the game, but Eden's decision to use it. It revealed a dubious aspect of character. She'd always excused it as legitimate and driven by a desire to win. Deep down, he reckoned it was a "get out", a way of making up for her self-doubts, losses of form or confidence. Yet it didn't matter what he thought, only that it had happened.

'It was in a game two years ago. Brooke was batting, and Eden, for whatever reason, decided to Mankad her.'

Eggs frowned. 'Shouldn't it be Womankad?'

'Yes, probably,' Matt groaned, feeling like Eggs was the last person who'd stand up for equality and political correctness. 'Anyway, Brooke was run out, and she was pissed off. Inconsolable. Her team lost the game, went out of the competition.'

'Shit happens, though. And it's not against the rules, this Mandad thing?'

'No. If it *was*, Eden and I... I don't know.'

'But you broke up.'

'Not over that. Although maybe over the... consequences of it. And me. And Eden being... Eden.'

'She's hard work, is what you're saying?'

'No. She has a tough job. She loves it and everything, but you put yourself on a pedestal. Create an expectation of form or results.' He shook his head. 'And when things dip, the knives come out. Some of these players are still teenagers, and getting interviewed on national TV. I'd be shitting a brick.'

'Not me,' Eggs said cheerfully.

'Well, pick up a bat and see how you get on.'

'Might do that. Think she'd give me a lesson?'

Matt shot a glower. 'I'm *hoping* you mean Brooke.'

'Course. I mean, look at her.'

Matt's attention was drawn to Brooke—her lithe figure, blonde ponytail swinging as she chatted with her teammates.

He shook that off, then assessed the interaction between the new housemates. Eden was putting a brave face on things, especially not having been picked in the XI again. Still, there was no frost in the air. She and Brooke weren't laughing and joking, but they weren't studiously keeping a safe distance.

Had Eden's gamble paid off?

13th Over

If it felt odd not to have her finger strapped up any longer, any emotional uplift was dulled by not being picked for the squad. Eden was finally fit, but her spot had been taken. That was always disappointing, worse now because her replacement was Brooke.

I have to cheer her on. The team is what's important.

She took her place on the bench, Day-Glo vest over her kit. The Scorpions were fielding first. As they fanned out into their positions, captain Danica tossed Brooke the ball.

Eden rubbed her fingers, wishing that the ball was in her grasp.

'Let's go, Harry,' called keeper Izzy from behind the stumps.

Beside Eden, the other subs clapped enthusiastically.

Taking a deep breath, she joined in. 'Come on, Tweed.'

Then she watched, with equal parts pride and despondency, as Brooke ripped through the opposition's top order batters. After 10 of the 50 overs, the Scorpions had the London Warriors on the ropes at 44-5. Brooke was bowling out of her skin, which meant two things—the team had hired well, and Eden would no longer be a first choice for the starting XI.

Her stomach tied itself in greater knots.

The Eden Palmer of six months ago would have excused herself to the changing room and thrown up. Now, she was a stronger, better person—yet not grounded enough to keep tendrils of black thoughts away. Like how it would be a shame if Brooke got injured.

She swallowed down the disgust at her own hatefulness.

'What're you feeding her?' asked George, a perennial benchwarmer. Being the second-choice wicketkeeper was tough, especially because Izzy was so good and seldom got injured.

Eden jolted from her introspection. 'Oh, you mean my new roomie?'

George leant in. 'I expected an undetectable toxin, but looks like your supplier accidentally gave you anabolic steroids!'

She inspected the girl's amused query. A resigned breath escaped. 'It's that transparent, eh?'

'However hard you try, Ede, you always wear your heart on your sleeve. You're *allowed* to be pissed off.'

'For six months?' she scoffed.

George rubbed Eden's shoulder. 'We all saw the Insta comment. We all felt sick to our bones. You can't control the *internet*.'

Eden's head dipped. 'Hell, I couldn't even control line and length for six bloody balls.'

'I bet that troll couldn't even hit a cow's arse with a banjo. Or get laid. Don't give him the satisfaction of ruining your career.'

She laughed. 'Pretty sure the boat has sailed on that.'

George grabbed Eden's hand. Firmly, no nonsense. 'Right. Enough of that shit. Come on, we're netting.'

Eden didn't need practice. She wanted a *game*. The same went for George, but those were the breaks, so they asked two other subs to cover their duties, tracked down a coach and headed off.

As they trailed along the pitch edge, the crowd to their right, game to their left, Eden's attention was drawn to the groundsmen's area. Dad sat perched atop the mower, clutching a familiar tired mug. Eggs and Alan were chatting. Matt was at Deep Mid-wicket, helping the fielder to realign the boundary sponge after she'd wiped it out in a vain attempt to prevent a 4.

The fielder pulled out her blonde ponytail and retied it. She and Matt shared a joke.

Yeah. Steal my bowling slot, and now you're after my man. Unbelievable.

Chill. There's no evidence of that. Stop being so bitchy and suspicious.

'Let's try some in-swingers,' the bowling coach said.

'Sure,' Eden replied, summoning enthusiasm.

The trio arrived at the nets and set up. George camped behind the wicket, fielding every one of Eden's deliveries with aplomb as she tried to beat an imaginary batter.

It was half an hour of intense concentration on technique—ideal for retaining muscle memory and distracting her from what was happening on the pitch nearby.

As they walked back to the pavilion, chatting about George's new girlfriend, Eden spotted a familiar face in the front row of the stands, so told George to go on ahead.

She leant on the railing. 'Hi, Lily.'

'Hey, Eden.' The girl pointed at the game. 'Thought you'd be playing.'

'Not today. Probably a good choice by Susie, though. Brooke's on fire.'

'Room for two seamers, though? Rose is playing.'

'Yeah, well, Rose wasn't laid up all winter.' Eden flashed a sober smile.

Lily patted her shoulder. 'It's only one game, coach. Long season ahead. Which is literally what you'd tell me.'

'True. Oh, how was the concert?'

'Like the best day *ever*.'

'Good. Downtime's important, especially if you work hard at your sport. Which you do.'

'Thanks.' Lily glanced round briefly, and Eden noticed a teenage lad a few rows back in the crowd.

Eden leant in. 'Secret admirer seems a bit less secret today.'

Lily blushed. 'Toby's... crushing hard. Can't deny.'

'And you?'

'Mum says fifteen's too young to have a boyfriend.'

'Mum needs to sort out her attitude. Want me to have a word?'

'No way.' Lily fiddled with her bracelet. 'I should, like, wait, right? Boys break your heart.'

Eden coughed. 'Not deliberately, usually. And it takes two to make it work... or not. But if Toby... or any boy... *gets* it, you'll be okay, Lily.'

' "Gets it"?'

Eden gestured around. 'All this. Pressure. Scrutiny. Hard work.' She chuckled sadly. 'Failure.'

Lily proffered her wrist, using a finger to show the legends written on two small charms. FOCUS. BREATHE.

'Stole the idea from Rose,' the girl admitted, wincing in amused embarrassment.

'Well, if you want a role model—'

Lily's hand went to her mouth. 'I mean, not that you're not—'

Eden took Lily's other hand. 'No offence taken. In fact, if I breathed more, counted to ten now and again, perhaps things would be different.'

'What happened to the coach who tells me, "Forget the last ball. Just bowl a better one next time"?'

Eden sighed. 'That coach would also say, "Do as I say, not as I do".'

Lily's brow furrowed. Then she unclasped her bracelet, gently took Eden's left wrist, and fastened it there.

'Lily, I can't—'

'I don't have an apple for teacher, so this'll have to do.' She grinned. 'Besides, you need it more than me.'

'If you expect me to go easy on you, good luck with that.'

'Whatever. I don't care. Go easy on *you*, Eden.'

Resigned to the gift, she pulled the girl into a shoulder hug. 'I'll try. Thanks for the pep talk.'

'No probs. See you at the club?'

'Definitely.' She lowered her voice. 'And don't let Toby kiss you *just* yet.'

'Oh, don't worry. I'm playing *very* hard to get. Elite athletes aren't supposed to be an easy ride, right?' Lily's eyes sparkled impishly.

Eden nudged her. 'You're a mischief, Lily Roberts. Now, I need to go before Susie hauls me over the coals for a bad attitude.' She scoffed. 'Unless the horse has already bolted.'

Lily raised a maternal finger in a gesture three decades beyond her teenage years. 'What did I literally just say about going easy on yourself?'

'*Yes*, coach.'

14th Over

If Matt knew Eden—and he used to think so—she'd be feeling low after the match, so he left her alone. Things did seem better between her and Brooke, but the latter's stellar performance would have riled Eden. It shouldn't, but if it were that easy to shake his ex from her funk, he would have done it months ago. He could only wait and hope.

At home, he ordered a takeaway, had a long phone call with Mum, then headed up to bed. So much for the rabble-rousing youth of a decade earlier. But then, life's travails grow you up.

He knew that taking his phone into the bedroom was a bad idea. An idle mind is easy prey for doomscrolling. He'd prefer not to be alone in the bedroom, have physical rather than digital companionship, and reading about far-off wars did little to distract him from the absence of an armistice close to home.

He tossed his phone onto the bed. It bounced on the pillow and leapt down the gap in front of the headboard.

'Bollocks.'

If the screen's cracked, that'll teach me. Or maybe it won't.

With a sigh, he left that issue for Future Matt and went to do his ablutions. A tired face stared out from the bathroom mirror. If only he spent as much time moving on as he did wishing Eden would do the same.

He picked at the dimple in his chin. Eden loved his dimple. *Had* loved.

In the bedroom, stripped down to his Calvin Klein's, he analysed the trapped phone issue. If he tried to snake a hand down the headboard gap and root around, his fat bicep would get trapped, or he'd whack his head against the wall.

He took the easier option. Grabbing the foot of the bed, he hauled the whole thing, mattress and all, three feet away from the wall.

If there's a six-inch spider checking out my Facebook feed, I'm sleeping in the spare room.

There wasn't. Instead, he found months' worth of dust, a couple of tissues, a USB-C cable, a screwed-up receipt, a phone... and a surprise. Or what had been a surprise nine months ago, until it had mysteriously vanished.

He gingerly retrieved the keepsake, tidied up the other things, left the dust problem for Future Matt, pushed the bed back, then sat cross-legged, fingering the necklace.

The small pendant was a conjoined bat and ball in sterling silver. A gift for Eden's 27th birthday. She'd missed it for a while, wondered where it could be. They reckoned it had been lost during the weekend at a local spa & conference hotel resort. Wharton Grange. Room 27.

Huge bed. Every inch of it explored...

Eden should have the necklace back. He merely needed to find the right time, and the right way, to return it.

As the following morning marked a day off, Matt headed to the gym.

From the changing room, he went to check if any of the bench press racks were available. As all were busy, he ambled along the line, assessing whether anyone was near the end of their reps. Reaching the last set of apparatus, he was drawn to a halt. A lithe blonde was effortlessly handling what he reckoned to be 150 lbs. Her outfit was an unfamiliar red-and-black sports top and shorts. Perspiration glistened on her forehead, and the raised band across her midriff tugged his heart as much as her figure spiked his hormones.

It's rude to stare, said a maternal voice in his head.

It's not staring, he wanted to reply. *It's indecision. I can't pretend not to have noticed her... can I?*

He glanced around. *But what if—?*

'Matt?'

He jolted.

Brooke sat up and licked her lips.

'Oh, hi. Small world,' he said.

She looked him up and down. 'Maybe not. You don't strike me as a reluctant, New Year's resolution type gym goer.'

'It gets me out of the house.' Which was a crass thing to say, given his job.

Had silly nerves created that reply? Not social—romantic—embarrassment, surely? Tongue-tied? That would be ridiculous. Being attracted to Brooke was dangerous, pointless.

She slugged from a Scorpions-branded water bottle. 'Saturday morning TV will do that.'

'Clearly, that's the only reason you come.'

'I mean, James Martin is one reason to surf the sofa, but,' she shrugged, 'the job, y'know?'

'Ditto. Oh, not the TV eye candy part—'

She chuckled. 'That would be some reveal, given your relationship history.'

He smiled sadly. 'Yeah.'

A clanging silence.

'Oh, sorry, did you want to...?' She tapped the bench.

'No rush. Athletes first. Lawn mowers, second.'

She covered her eyes. 'Thanks for that.'

'I've been called worse.'

'We've all been called plenty worse, I can tell you.'

'Amen.'

Brooke's midriff beeped. She pulled up her shirt, exposing a flat stomach, and eased the phone-sized monitor from its waistband.

He half looked away, not wanting to pry... or imagine what more of her torso looked like.

'Okay?' he asked with feigned casualness.

'Low reservoir.'

'Right.' Their eyes met. 'Sorry. Not my business.'

She angled her head. 'It's kind of everyone's, unfortunately.'

He frowned. 'How?'

She shuffled along the seat and indicated the space beside her. After a beat, he sat. She lifted a crossbody bag from the floor, pulled out a sweet packet, popped a handful of gummies into her mouth, and offered him the bag. He took a couple.

'Guilty pleasure,' she explained. 'And an occupational hazard.'

'If I lived on those, I would be *so* fat.'

'I don't *live* on them, mate! Anyway, there's not an ounce of fat on you.' She prodded his bicep. 'You're fit.'

His cheeks warmed. 'It is a *big* lawn to mow.'

She nudged him. 'Can you at least *try* to let me live that down?'

'Sorry. You have enough to cope with.'

She tapped the belt pack. 'This? Yes, it's a pain in the arse. *Literally*, with the needle, but you get used to it. There are ways to mitigate it. Medical science is amazing. And Bluetooth. Harder to find a machine that keeps *depression* at bay.'

'I find the Xbox works well.'

'You're not depressed... are you?'

'No. Time will be a healer,' he said, trying the platitude on for size.

'Definitely. Although I doubt I'm helping. Probably the last person she wanted around this year.'

'You still would have played against her, right? Maybe it's better this way. She can't be your... nemesis again.'

Brooke bit her lip. 'I hate that I was, or she sees me that way, but, yeah, better to work together, get back our friendship. Hopefully.'

'And good to have her close by, I expect. With your... condition.'

Brooke rubbed her belt pack. 'I suppose. No, *definitely*. Like I said, people have to know. In case of... issues. Not that I'm asking for a chaperone, a paramedic, a guardian angel. From you or anyone.'

He nodded. 'So I'm *aware*.'

'If you want to be, Matt,' she said quietly, almost tenderly.

His heart thudded. 'Whatever you did or didn't do, deliberately or accidentally, whatever the fallout on Eden or me, I'd never stand by and watch any person suffer, fall ill.'

'I don't intend to keel over. But I'm not perfect... much as Ede thinks I am.'

'She knows you're not. And if I had to guess, I'd say she offered you a room partly because she's been on this journey with you.'

'Hmm.'

Someone coughed. Matt looked up. A tattooed guy wore an enquiring expression.

Brooke stood. 'Sorry. We're hogging the space.'

Matt rose. Suddenly a workout felt like the second priority behind this conversation—whatever it was or wherever it was heading. 'Go ahead, mate.'

'Cheers.'

Brooke scooped up her bag and ushered Matt towards a vacant bench seat. When they sat, she surveyed his face for a few seconds, as if weighing something, then gave the full "Welcome To My Type 1 Diabetes" tour. The sensor, the monitor, the function of insulin, high and low blood sugar, side effects. How she needed to assess the carbohydrate load of every meal or snack and put data into the machine so it knew how to meter out her dose.

What a ball-ache. What an albatross around her, or anyone's, neck.

She showed him where the drip entered her shorts, saying the needle site was in her backside, but it was probably a bit much to drop trou in the middle of a crowded gym. It didn't stop Matt wondering what her poor bum cheeks looked like...

'So now you know. In case the whole knight-in-shining-armour thing is ever needed.'

He exhaled from a heavy chest. 'Don't rely on me, Brooke. I'd screw it up.'

Brooke folded her arms. 'Do I have to dig *you* out of the pit as well as Eden?'

'That's not your responsibility. You didn't come to the club as a psychologist. You came as a leading wicket-taker.'

'True. So you do you, and I'll work on her. Okay?' She met his gaze, and he was drawn into her beautiful blue eyes. 'Or, better yet, we do it together. Because... we're friends now, right?'

'No question.' He noted the running machines. 'But who's faster over five miles?'

She patted his hand. 'Oh, me, mate. Every day of the week.'

15th Over

Eden's rest day was spent doing chores. Brooke had gone to the gym, then was meeting a friend for lunch before hitting the tiles. Brooke, the social butterfly, had settled into the Scorpions, and her new playing arena, with typical ease.

On one side, Eden envied her friend. On another, she was guiltily happy that they weren't in the house all hours, as it made the wound healing easier. In fact, she wished one of Brooke's evenings out resulted in a boyfriend... one who wasn't Matt. She wasn't being possessive. No. Things between them were done. She merely didn't want things to get complex, especially as there were green shoots of hope in the Garden of Eden.

At six o'clock, she pulled on less slovenly clothes and drove to Dad's. They hadn't properly spoken in a couple of weeks. Life, and trying to re-integrate Brooke into it, logistically and emotionally, had been busy. Dad knew the early part of the season was tough, and he never berated her for the infrequent visits. Deep down, though he never said it, he was grateful that she'd returned to the town to support him during his own dark spell. Now, with the house move imminent, there was light at the end of the tunnel.

Good thing Mum wasn't around to see my bad turn. She'd have loved saying "I told you so."

Eden hated thinking that. Although, of the two parents, she'd wound up with the better cheerleader close by anyhow.

Dad greeted her at the door, the usual peck on the cheek. He hadn't shaved.

Perhaps at 59 you've basically given up on celebrating your age? Maybe next year.

'What are we eating?' she asked, stepping into the hallway.

'Since when am I cooking on my birthday?'

'Do I at least get to choose which particular Deliveroo provider I have to answer the door to?'

'Anything for you, daughter dear.'

They sank onto the sofa, he with a groan, the t-shirt riding up over his belly.

She tugged it down. 'You want to lose weight, Dad.'

He gave her the side-eye. 'You want to forgive Matt, Eden.'

She didn't dignify that... yet. Instead, she handed over the small bag of gifts.

As Ray unwrapped them, she wondered whether the half-empty glass of beer on the coffee table was his first, or second, or *unspecified*. To save him, his liver, from the tiniest amount of additional abuse, she picked up the glass and drained it. He didn't say anything. Instead, he unwrapped the presents, then picked up the whisky bottle and scrutinised the label.

He shot her a glance.

'I know, I know,' she said. 'One minute it's "Stop drinking so much, Dad", and then it's, "Have some expensive booze".'

'I drink the *expensive* stuff slowly.'

'If it's not empty by your sixtieth, I'll buy you something properly expensive as a present for doing well with your last present.'

He extended a fat hand. 'Deal.'

'Deal.' She shook, not believing for a second that she'd have to fork out again.

'The lad got me a nice thing.' He pointed at the mantelpiece.

She went to investigate. Inside a small, transparent plastic cube was a cricket ball. She recognised the signature across its surface, because she had a ball signed by the same England legend. Stuart Broad was always Dad's favourite.

Wow. Pushed the boat out there, Matt. Trying to regain Dad's favour? Doubt it. You're not that scheming.

'He's not just a pretty face, eh?' Ray said.

'Anything you want to tell me?' She smirked. 'Mum turned you off women?'

'Like I'd take your sloppy seconds.'

Her mouth fell open. 'Wash your mouth out, Raymond Palmer.'

'Alright if I do it with masala sauce?'

'I'm curious how this cordon bleu soirée is different to most other nights in this house?'

'*You're* here, daughter.'

'Is that a jibe?'

He patted the sofa. 'Never.'

She sat. 'I'll come to the new place a lot more. If you want.'

'To pick out soft furnishings, I suppose.' He raised an eyebrow.

'Or you could sit on deckchairs on cold wooden floors. I'm easy.'

'Busman's holiday.'

'You want me to come to IKEA with you?' she offered.

'Fuck IKEA.'

'John Lewis? Are they paying you that well?'

'I'm not *burning* everything in this place, Edie.'

'Pleased to hear it.'

'Matt was after that painting, for one.' Ray pointed at the wall.

Mum and Dad had bought it in an art gallery in Barcelona during their honeymoon. Odd that Matt liked it, but at least Dad wasn't giving it away to a charity shop.

'Will there be *any* of my inheritance left over?'

'Talk to your mother. *She's* the high-flier.'

Eden scoffed. 'As if we could forget.'

He enveloped her hand in his rough palm. 'It was only done out of love. Like everything, out of wanting the best for you.' He looked away. 'Even the lad tried his best.'

Ah. Here we go.

'Shall we order?'

They ordered moped-facilitated food, then she got them beers from the fridge. All throughout, something prickled at the back of her skull.

'Dad?'

'Daughter.'

Deep breath.

'What does he say about me?'

He took a modest mouthful of beer. 'Ah. Miss Bighead thinks she's the hot topic amongst the lads.'

Eden scoffed. 'The hot topic is probably Brooke.'

Ray's look was openly judgmental. 'Jealous much?'

She laughed. 'You're a teenager suddenly?'

'No.' He drank again. 'But you're stroppy like one.'

She snorted. 'Says the expert.'

'I've been through your teen years. Once is more than enough.'

She folded her arms. 'I was a perfect daughter, thank you *very* much.'

Ray's mouth opened on a comeback, then closed. 'Yes,' he said with feeling. 'You studied hard at your exams and at cricket. Your mother and I were blessed.'

Her eyes narrowed. '"Were"?'

'Still are.'

'Even today? Me throwing a strop at my best friend?'

He scratched his chin. 'I thought you were sworn enemies now.'

'We're *teammates*.'

'That doesn't answer the question.'

'Housemates too,' she added.

'Politician's answer.'

She sighed hard. 'Okay. We're working through it, and we haven't come to blows yet.'

Ray let silence hold sway for a moment. 'Move on, daughter dear. Susie won't be happy, and if you get a reputation, England will take a dim view of it. Try to play nicely with this squad.'

'I've played nicely for years,' she protested.

'*Today's* squad.'

She jabbed his arm. 'I invited Brooke into my house, for fuck's sake! That's playing *unbelievably* nicely.'

'In Parliament, Conservatives and Labour sit under the same roof. It doesn't mean they are *friends*.'

'*Very* insightful.'

'Don't be pig-headed or hold a grudge. I know the Cup was a bad experience, but don't blame her for that horrible trolling, your breakup with Matt, and certainly not for busting your finger.'

'Why not? She was the butterfly who flapped her wings.'

'*Innocently*, like that proverbial butterfly.'

'Didn't we already do this? At Christmas? I'm still pissed off that I didn't get to eat my figgy pudding.'

'You're the one who stormed out. And the brandy I flamed was a wedding present.'

A cruel smile hit her. 'That's some metaphor.'

His bushy eyebrows knitted and then raised. 'I suppose so.'

The doorbell rang.

She collected the large paper bag from the moped rider and met Dad in the kitchen, where they assembled the dinner onto plates and took it to the small dining table. He ate pensively, as if distracted.

'Penny for them,' she said.

He played with his rice. 'It's like this,' he began.

'Ah. Socrates Palmer.'

He shot a paternal glower. She blew him a kiss.

'Relationships are like gardening. Sometimes you find a big stone, or a real bastard of a tree root, and you have to work hard to get it out. It's back-breaking work. Team effort is best. And then? The garden grows better.' He met her eye. 'Everyone expects... artificial grass. Something you don't have to work at. Love's not like that.' He shrugged, then dug into his tikka masala.

She wiped condensation from the neck of her beer bottle. 'A weed is just a plant growing where you don't want it to, right?'

'That's the case.'

She ate for a while. Dad had understood the remark.

'I'm proud of you, Edie,' he said.

Her brow lifted. 'Generally, or specifically?'

'For giving her a room.'

'Renting. I'm not a charity.'

'How are you two doing with that?'

She reflected. 'It's not the glory days yet. But the language is only PG-15.'

'And I don't see any scars.'

'Oh, all the bruising's on the inside.' She winked.

'The sooner you laugh about it, the better for all of us.'

She pushed her knife and fork together on the empty plate. 'The stone's gone. Garden's growing again, Dad.'

'This would be the garden of... Eden?' he joked.

'If you don't drop that old chestnut, next year I'll buy you a bottle of bleach.'

'I was hoping you'll be off on tour with England and won't have time to buy me a present.'

She snorted reflexively. 'The impossible, I'm working on. Miracles take a little longer.'

He put his elbows on the table and interlaced his fingers. 'You'll get there.'

'Which one?'

'Both.'

'Thanks.'

He angled his head toward the kitchen. She took her plate and followed him. They loaded the dishwasher, then she took two more beers from the fridge.

As she did, gentle hands rested on her shoulders. A kiss was pressed to the top of her head.

'I love you, Edie.'

'I love you too, Dad.'

And I will try harder. I promise.

16th Over

In the morning, Matt lingered in the shower, his thoughts turning to Brooke. The theme wasn't romance, only reflection.

For too long, he'd viewed her as if through Eden's eyes, with resentment holding back an ability to take Brooke at face value. Now, that judgement wasn't clouded. Eden's burden was temporary, but Brooke's was permanent. Yet there was no mileage in feeling *sorry* for her—she was a strong character. Probably stronger than Eden, more resilient. Perhaps a refusal to be cowed by diabetes had caused it. Nevertheless, being harangued online by faceless morons is uncontrollable. Medical science can't mitigate for that. Nor the fallout for friendships, either.

As he towelled down, he recalled yesterday. Both had finished the good-natured run challenge coated in sweat. He'd asked whether perspiration affected the needle site, and then how bathing worked. That had led his caveman brain to visualise her in the bath. Now, despite having shaken off the pang of desire before, his libido spiked again.

Get a grip. It's impossible. Verboten.

Right?

Eggs collected Matt at ten o'clock.

He'd agreed to help out with another Man & Van job. Something had happened to Eggs in the last week—perhaps a bump to the head—because Eggs now *owned* the van.

Matt didn't know what to make of the situation. Whilst it was unfeasibly entrepreneurial of Eggs to set up his own business, this was tempered by reflecting on the vehicle he'd chosen. Yes, it had been washed since last time, but Matt reckoned its chances of passing the next MOT were still as slim.

Surely there were mitigating reasons for Eggs' decision? Naturally, as a casual summer worker, the lad needed something to fall back on over the winter, but he hardly exuded the impression of a careful and trustworthy removals operative. Perhaps he'd spied the possibility of doing more work for attractive, young, blonde athletes. Matt wondered whether that was *Ben & Van*'s marketing strategy...

Today's client was very unlike Brooke Harris. She was an upper-middle-class divorcee with a chest you could ski down. The job was to move sundry effects out of the former marital home, due to a snafu with the main removal lorry the previous week.

Geraldine (never 'Geri') brewed them a cuppa as they loaded the van, then shadowed them for the last five minutes, curious rather than overbearing. More than once, she commented on how lovely it was to have "two such fine young men" helping out.

Mercifully, she had a car—a soft-top Mercedes—so didn't need to share the van's bench seat with Matt. He feared wandering hands, and not those of Eggs...

They headed off to the destination property.

Halfway there, roadworks brought ten minutes of stop-start. Eggs used the handbrake effectively, didn't impatiently rev the tired diesel engine, or make salubrious comments about Geraldine's forty-something curves. Matt was beginning to reevaluate the guy.

Then, in a two-minute stationary spell, Eggs pulled out his phone, scrolled, and showed Matt the screen.

'Seen this?'

It was an Instagram post by Brooke, with the caption "Best winter ever". The selected photo showed her on a beach, probably in Australia, in a bikini. She was much more relaxed about social media exposure than Eden. A more outgoing, sharing person. Eggs, however, had only just discovered this goldmine.

'No,' Matt replied flatly.

'Hot, right?'

'Almost certainly. Forty degrees sometimes in Sydney.'

'No, *her*.'

'She's a nice girl.' Undoubtedly, Brooke looked very fine in swimwear, as she had in gym wear, but long-term relationships demand more than skin-deep lust.

Eggs quickly pocketed the phone, engaged first gear, and trundled them forward a hundred yards.

'Oh, she's nice alright. Not your thing, though, mate?'

Matt deflected. 'It's still too soon.'

'Dunno about that. Got to get back on the horse.' He shot a knowing look. 'You saying you're not interested?'

'Beauty needs to be more than holiday snaps.'

Eggs pulled out his phone. 'What's Eden's username?'

Matt scoffed. 'You won't find anything like that from her. And I wouldn't want to see anyway.'

'Don't need to. You've seen the lot, mate. Loads of times.'

It was pointless to reiterate that nudity wasn't the decision criteria for a deep romantic bond. Still, initial physical attraction *had* been a factor with himself and Eden.

His attention drifted to a playing field beside the road.

For a few months, the season before last, his and Eden's paths had repeatedly crossed in and around the Aurora stadium. Nothing more than the natural interplay of their roles. Then, in July, he'd been loitering near the boundary—a rain shower was expected—when an opposition batter had bludgeoned a 6 in his direction. The ball sailed over the head of the nearby fielder, and he managed to catch it.

He milked the applause of the spartan weekday crowd, then tossed the ball to Eden. Hilariously, she dropped it. After scooping it from the turf and lobbing it to the keeper, she called, 'Perhaps you should be fielding here instead of me!'

They laughed.

Then, half an hour later, she took a brilliant catch nearby. He applauded in unison with the crowd.

She cheekily bowed, then winked. 'Maybe we should stick to our jobs after all.'

If that hadn't endeared him to her, bumping into each other in the car park after the game did. It was serendipitous.

At training two days later, she was practicing in the nets, and they chatted during a rest break. Something in her beautiful brown eyes gave him the courage to ask her for a drink that night. She accepted. He didn't make it back to his bed. The rest was history... until their relationship became history.

But those good times—not merely the bedroom ones—were gone. Some pea-brained grunt had destroyed her mental health, her confidence, and her love life.

When they arrived at Geraldine's new address, she was on the driveway, two steaming mugs in her hand.

Matt's instinct throughout this had been to take charge, as he was three years Eggs' senior and credited himself with better customer service manners. However, it was the lad's enterprise, and Matt needed to let Eggs make his own mistakes... or create his own successes.

So he chatted to Geraldine as Eggs unloaded a few boxes into the house. Every time he went through the front door, he wiped his feet. Did Eggs have an identical twin?

If so, the twin was a clumsy one. During the next back-and-forth, Eggs tripped over his feet and the cargo of two brown boxes was catapulted onto the tarmac drive. Matt winced, anticipating the breakage of a grand's worth of bone china. Luckily, Ben & Van was spared that insurance payout, but not an ounce of embarrassment.

The top box split open and the contents were strewn across the ground. Matt's cheeks flushed scarlet.

'What the...? Oh,' Eggs managed.

Matt didn't know where to look. He wished Geraldine was moving into a house adjacent to the sinkhole, as this would have enabled the ground to literally swallow him up. And Eggs. And possibly her too.

'I'll... er... just...' Eggs fumbled.

Matt risked a glance at Geraldine, who wasn't about to go off like a rocket. Neither was she a delicate shade of beetroot.

'Don't worry,' she said. 'Accidents happen.'

Eggs, crouched down, paused, one toy in his hand. 'Madam, I'm *so* sorry.'

She stepped over, reaching down towards him. Instead of allowing himself to be helped up, Eggs passed her the cylindrical object. One of maybe a dozen in different shades and shapes. She hastily secreted it in a deep skirt pocket.

Eggs stood. 'We'll pay for any damage, of course.'

She patted his upper arm. 'Let's not fret, young man. We'll say no more about it. But perhaps a glass of wine one evening will be sufficient apology,' she purred.

'I... um... If you think that's...'

'No need to make this all litigious, is there?'

Matt was rooted to the spot, begging that she wouldn't extend the invitation to him too.

'Dunno what that word is,' Eggs said, 'But how about I crack on and you can tell me afterwards if anything's... broken.'

Do these things break? And could you tell? Would Geraldine have to use all dozen in quick succession to validate their continued effectiveness?

Matt swallowed.

Or will she wait until the evening with Eggs and ask him to test them all out on her?

To avoid getting an image, he hastily downed the mug of tea and resumed the removal task. If Eggs *had* started the business as a lame excuse to hook up with women, he was on the verge of reaping the whirlwind.

'What do I do?' Eggs hissed when they were pulling the last items from the back of the van.

'It's your removal business, mate.' Matt patted the lad's shoulder. 'But I'd hope her ex-husband isn't the jealous type.'

17th Over

It was like days gone by, yet oddly different.

Eden and Brooke had travelled to many games together in the past, but today didn't have the easy camaraderie of their Loughborough and post-Uni days. They were sharing a car because it was convenient, because they were teammates and housemates, not because they were revelling in each other's company.

Still, it was a watershed.

Certainly, today's match would be easier to bear, because Eden had been selected to play. This would have been a real confidence boost if the decision had been made on merit, but it was out of necessity as Rose had picked up a knock in training. Still, Eden had to consider it a win. There wouldn't be the jealousy and bitterness of warming the bench while Brooke plied her trade on the pitch. They'd be working together for the common good, which was what the coach and team needed. Hell, if it helped to rekindle the friendship, even better.

Actually, Eden had missed driving to the stadium with a teammate—the banter, camaraderie, and pre-game analysis.

As Eden's hand rested on the steering wheel, Brooke pointed. 'Will Rojo mind you nicked her idea?'

Eden glanced at the bracelet. 'I'll say it was a gift from a fan. Then she *can't* have any beef.' She winked.

'So long as it works, right?'

'At this point, I'll try anything.'

'Not sure you need to. I swear you're a yard faster than last season.'

Eden looked across. 'Speed wasn't the issue. It was control.' She sighed. 'And not just of the ball.'

Brooke patted the seat bolster. 'Come on, Ede. None of that. Game time. Game face.'

Eden's stomach twisted. Could she take this opportunity to get back on the horse, prove to herself and others that she deserved her place? Pressure had been her undoing before. Would it happen again?

'Definitely,' she mustered.

'You watch. I'll bet you beat me to the first wicket.'

Eden's laugh verged on a scoff. 'Is this you trying to get a night off from cooking again?'

In happier years, they regularly had a bet that whoever came away from a game with the poorer bowling figures would make dinner. Invariably, Eden wound up in the kitchen.

'Not if you're going to make me a roast with *mash* again. Who has Sunday lunch without the roasties? Oh, I remember, people whose friend boils the potatoes dry before they even get a chance to hit the duck fat.' Brooke sniggered knowingly.

'Alright, it was an epic fail. But in my defence, you did drag me into the living room to point out how hot James Martin looked.

Anyway, if you think I'm spending the evening after a one-dayer shoving stuffing up a chicken's arse, jog on.'

Eden guided the car through the gates of the Aurora Stadium, waving at the security guard as they passed.

Time to go to work.

An hour later, the Scorpions warmed up on the pitch. Eden inspected the wicket. It was her second favourite strip, one to the immediate left of centre. She looked over at the groundsman's compound, wondering whether Dad had prepared the playing area even more diligently than usual, knowing it was her first game back.

As she, the team, the opposition, the match officials and staff milled around, Matt approached. Tension stiffened her joints.

'Hey,' he said.

'Hey.'

'Ray says... play nice in his garden.' The amusement in Matt's lovely eyes was unmissable.

'I'm playing, which is a start.'

'True.' He nodded. Slowly, awkwardly, guardedly. 'So... go well.'

'Thanks.'

He shrugged his strong, defined shoulders. 'It's a day for seam.' He smiled. 'I mean, I'm no expert, but...'

She examined the sky. 'Let's hope, eh?'

A familiar piercing whistle cut the air. Dad was beckoning from across the pitch.

'Better go.' Matt jogged away.

She watched his toned backside, sighed, then went to the pavilion to change.

Half an hour later, Eden and the team walked out. Her heart swelled. The ups always outweighed the downs... didn't they? The crowd was applauding, the music blaring, flame jets belching. The stage was set. Hopefully she could perform, not fluff her lines.

The Scorpions fanned out into their fielding positions. Team captain Danica tossed Brooke the ball.

From her position at Deep Backward Point, Eden watched as Brooke bowled a faultless first over. Swallowing down nerves, she jogged to the middle, patting her friend's shoulder as she passed.

'Bowled, Tweed.'

'Thanks, babe.'

Danica handed her the ball. They discussed field settings.

'Let's go, Edie!' Wicketkeeper Izzy clapped her huge gloves.

The announcer's voice rang from the speakers. "Bowling from the City End, number 9, Eden Palmer."

She took a few deep breaths, paced to her mark, turned and paused. The batter took guard. She rubbed a thumb across the ball's stitching.

Finally. It's been too long. Let's do this.

Eden ran in.

The delivery was short and wide. The batter slashed it for 4.

Shit.

She trudged back to the start of her run-up, plucking the ball out of the air as Bryony lobbed it over. She gripped the ball, took a breath, and accelerated in.

Not short this time, but Leg side, on the pads, and clipped away for another 4. Applause from the visiting fans.

Shit.

As Eden walked back to her mark, a familiar dependency took told. Would this over go for 17, as it had in the Final? Was the monkey still on her back?

Breathe, dammit.

What would Lily say? "Go easy on *you*, Eden."

A small scoff escaped her lips.

Here I am, a pro athlete, asking a teenager for advice. What a mess.

As she caught the ball in her left hand, the bracelets clinked.

She slowed to a halt, fingering the beads. Despite curiosity at Rose's bracelets, Eden had never felt in need of an emotional or mental support mechanism, a touchstone.

The past winter had proven that to be a lie. She wasn't as resilient as she'd believed. Whilst teammates had rallied around, offering support, telling Eden that she hadn't single-handedly cost them the game, it never sunk in. Even sessions with the team psychologist hadn't been a magic cure-all.

If she'd had this motivational, grounding jewellery on that godawful day, would things have been different? It was odd and crazy to think that a few lettered trinkets could have saved a lot of heartbreak... and her relationship. But there was no point in dwelling on the past. Moving on was the only way.

It was time to do it *now*. Proof that you can train regularly, work on your fitness and technique, but that was only part of the game, of the job. She didn't want to fail under pressure again. Disappointing the team and the coach was one thing, but the emotional derailment was worse, because it had hurt people she cared about.

FOCUS. BREATHE.

Eden studied the batter, her stance. Replayed yesterday's pre-game briefing. Adjusted her grip to fashion a wobble seam delivery. Tightened her jaw. Ran in.

The batter played and missed... by millimetres. Izzy's hands came to her head in anguish.

Dani clapped hard. 'Bowled, Edie!'

Eden paced purposefully back to her mark, fingering the beads. *Another one of those, please.*

But the next delivery was on the bowler's pads and defended with a straight bat. Ditto the next. The last ball of the over seamed beautifully, and for a split-second Eden thought it would be nicked, but the batter left it alone.

With her chest heaving in effort and pride, Eden collected her cap from the umpire, threaded her dark brown ponytail through the fastening, and jogged towards her fielding spot.

Brooke crossed in front, raising a palm. '*Bringing* it, babe.'

Eden high-fived. 'You too.'

Then, as if to prove the fact, Brooke's next delivery, her seventh of the day, was a missile that tore through the batter's defence and ripped out her middle stump.

Looks like I'm cooking tonight.

Do I care? Hell no. But I'd like at least one scalp.

And in Eden's next over, she took it.

For the first time in a long while, life wasn't a pile of shit.

18th Over

Matt punched the air. 'Come on, baby!'

Then he cringed, shoulders hunching. Luckily, there was nobody within earshot—he'd gone walkabout from the groundsman's area.

She's not your baby. She's nobody's.

Nevertheless, the sentiment stood—he was pleased that Eden was back in the groove. However hurt he'd felt by being unceremoniously dumped, he still wanted the best for her.

He circumnavigated the pitch, waving to a few familiar faces. At Deep Backward Point, he gave Eden a double thumbs-up.

'Thanks,' she mouthed.

Back at the familiar pitchside home, he climbed onto the roller—a favourite vantage point.

Eggs wandered across and passed Matt a mug of tea. He leant on the machine, attention fixed on the nearby fielder.

'What's up with her belly?'

Eggs' detailed scrutiny of Brooke's frame had apparently moved away from the chest and backside, which counted as a win.

'Yeah, I noticed that,' Matt replied. 'I think either she's a human cyborg from the future, or it's an insulin pump.'

Please, Eggs, don't say you'd like to pump her full of something besides insulin.

'Ah. That's a bugger.'

'I'd imagine so.'

'Her bloke must be a really understanding sod,' Eggs said.

'Pretty sure she doesn't have one.'

'Result.'

Matt shot him a look. 'Won't Geraldine get jealous?'

Eggs threw a fake punch. 'I'm not into cougars.'

'She's a sure thing,' he teased. 'And she'll give you a good Google Review...'

'Sod off.' Eggs drained his mug. Then his face lit up. 'Hang on. You think Brooke would give me a Google Review? For the removal what we did for her?'

Matt shrugged. 'Why don't you ask her?'

Eggs puffed out his chest. 'I will.'

A few minutes later, there was a break in play when the batter asked for a new bat. Brooke was loitering nearby, retying her laces.

'Hey, Brooke?' Eggs called.

She turned. 'Hey.'

'Can I ask you a favour?'

'Washing my hair.'

Matt held in laughter.

'Eh?' Eggs said.

'Sorry. I'm not around that evening.'

Eggs frowned deeply. 'What evening?'

'Whatever evening you were thinking of.'

Eggs looked at Matt, open-mouthed, utterly lost. Brooke offered Matt a wink. He returned the gesture.

The stadium PA boomed. "Returning from the Pavilion End, number 9, Eden Palmer."

Brooke returned her focus to the game.

Eggs shot Matt a query. 'What was that about?'

'She doesn't want to spoil you for Geraldine.'

'I wasn't—'

'I know, mate. But why don't *I* ask Brooke for the review?'

Eggs snorted. 'Yeah. She likes *you* well enough.'

Matt spread his arms. 'What's not to like?'

'What happened to "Cricketers are a pain in the arse"?'

'I never said that! Eden had a tough time, that's all. Besides, so what if Brooke and I get on?'

Eggs grinned suggestively. 'I bet she wouldn't be *washing her hair* if you asked for a Google Review.'

Matt frowned. 'I *said* I'll ask her.'

'Why not ask her out, n'all?'

Matt laughed. 'It's a hiding to nothing.'

'How come?'

'It will piss Ray off, it will piss Eden off, and there's the whole "once bitten, twice shy" thing.'

Eggs scratched his chin. 'You said those two aren't the same. Don't even look the same. One's a fit blonde, the other's a fit—'

'Alright. They're not peas in a pod. But if I dated Brooke, Eden would have an issue.'

Eggs snorted. 'What do you care? She dumped you. She had her chance. Come on, Matty, you can't worry about that.'

Matt hopped down from the roller. 'They're best mates, okay?'

'Not any more, seems like.'

Matt debated that. The girls appeared to have mended their split, but weren't yet at the stage of having the stitches removed.

'Look, thanks for the nudge, but the last thing I want to do is drive a wedge between them.'

'Why not? Brooke already did that to you and Eden, by smacking her round the park.'

Matt's stomach bottomed out. 'It wasn't that.'

'Well, no. Eden caused it by bowling like shit. Right?'

The harsh truth, spoken aloud, hit Matt like a cannonball. Words he'd never dare say to Eden, even with the best intentions. That would have been a red rag to a bull, certainly when her gloom was deepest.

But surely Eden knew she'd brought the house of cards tumbling down. If not last September, then certainly the previous year, when she'd essentially cheated Brooke out of her wicket with a Mankad borne of frustration.

Would Eden realise that she, not he or Brooke, was at fault? Only that admission, and self-forgiveness, might mend things between them all.

When the game finished, the Scorpions coming out on top, Ray did something uncharacteristic. He invited Matt to the pub. In three years working together, this was only the second time they'd socialised.

The first occasion was last June, for Ray's birthday. The Ground Staff team had gathered to raise a glass to the boss, then drifted away, one by one. The last two men standing—or sitting, gradually more sloppily—were Matt and his girlfriend's father.

As those halcyon days had passed, what could have precipitated today's extracurricular visit? As Matt entered the Rose & Crown, it was hard to suppress worry.

Ray was at the bar and insisted on buying. To start, there was small talk about the day's game, Eggs' hilarious strikeout with Brooke, and the workload for the coming days.

Matt sensed the guy was marking time.

Silence fell.

Ray sipped his pint. 'A while back, you were talking about moving away.'

Matt swallowed hard. 'Yeah. I was.'

'And now?'

'Not necessarily. But if you want me to, I will.'

Ray frowned. 'Why would I?'

'Because I made Eden's life worse.'

Ray nodded slowly. 'Maybe. But I think the blame is equal.'

The man was only using the information he had, which, at the time, was probably a tirade from Eden about how Matt had been AWOL, insensitive and unhelpful. But a father will always protect his daughter.

'What could I have done differently?'

'You wish you had?'

'I wish I hadn't lost her,' Matt said.

Ray drank. 'You still care about her?'

'I can't turn my feelings off like a tap.'

Ray smiled. 'Same as my Eden. You two are more alike than you think.'

Matt's head dipped. 'It's the helplessness. Not being able to pull her out of the quicksand. Maybe I was naïve to expect love would be enough, a spell to ward off bad things.' He fingered the wooden tabletop. 'Or more likely I believed I was good enough for her, could handle her.'

'You did okay for a year or so.'

Matt scoffed. '"Okay" is not enough for someone like Eden. She needs "brilliant" or "perfect".'

Ray exhaled heavily, gripping Matt's shoulder. 'Fuck, son, you really loved her, didn't you?'

Matt's chest swelled. From memory, this was the first time Ray had called him "son". Yes, it was a casual term, but he had always thought of the man as a surrogate father. Either way, this didn't sound like the language of a man who was ready to sack him, suggest he left the ground, demand an apology, or ban him from being around Eden ever again.

Ray had hit the nail on the head. Matt had loved Eden. Deeply.

'I'm young and reckless, I know.'

Ray laughed sadly. 'I married her mum when I was younger than you. And we had thirty great years.' He toyed with his pint. 'It's like Eden's coach said when she was selected for her first senior game at seventeen. "If you're good enough, you're old enough".'

Matt snorted. 'Lasting not even two years means I'm not good *or* old enough.'

'Christ, you've caught the wallowing bug off her.'

'Would you rather I brushed it off? What if I'd come back to work, the day after, and been all sunny, as if breaking up with Eden was no big thing? You'd suspect I never loved her that much if I was able to say, "What the hell" and start looking for the next person.'

Ray shot a knowing look. 'Seems like you're looking for the next person anyway.'

Matt arched back. 'Brooke? Well, if you want to look down your nose, go ahead.'

'Not my business.'

'Why not? It concerns Eden. So which is it? I should move on, or I should wallow? When is it okay for me to be open to another relationship?'

Ray scoffed. 'Why the fuck are you asking me? I'm not your dad. And I'm hardly the best person for relationship advice.'

'Thirty years says so.'

Ray shook his head. 'If you're expecting me to say, "Talk to Eden and work it out" or "Stay the fuck away from my daughter", I'm giving you neither. You're a grown-up, Matt. A lot more than... some people.'

'You didn't hire Ben for his emotional maturity.'

'No. I hired a worker. No different from you.' Ray scrutinised Matt's face. 'But you've really stepped up. One of my best ever hires.'

'Thanks, Ray. That means a lot.'

The man tossed up a hand, as if dismissing a foolish, unmanly, emotional outburst. 'What I'm saying is that you and Eden, whatever happened, whatever might still happen, doesn't go on your work record. Doesn't... hurt your chances.'

Matt's heart skipped a beat. 'Right. Thanks.'

'I hope you'll stay. Especially with Alan leaving. If you get my drift.'

Under the table, Matt clenched a fist.

Things with Ray were square. He and Brooke were in a good place. If the relationship—friendship—with Eden could be recovered, all would again be rosy in the garden.

19th Over

Eden was in mixed spirits as she drove home from the game.

Whilst she was pleased with her performance of 2 for 55 from 10 overs, the voice at the back of her head wouldn't go away. Brooke had declined a lift, saying she was staying behind to chat to someone. Little Miss Scratchy put two and two together and reckoned Brooke was meeting Matt. After all, why say "someone" rather than specify a name? You only do that when you're hiding something.

That put paid to any hope of a convivial evening in. Even stranger, given that Brooke had won the bet and was entitled to be the beneficiary of Eden's cooking.

It seemed like "two steps forward, one step back" in their reconciliation.

At home, as Eden sat on the sofa, eating dinner, the conflict in her head didn't abate. The last two weeks with Brooke in the house had made life more bearable, and she missed her friend. Reliving the day, laughing about it, maybe dissecting the reasons for their success or failure against certain batters, ushering each other onto better things.

At the same time, evenings without Brooke were par for the course. The social butterfly would always prefer a café, bar, or club. Never overdoing things, but somehow being *more* than Eden, in every way. Yet, despite knowing that this was who her best friend *was*, the green-eyed monster wouldn't go away.

Matt would tell me I'm being silly. I hope I am.

Of course, there was someone else who'd tell her the same. A neutral voice. Someone she owed a drink.

An hour later, she met Phoebe at a bar in town.

'What do you want to drink?'

Phoebe raised a hand. 'Oh no. I still owe you one. Giving me a heads-up that a house was coming on the market is one thing, but Ray's place? I mean, it's nuts, isn't it?'

It felt a lifetime ago that she'd told her teammate that Dad was selling up—probably because a torrent of water had passed under the bridge in the last few months. It was a miracle that the bridge hadn't been washed away.

Whilst it was a circumstance filled with joy—that Jade and Phoebe were getting a place together, and the timing was perfect—it felt odd that her childhood home would now belong to friends.

'A *good* crazy, though,' she replied.

Phoebe pointed at the row of optics. 'Yeah. So?'

'Virgin Margarita.'

Phoebe led her to a table, and they sipped their drinks.

'Look, it's nice to finally chat, but I won't rake over things, Ede. You're trying to put it behind you. And your spell today shows you're nearly there.'

Involuntarily, Eden snorted. 'Hmm.'

'You're *allowed* to paddle like hell underneath. At home or at work. You think I'm not a tiny bit worried about what Jet and I are doing?'

Eden smiled inside. Phoebe calling her girlfriend "Jet", the squad nickname, was a small curio. Everyone called Brooke "Harry", but Eden used a pet name because their friendship was close. While Jet was a brilliant moniker for Jade Black, Eden suspected that an un-revealed, more tender name was used at home. A home that was soon to change, with the two surely on a path to marriage.

'I'm not worried, Phoebs. You've been going, what, three years?'

The girl stirred her drink. 'There are never any gimmes.'

'No shit,' Eden murmured. She shook her head. 'Sorry. This isn't about me. And don't you dare break up. One split in that house is plenty. I'll have it de-hexed, if that helps.'

Phoebe chuckled. 'Yeah, the last thing you need is any more guilt.'

She clamped her mouth over a rebuttal. Phoebe's comment was a throwaway—just a shame that it resonated. She slurped her mocktail.

Phoebe laid her hand on Eden's. 'What? What did I say?'

Eden sighed. 'Nothing. It's me.'

'Then spill. Permission for it to be about you for a few minutes. Come on, Ede. I wish to hell you'd leant on me earlier. Do it now. Please.'

She didn't point out the girl's absence from the UK for most of the closed season. Phoebe had won a franchise title in Australia and been on an England Development camp in Oman. She wished that Phoebe had been around, a shoulder to—literally—cry on. It was a futile wish. The lives and careers of teammates had to carry on. Besides, she'd had Matt's shoulder... until she shoved it away.

'I came *this* close to giving up. Stupid, right?'

'Hell, yes,' Phoebe said firmly. 'You're stronger than that. Lesson One is to ignore the dickheads.'

Her head fell. 'Well, I failed that test. But, y'know, maybe guilt is allowed.' She took a deep breath, then a long, slow sip of drink. 'I'm good at what I do. I know that. But one more troll from hell and I might have stopped believing it. If I'd jacked it all in, that Scotty fucker would have won, and you can't give those people the satisfaction.' She scoffed, clenching a fist. 'He already had me on my guard any time I went out.'

'I'm not surprised.'

Waves of memory, salty and stinging, crashed through Eden's skull. 'I didn't do it right, Phoebs. I thought I knew better, was stronger. Going to training with you all, putting on a brave face, but inside I was dying. If I'd had any fucking sense, I'd have deleted Insta from my phone *the second* we walked off that pitch.'

'You weren't to know.'

'No. And I'd have hated to throw away all the good stuff. To vanish without a word.'

Phoebe nodded hard. 'Exactly. You're a role model, Eden. I've seen your feed. People love you. Girls like Lily look up to you.' Her smile was reflective. 'But the bad apples can spoil all that. It's inevitable, sadly.'

She sighed, rubbing her eyes. 'I should have gone to the team psych earlier, not tried to bottle it up, to deal. I shouldn't have leant so hard on Matt.'

'Hindsight is a wonderful thing, Ede. But you got through it somehow. You've got balls, girl.'

She met her friend's eye. 'What actually stopped me, in a funny way, is Mum. Oh, the irony. If I hung up my pads, it would make the tug of war between her and Dad redundant. And it cost them the marriage. If I gave up cricket because I failed one test, that would be weak. And I couldn't bear the guilt of the divorce, which was pretty much my fault, being avoidable. I stood up to my parents about my career. I should bloody well be able to see off some cowardly, sexist bellend.'

Phoebe gripped Eden's hand. Her eyes were moist. 'Absolutely, babe. And here you are.' She raised her glass in a toast.

'But with casualties strewn behind me, right? Brooke, and Matt, and almost Dad. I bet he knew, too. He fought my corner with Mum, and he'd look an idiot if I took the easy way out.' Dark humour spiked into her mind. 'I suppose there's a silver lining. You get to live in the old sod's place. Those blue plaque people will probably be along in a while, wanting to put up a sign because "the great and mighty Eden Palmer once lived at this address".'

Phoebe laughed, spraying droplets of dirty martini across the table. The levity caught Eden, and quickly she was chuckling.

Enough of this navel-gazing. Let's just have fun.

And she did.

At breakfast, Eden studiously avoided asking what Brooke had done the previous evening. Instead, they debriefed the game and then discussed the day's activities. A few players were doing a community outreach session at a local school—one of the club's regular initiatives. Eden had done a couple before, but today's had a special meaning.

They arrived at Grove Lane Primary at ten o'clock and met up with Jade and Ellie, plus a couple of Scorpions coaching staff.

A lot had changed in the sixteen years since Eden left, yet the place lived in her heart. Mr Sutton, her gym teacher. Jack, the boy she loved playing catch with. Rushing to the gate at the end of lessons to see Dad.

Someone made a beeline for Ellie Waites, who took the girl in an embrace.

'What gives?' Brooke asked.

'That's Grace,' Eden replied. 'She's... pretty special, person and player.'

'A future Scorpion?'

'Safest best since yesterday's.' Eden winked.

'Oh. Yeah. Missed my winnings. Mac 'n' cheese tonight?'

'Want any mash with that?' Eden joked.

'Nah. You're alright.'

'Come on, let's go.'

'Yes, *coach*.'

There was a gentle teasing in Brooke's tone. Surely she wasn't envious? She'd never been too interested in connecting with the next generation of female cricketers. She wasn't as inherently nurturing as Eden, as maternal. Or maybe she hadn't had the time or opportunity to find someone she wanted to guide, to mentor.

Clearly, Ellie and Grace had a bond, as did Eden and Lily. So what if Brooke didn't lean as hard into paying things forward? Everyone was built differently.

The team coaches, along with a couple of teachers, escorted the dozen Year 6 girls to the playing field on one side of the school campus. Ellie walked alongside Grace, deep in conversation. Jade chatted to the Head of PE.

On the field, the staff set up a couple of wickets, then the girls were gathered together and Ellie introduced everyone.

'This is really cool,' Brooke murmured.

'They must do this at the Stars, though?'

'Started last season. I never got asked. Don't know what that says about me.' Brooke looked sheepish, downcast.

'You're too good, Tweedie. That's the problem. Can't put the star performer in front of impressionable girls. They'll think, "How can I ever be that good?"' Eden nudged her.

'Stirrer.'

'What, you're worried we'll fall out? Been there, got the t-shirt. Hoodie. Mug. Tote bag.'

Brooke looked her straight. 'At least you're joking about it.'

'We never fought in the playground. Silly to start now.'

'Not sure we were ever *in* a playground.'

'Club, pitch, hall of residence. You know what I mean.'

Brooke squeezed Eden's arm. 'Salad days.'

'Every day is a salad day when you have this.' Eden tapped the device in the small of Brooke's back.

Brooke laughed. 'Well, maybe not with a roast.'

'Ooh, that should be my next cookery faux pas.'

'I think that's something we *would* fight about.'

'Let's leave fighting for a while, eh?'

'Always, Ede.' Brooke pointed. 'Come on, show me the ropes.'

'Okay,' she said earnestly. 'There are two teams. One is what we call the batting side, the other—'

Brooke slapped Eden's shoulder. 'Now you *are* stirring.'

'Sorry.' She painted on a serious face. 'Oh, FYI, Grace has autism, so go easy, okay?'

Brooke's smile faded. 'S'ok. So does my nephew.'

'Yeah, but does he know your economy rate?'

'Doubt it. He's not into cricket.'

Eden beamed. 'Good. Don't need *boys* in the sport, do we? Ugh.'

The children were split into four groups of three, with Ellie, Jade, Eden and Brooke working with one group each. Ellie and Jade did batting exercises, Eden and Brooke handled bowling.

Occasionally, Eden checked how her friend was getting on. At one point, Brooke was kneeling down and showing a redheaded girl the insulin sensor on her upper arm. Then the girl tugged up her sleeve to reveal a similar small white disc.

Eden's soul creased.

You have a hell of a ride ahead, sweetheart. But if you can be as fearless as my friend, the world is your oyster. She doesn't let a lifelong illness define her actions, yet six bad balls haunted me for months.

Eden eyed the girl, who was being given a tour of Brooke's insulin pump.

Yeah, sweetheart. She's a lot better role model than me, in many ways.

Then Brooke beckoned, and Eden walked over.

'Eden, this is Sophie. She's been dying to meet you.'

20th Over

On Thursday morning, Matt headed to the ground with a spring in his step. He'd resolved to recommit to his role and end the emotional flip-flopping about the benefits of staying versus the heartache of seeing Eden every day.

He needed to live the mantra that he'd failed to instil in her—move on.

It was a team training day, and the players were scattered across the pitch, engaged in various activities. For the Ground Staff, it was a day for equipment maintenance and preparing a strip on the nursery pitch.

Matt was in the stadium building, emerging from the Gents, when Brooke crossed his path, a kit rucksack on her back and a smaller plastic bag in her hand.

'Hey, Matt.'

Did I zip? Please say I zipped.

'Hey. How's it going?'

'Good. Gummy?'

'Always.'

Brooke tipped the packet over his palm. A single, last sweet plopped out.

'Thanks for looking after *my* blood sugar,' he joked.

'Sorry. Must have given away too many at the school yesterday. I met this girl...' She waved it away. 'Not important. Tell you later.'

'Sure. Have a good session.' He chewed the gummy.

'Enjoy my last Rolo!' She winked.

His neck prickled. That reference had only one meaning—a romantic gesture.

Don't do this to me, Brooke. Especially not when you're sashaying away like that.

Still, he stopped chewing and sucked languorously.

Four hours later, he was perched on the roller, cuppa in hand, scrolling through a webpage on his phone. Ray had asked him to research something.

The players had ebbed away towards the pavilion, but Brooke was heading his way. She was moving slowly, scanning the ground ahead. Had she dropped an earring? A bat or a ball is easy to spot.

'What's up?' He slid down to the turf, not spilling a drop of tea.

'Have you seen my med bag?' she asked, uncharacteristically mousy.

He glanced around. 'It was never here. Was it?'

She leant on the roller. 'Shit.'

His eyes widened. 'Are you okay?'

'I will be.' But her face was pale.

He guided her to sit on the roller's side step. Her arm quivered.

He crouched. 'Brooke, what do you need?'

She licked her lips. 'Think I'm low.'

'So, check.'

'Yeah.' She pulled up her shirt and winkled the monitor from the wide belt band.

His pulse raced. He surveyed the area. The pitch was deserted. Ray and Eggs were at the nursery ground.

She looked at the screen. 'Yeah. I am.'

He raised a finger. 'Gimme a second.'

He pelted to the groundskeeper's hut, feverishly scoured around, located an unopened packet of chocolate digestives, and raced back to Brooke. Collapsing to his knees, in a pose that could have appeared like a marriage proposal to anyone looking, tore open the packet and pressed it into her hands.

Brooke ate hungrily. 'This is okay, but I could really do with a juice. Or a Coke.'

'Okay, wait there.'

'I was going to practice a few run-ups, but...' She smiled weakly.

He jogged back to the hut, grabbed two cans from the fridge, and pelted back to Brooke.

She cracked open the can and slugged down the sweet soda.

'Thanks, Matt.' She shook her head. 'My fault for giving sweets to kids.'

'If diabetes hates generosity, then it's even worse than I thought.'

She smiled. 'No. I pushed too hard today. Worried about Rojo coming back next game. Don't want to lose my spot. Should have eaten better when I noticed all the sweets were gone.'

He shrugged. 'We all make mistakes.'

'Lucky you were here.'

He patted the roller's seat. 'Best view in the house.'

'You've obviously never been on the Member's Balcony.'

'Bit fancy for a gardener.'

She covered her eyes, peeking through her fingers. 'Sorry.'

'No. I should let it go.'

She gazed around. 'Can I?' She pointed at the seat.

'Providing you don't fall off, in your weakened condition.'

She flapped a hand. 'You can always give me the kiss of life.'

'I'm no paramedic.'

'Still, you could give it a go.'

His palms moistened. 'I think Eggs would be over here like a shot, waving fake First Aider credentials.'

She eye-rolled. 'Doesn't surprise me.'

'He's... maybe not as bad as he appears.'

'Well, he'll need a shit ton of luck and two bottles of Prosecco inside me. Or crashed out in a diabetic coma.'

Matt laughed. Then it didn't seem funny. 'Don't do that, Brooke. This is bad enough.'

'Aw, it's nothing. But thanks for your help.'

'No worries. Still want to try the Dress Circle?' He indicated the seat.

'Sure. Hopefully, this pro athlete can manage the step up.' She gingerly climbed onto the roller and eased into the single seat. 'Wow. I can almost see my house from here.'

He perched on the vehicle's side bolster. 'Very funny.'

She munched another biscuit. 'Do you sit up here and watch Ede?'

'You mean watched, past tense?' His forehead pinched.

'Don't tell me you refuse to now.' Her expression was sympathetic.

'No. I mean it's... different between us. Night and day. You two are hardly the same as you were... before.'

Brooke nodded sagely. 'We're not braiding each other's hair quite yet.'

He thought for a second. Would these words break a confidence? What if Brooke relayed them to Eden?

Sod it. We're already broken up.

'For what it's worth, I'm on your side about the Mankad... or Womankad as Eggs calls it.' He eye-rolled theatrically.

Brooke smiled, groaning. 'Hilarious. Tell Eggs not to give up the day job. But... thanks.' She tapped his knee.

'I'm not sure what's worse, that she felt the need to do it, or the fallout.'

'The fallout, definitely. So I lost my wicket? Shit happens. Was I pissed off? Hell yes. So I know how she feels about the Cup game. But it wasn't *personal*, by either of us. I'd never hurt Ede.' She chuckled sadly. 'Seems like she's good at doing that herself.'

Matt grimaced. 'Yeah.'

'How... did she do it? Break her finger, I mean. She's been very cagey.'

'Embarrassed, probably. She never told me, but Ray got the headlines.' He sighed. 'After she kicked me out of the house, she took her frustration out on the wall.'

Brooke scoffed. 'Fucking stupid idea.'

'I guess she flew into a rage. All the wheels had come off. She'd lost you, lost me, and lost her mental health, her equanimity.' His chin fell. 'All because I was a useless boyfriend.'

She took his hand and squeezed it. 'No. My batting did that. I'd give everything if it had been someone else I'd hit over the boundary. But it wasn't. It was Ede. And she forgot the first rule of cricket.'

'Is that "You don't talk about cricket"?'

She laughed, a spike of levity that vanished as quickly as it came. 'No. The rule is that when you walk off, when you cross the rope, the rivalry is over and it's back to being mates again.'

'But she's normally good at that. What changed?'

'Honestly? Pressure. Her first Final. A big stage. England scouts in the Press box. And we all want that phone call.'

He frowned. 'She never really talked about the national squad.'

'Typical Ede. Never believes she's good enough. Which is bollocks. We may be mates, but we're always competing, deep down.' She eyed him. 'And you know the irony? Ede is the one with the natural talent. I have to work hard at it.'

He blew out a slow breath. 'Wow. That took some admitting.'

'To myself? No. To you? Not particularly. You're... easy to talk to. Be with.' She looked down. 'I see why Ede... Never mind.'

His heart rattled. 'But I fucked up, Brooke. *That's* the takeaway. I tried to help her through the worst times... and I couldn't do it.' He smiled forlornly. 'She needs someone stronger. So maybe everything that happened was for the best.'

She clasped his knee. 'It was a blip, that's all. I've known her ten years, and she was never that low. Life bowled the two of you an unplayable delivery. They're pretty rare, believe me. I have experience.' She winked. 'Next time, you might hit a six. And there's nothing better than a perfect connection, when you feel on top of the world.'

'Especially when you bat at ten or eleven.' He beamed.

Her mouth formed an O. 'You cheeky sod!' She shoved him. 'I've hit my share of sixes.'

'Hmm. How many?'

'Honestly?'

'I can always look up the facts. Or ask Eden.' He shot a knowing look.

'Spoilsport. Okay, I've hit three. One at Uni, one at a charity event, and one in a warmup game.'

'But none professionally?'

She whacked his thigh. 'Rub it in, why don't you?'

'I bet Eden already does that.'

'Because she's hit four, professionally? Yeah, it's cropped up once or twice. She's better with the bat *as well as* the ball. For a best friend, she's *really* fucking annoying.' She laughed.

'Amen to that.'

His sentiment was the same as Brooke's—Eden had her faults, but she was also amazing and utterly adorable.

Quite like Brooke, in fact.

21st Over

Eden was glad that she and Brooke hadn't travelled to the stadium together. She needed time and space to process what she'd seen.

Part of it was clear as day, if you knew the signs of diabetic distress. Actually, she was pleased that Matt had intervened quickly. Proud, actually, of her ex. That's the type of guy he was—laden with compassion.

Watching from the pavilion, she'd been tempted to pelt across the field to help, but it would have partially been done out of nosiness, a sense of protection—which wasn't helpful. Little Miss Scratchy needed to be put back in her box.

But it was hard. Even harder with every passing minute, watching Matt and Brooke deep in conversation, laughter and, at the end, a hug.

A hug of gratitude on Brooke's part, surely? She wouldn't be so tone deaf as to make a pass at Matt, given how finely balanced things are between all three of us. Would she?

Unless Brooke was on a crusade, as in the Cup Final. None of this was anti-Eden, only pro-Brooke. Different perspective entirely. Still, the outcome was the same.

Eden drove home feeling aggrieved. The two people who'd contributed to months of malaise were teaming up to drag out the pain. Just when she and Brooke had patched things up, Casanova Matt was driving a wedge between them. His insensitivity during the winter wasn't a blip. It was a portent.

Brooke arrived home while Eden was making dinner.

She plopped supermarket shopping bags on the kitchen floor. 'Hi, Ede.'

'Tweed.'

Brooke left, returning with her kit bag, which she dumped in the living room. Then she proceeded to put items in the fridge and cupboards.

Eden forced down a spike of resentment. 'You okay? You looked a bit peaky at the end there.'

Brooke leant on the worktop. 'I messed up my levels. Forgot I'd moved my med bag. But Matt was a star.'

'Oh, yeah?' Eden feigned ignorance.

'He was right on point. Lucky your dad's a biscuit addict.'

'Hmm. Less lucky for his arteries, though. But this isn't about Dad.'

Brooke folded her arms. 'What's it about?'

Eden had failed to mask her suspicions. 'Nothing. Just pissed off you didn't call me when you crashed.' That was partially true.

'Like I'm going to run around the place looking for you.' She tutted, stacking the fruit bowl. 'What happened to this being a team game? You're not the only one who knows about my condition. I didn't join the Scorpions because I needed you there as a safety net. I managed for long enough, thank you.'

'Suddenly it's wrong for me to give a shit?'

Brooke peeled a banana like she was ripping off wallpaper. 'You gave a shit *so much* that you didn't even wait for me to come back to the locker room and check I was okay?'

'Clearly you were okay because you had Doctor Matt on hand.'

'Actually, yes, I *was* okay. I'd told him about the disease... before,' she looked away guiltily, 'So he had an idea what to do.'

A lump caught in Eden's throat. The desire to interrogate Brooke about "before" was strong—but also the recipe for an argument. What if Tweedie said something *was* going on between her and Matt? That would be a dagger to the heart.

No, not the heart. The back.

Better not to know. 'Well... good. I suppose.'

Brooke slowly shook her head. 'So much for the accountant. Two plus two equals four, not five.'

Eden frowned. 'What's that supposed to mean?'

'I'm not fighting you for a *guy*, Ede.'

Eden put her hands on her hips. 'Who says I'd fight you?'

Brooke circled a finger around Eden's face. 'This.'

Eden scoffed. 'Maybe *you've* added up and made five. Ever think that I was worried about you, and annoyed that you didn't lean on me?'

'There's always *something*, isn't there?'

'You'd rather I didn't care? You want us to go back to how it was before? No WhatsApp's for six months?'

'I think that was your problem, not mine,' Brooke said.

'Hell yes, it was my problem. I had a million of them.'

'And I understood, absolutely. Which is why I gave you space. And no, before you say it, *not* out of guilt. Out of reading the room. Was I hurt that you didn't ask for my help when you got the death threat? Damn right. We're *mates*. You can't shut yourself away and try to deal with it on your own.'

'I wasn't on my own,' Eden protested. 'I had Matt.'

'Yeah, and look how *that* worked out.'

'Great. Thanks a bunch.' Eden turned her back.

Brooke sighed loudly. 'All I meant was that if you'd called, I'd have been here in a shot. And who knows you best? Me or him? Huh?'

'I can't drag you halfway across the country to cry on your shoulder.'

'But I should have called you down from the changing room to bring me some food, instead of asking a guy who was six feet away? Come on, Ede! Get some perspective.'

Eden slouched against the fridge, the wind taken from her sails. 'Yeah.'

'I'm grateful you care, babe. But you already gave me a room. Matt brought me a drink. That's it.' She clasped Eden's wrist. 'And I didn't take him into the groundsman's hut and shag him afterwards. Either to thank him, or piss you off. Neither of those is necessary or sensible.'

Eden's eyes were saucers. Brooke was always the more brazen of the two, but this deep insight into Eden's mind was alarming. Scary, yet heartwarming. She felt seen *and* reassured.

Something else was apparent. The two of them were far from being back on an even keel. Eden would never normally consider her friend guilty before being proven innocent. She'd never instinctively think bad of her—but was doing it now.

'Okay,' she conceded.

I still have some way to go on this. Me and her. Me and Matt. Her and Matt.

Six bad balls caused all this. Christ.

But then, I got over two bad balls yesterday. I flipped the switch. Maybe next time, I can get over three bad balls. Then four.

Today, she had to ignore the fact that her teammate was talking to one of the Ground Staff, and letting him help her not to pass out. She didn't want Brooke to ever pass out... or worse.

'Tweed?'

Brooke, who was boiling the kettle, turned. 'Yeah?'

Eden bit her cheek. 'Remember how I used to have a login to your monitoring app?'

The girl's face lit up . 'Yeah.'

Any trustworthy friend, partner, or family member could download an app that allowed them to remotely monitor a diabetic's blood sugar levels. All part of the hardware and software ecosystem. A safety net. A buddy.

When, a couple of years ago, she and Brooke had taken a fortnight's winter break to Tenerife, Eden had assumed the mantle of 'significant other', as both were single at the time. One night, when Brooke had hooked up with a guy in a bar, and Eden had bailed. Returning to the hotel, she'd logged onto the app and spotted that Brooke's blood sugar was dropping.

Hoping it wasn't due to a sudden bout of *physical activity*, she texted Brooke to check up on her. The reply was immediate,

"Just sitting down to eat. Prawns look amazing!"

Brooke didn't have an impending issue. Neither did she get laid. The worst that happened was she failed to apply enough Factor 50 and came home looking like she'd fallen asleep on a sunbed.

Eden had felt closer to her friend than ever before. They'd shared tens of cricket pitches, locker rooms, hotels and bars together, but looking after someone's welfare was special.

Of course, last October, she couldn't give a shit about Brooke's welfare. She was too busy struggling with her own. She may not have removed Brooke's contact details from the phone, but she'd hastily deleted the diabetes app.

Now? It was time for olive branch number two.

'You mind if I have the login again?'

22nd Over

Matt pushed the necklace around his palm.

What should he do? It wasn't always straightforward to judge the correct move with Eden, the best gesture, the perfect thing to say. Not too hard when things were fine between them, but seemingly impossible when the atmosphere was strained.

And now, where were they on that spectrum? Nowhere near cosy, for sure. Still, was returning the necklace fraught with danger? Would it be an unwelcome reminder of a relationship she'd clearly moved on from... certainly much more than he had? If that argument, those marching orders, had been a blip, a regret, Eden could have sought reconciliation, but she hadn't.

He needed to get the necklace out of the house, out of his life. Perhaps then he'd realise that the book had closed, that it was ridiculous to expect her to crawl back, apologise for being impossible, for overreacting.

Yet it had happened once before. At college, he'd dated a girl for six months, then she'd given a lame excuse that he was "too perfect", and felt guilty seeing him when he deserved better. He was poleaxed.

Dumped for being a good boyfriend. Unbelievable.

Mercifully, she'd come to her senses a week later, and they continued dating until graduation, when she announced she was going travelling for a year. He'd got a job as a groundsman at the local football team, a first step on the employment ladder.

So that was that. In different circumstances, they might still be together. But then he wouldn't have met Eden. And, in different circumstances, they too might have continued on. All but for six slaps of willow on ball and one cowardly internet troll.

Don't forget what you did too. Blame where blame is due.

Except he couldn't rewind history, unmake his decision, or reverse the result of that game. What he could do was drive to Eden's, return the necklace, and hope it was another step towards gaining a friendship from the ashes of a deep love.

With a tentative finger, he rang Eden's doorbell.

The face that answered was the wrong one, but still familiar.

'Oh,' he blurted. 'Sorry. I was after Eden. Obviously.'

Brooke's forehead pinched. 'Obviously? What, you'd never come to see me?' She winked.

'Oh, no... I mean... I might, but that would be pretty awkward.'

'Because of Ede? And you two being... what you are, and me and her being... a bit between what we were and what we are. And you and I being, well, friends?'

He sighed. 'Am I worrying too much?'

'Nothing's on a knife edge, if that's what you mean.'

'Then, good.'

She stepped aside. 'The landlord's not in, but the tenant can make you a cuppa. If that's alright? If you have time.'

He hesitated. 'You don't have anywhere to be?'

'No. Ede's having lunch with George, then coaching. I was knocking-in a new bat. Which is boring as fuck. So *please* come in.'

He followed her inside.

'Tea?' she asked, disappearing into the kitchen.

'Always.'

He ambled around the living room. The piano lid was closed, but the music book was open at a familiar tune. One that Eden had played on the morning after they'd got together. He remembered thinking, "Athletic, talented, funny, brainy, pretty, great in bed... and musical too. I am batting well above my station."

He sank onto the stool, laid the necklace on top of the piano, and stroked the lid.

They'd both been in underwear that morning. She'd asked if he played. He'd said, "Not with these fat fingers". She hadn't taken no for an answer. Reluctantly, he'd let her teach him Chopsticks. Then she'd played for him. Then they'd gone back to bed.

He lifted the lid.

During the following year, Eden had taught him a couple of tunes. It turned out he had an ear for it, and those groundskeeping fingers were exactly as dextrous as she expected.

He stared intently at the pattern of black and white, trying to dredge up a sense memory. His fingers moved over the keys, rehearsing.

'Here you go.'

He jolted, narrowly missing the mug Brooke was offering.

'Sorry.' She grimaced. 'Did I interrupt... something?' She set the mug on the piano.

'No. Just... Nothing.'

'Didn't know you played.'

Why would she? They weren't close. He knew she liked sweet tea and gummies, could outrun him, felt like she lived in

Eden's shadow, had a beautiful laugh and a great backside, and occasionally needed a white knight.

What did Brooke know? That he mowed the grass, was passable at keepy-uppy, and had dated her best friend.

'I'll never trouble the Albert Hall,' he replied.

'Still. I suppose everybody has a secret talent.'

'And what's yours?'

She shrugged. 'Don't know.'

'Come on. You don't seem like the modest type.'

She folded her arms. 'Not sure how to take that.'

He winced. 'With the best intentions?'

She scrutinised him for a moment, then a smile broke. 'Okay.'

He drank the perfectly made tea. 'Please tell me you're not Grade 8 piano, or a nuclear physicist, or once water-skied the length of the Amazon.'

She laughed. 'Hardly. I'm also not the brainbox that Ede is.'

'Can you rub your tummy whilst patting your head?'

What am I prattling on about? When did this become "Show me yours and I'll show you mine"?

Brooke mused. 'Not that, but...'

She looked around, then went to the tall corner bookcase. Eden jokingly called it her trophy cabinet. On display were a few medals, two tiny cups, framed photos, and an array of cricket balls on stands. These were invariably souvenirs from memorable games, a few 'match' balls presented for good performance, and one signed by England legend Stuart Broad.

Brooke plucked three balls at random.

Matt's skin prickled, as if someone was walking over his grave. Would Eden mind that her housemate and sort-of-but-not-quite bestie was messing with valued possessions?

What she doesn't know won't hurt her. Right?

Brooke weighed the balls, gathered herself physically, zoned-in mentally... and began to juggle.

This was catnip to Matt. As well as being drawn to Eden's looks and personality, her athleticism was hugely appealing. Brooke also possessed those attributes, with added dexterity.

He watched, mesmerised, as ten then twenty seconds passed. Whilst he hadn't played a note for Brooke, it felt like this was her performance for him.

Myriad thoughts crossed his mind. He considered shouting encouragement or applauding. Then he debated distracting her by pulling faces or pretending to reach for a ball. Then he pondered taking a picture, tickling her, or grabbing a beer and pulling up a seat.

'Ah. The circus is in town,' came a voice.

23rd Over

Eden let her shoulder bag slide to the floor. Brooke collected the three balls out of the air. Matt's face reddened. The air crackled.

Seducing him with cabaret acts, Tweedie?

She glanced at the bookshelf.

Good thing you didn't use the Stuart Broad ball.

Brooke grimaced. 'Sorry, Ede. We just... I mean...'

Matt wrung his hands. 'I came over. Popped in. To drop something off. And you were out. Then Brooke kindly made me a cuppa and...'

There is a LOT of guilt around here. Still, his fly is zipped, so I'm overthinking again.

Brooke carefully put the balls back in their place. 'How was coaching?'

Great deflection, babe.

'Good, thanks,' Eden replied, heart thudding.

'Want a cuppa?' Brooke asked.

Eden swallowed down discomfort, resentment, and a million questions. 'Um... no, ta. Actually, I'm heading off out again.'

'Okay, no worries.'

Matt went to the piano and collected an object.

His expression was sheepish, the smile forced. 'I found this. Finally.' He gently took her hand, lifted it, and placed something there. 'So I thought... bring it over. Why not?' His voice was soft, yet trembling. Nerves? Embarrassment?

She looked at the necklace. The glowing coals in her heart caught alight.

'Oh. Good. Wow. I'd completely forgotten.' She met his eye. 'Thanks.'

His broad shoulders lifted. 'Melt it down, maybe. I hear the price of silver is on the up.'

A snigger escaped her throat. She wished it hadn't. She wanted to be angry at him, at both of them, for getting up to whatever they'd got up to... which was probably nothing, but her hackles were up and she hated that.

'I'll bear it in mind.'

His smile was full. 'I should go.'

She found herself squeezing his hand. 'Thanks. Stay if you want. I think Tweedie's next trick is the high wire. Or sword-swallowing.'

Over Matt's shoulder, Brooke gave her the finger.

Upstairs, Eden hastily called her friend Niamh and arranged to meet for a drink. Now, she wasn't lying about plans to go out.

They met at a tapas bar in town. On the bus, Eden's claws had retracted, but she was still looking forward to a heart-to-heart.

This is good. I didn't stew. I needed to get out of there and not cause a scene. And the first step to curing a problem is admitting it.

Niamh pulled her into a hug. Niamh was a rare and valued thing in Eden's life—a friend outside of cricket. An independent voice.

An umpire. She was a counterpoint to Lily's youthful sass, a voice of reason, a bearer of uncomfortable truths.

As the HR Director of the accountancy firm where Eden had done a spell of maternity cover for one of the administrators, she was a people person. They'd hit it off immediately, partly thanks to Niamh's fiancé's interest in cricket and the women's shared modest ability at the keyboard.

Eden explained that as there was a game tomorrow, it was a no-booze evening and an early night. She was saying this partially as an affirmation, knowing that tipsy ranting was a bad idea, both for her mental health *and* her place on the team.

When the drinks and first plates of food arrived, Eden got down to brass tacks. Stirring her spritz, she recounted all the episodes that had got her hot under the collar—Matt and Brooke in the car park, on the roller, and today's discovery.

'I know what you're going to say. "Why are you so suspicious?" But they seemed so guilty today, so caught in the act.'

Niamh frowned. 'Could it be because they know you're hypersensitive about everything?'

'So it's *my* fault?'

'It sounds like you're desperate to uncover some impropriety, so you can go off on one. You're looking to pick a fight.'

Eden shrank back, distaste in her mouth. 'Thanks a bunch.'

'I'm only saying that you're a glass half-empty person. Look at the last six months. You've been focussing on the breakup and the injury.'

'What else is there? Those were a big deal.'

'Didn't you get another coaching badge? And you did loads of studying. You passed your Certificate.' Niamh put her hand on Eden's. 'Perhaps breaking up with Matt was a blessing in disguise.'

'Fucking good disguise,' she spat.

'Hey. I know it wasn't a fun time, but if it showed you weren't compatible, isn't it better to discover that now than during the marriage?'

'You presume we would ever have got married.'

'I'm trying to show you some perspective. So if he'd asked, would you have said yes?'

Little Miss Scratchy knocked at the inside of her skull. 'Why does it *matter*?'

Niamh leant in. 'Because if you would have said no, it means there *never* was a long-term future for you two, and you're grieving and grouching and blaming and feeling guilty for *nothing*. You're wasting your anger towards him and Brooke.'

Eden arched back. 'I wanted support, and he annoyed me. That's all.'

'Maybe you annoyed him too. Temporarily, I mean. You were happy with him, right? You just had a bad spell.'

'Okay, yes, agreed. But the acid test of a relationship is the bad times. And we *failed*.'

Niamh shook her head. 'You had an *argument*. *We've* had arguments, and we're still friends. You throw in the towel too easily. That's your problem.'

'It's the way to stay sane in this game. We have to be pragmatic, move on from a failure.'

'But you don't move on! You harbour grudges! Do you do that with every umpire that gives you an iffy LBW decision?'

'You don't *get* it, hon. Love and friendships are not the same as cricket. I'm allowed to *care*.'

Niamh's face was sober. 'If only you cared as much about yourself as you do about what other people are doing. You know what this sounds like? You're worried that Brooke's moving in on your territory.'

Eden put two and two together in a microsecond. 'Matt is not my *territory*. He's my ex.'

Niamh raised an index finger. 'Exactly. He's a free agent.'

'Doesn't mean he's free to flirt with Tweedie and rub my nose in it, like, "Look, I found someone better and who isn't a basket case".'

Niamh laughed. 'You aren't a *basket case*. Someone threatened to kill you. You went off the rails. Matt was in the wrong place at the wrong time. It could have been *me* you had a slanging match with. Or Brooke. Somebody was going to get caught in the shrapnel.'

Eden's chin dropped. 'Yeah. That's fair.'

It *wasn't* fair that such a relatively private person online was singled out for abuse, and a social media darling like Brooke only ever attracted heart emojis.

The world is the basket case, not me.

Matt would have to accept that. If he wanted Brooke—or another cricketer, an elite athlete in his life—he'd need to go into it with his eyes open. He'd have to share the physical, emotional and mental struggles... and be able to cope. If he'd realised he couldn't handle the low spells, he'd steer clear of Brooke, which would be a great result all round. Nobody would get hurt.

She smiled reflectively. Apparently, it was possible to be at loggerheads with someone and still want the best for them. If her Uni boyfriend Dan was torn apart by sharks, she wouldn't cheer, even though he'd dumped her by text message.

'How's Ray?' Niamh asked.

Eden was grateful that the woman had moved the topic on. She said he was fine, and they were both looking forward to him moving into the new place, drawing a line under the divorce and hopefully taking care of himself a bit better.

Maybe the apple doesn't fall that far from the tree. It took him two years to regain his sparkle, so surely I'm allowed six months of wallowing?

Yet holding a mirror up to her situation revealed another inconvenient truth. Firstly, she'd tried hard to help Dad move on, but he did it reluctantly and at his own pace. Secondly, she had a window into Matt's challenge, because he'd failed to catalyse a miraculous recovery in her. If she'd naively expected Dad to wake up one morning, bright and carefree, and say, "Enough of that, time to move on", why imagine that *she'd* ever have such a hard-edged epiphany, or expect Matt to know the magic formula for an overnight cleansing of the mental slate?

Idiot.

'Does he still call it the Garden of Eden?' Niamh asked.

'Only in private. He's had enough of embarrassing me.'

She struggled to recall at what point it had ceased to be funny and endearing. Now it was more of a private joke. Dad did it because she was always his little girl, from the first day he'd applied the jokey term to their lawn at home.

Always the gardener, a hobby which informed his career, Dad landscaped the rear garden when Eden was still a toddler. He child-proofed it for her, the apple of his eye. Mum couldn't have a second child, so Eden got every ounce of their love.

Mum had always wanted Eden to follow the safe path into accountancy. If she'd joined Niamh's firm two years ago, rather than doing placement work, cricket would be history, as would the dark shadows of modest fame. Did that mean she should bail on a job she loved? Take the cop-out route, turn her back on her friends, and give Mum the satisfaction of 'I told you so'?

No. She hadn't given up in October, and wouldn't now.

Eden had to carry on, rebuild her career and her private life.

24th Over

Matt's head was all over the place.

It had been a night of tossing and turning, contemplating whether he'd annoyed Eden the previous day. She hadn't been snippy—in fact, she'd accepted the necklace with good humour, tender grace—but something was bubbling beneath the surface.

He'd debated texting her, "Are we okay?", but that covered a lot of ground, and he didn't want to spoil the evening with her friend. On top of this was an apprehension tinged with disappointment on her behalf. Rose had returned from injury and regained her place on the team, thereby consigning Eden to the bench again. Brooke, naturally, kept her spot.

As he circumnavigated the pitch, setting out the boundary sponge, he noted a downbeat edge to Eden's demeanour. Surely she would be aggrieved that her friend had joined the Scorpions. Yet Eden was not a bad person. He wasn't in the habit of falling in love with mean, bitchy women.

Brooke was as sunny as always. During the warmup, they had a quick chat. Matt couldn't help constantly scouring the field for signs of Eden watching, devil rays shooting from her eyes. His stomach roiled, torn between wanting to chat to one beautiful and engaging woman, and not wanting to offend another.

How long would this go on? The trio had to coexist here, and something needed to change. Of course, the easy way out was to tell himself he didn't fancy Brooke, she didn't fancy him, and they didn't get on. Sadly, none of those were true.

The final thing messing with his nerves was that Eggs hadn't shown up. True, he wasn't the lad's keeper, but if he did wind up being promoted to Assistant Groundsman, he'd have an axe to grind. It wasn't acceptable to roll in three hours late on a match day.

Ray had been grouching since eight o'clock. Matt had texted Eggs but received no reply. He hoped the explanation was as simple as a puncture and a dead phone battery.

Then, as the game was about to start, a hoodied figure loped across the outfield. The big screen countdown ticked through 10-9-8-7..., as if Eggs was on a spy mission to save the world before 0 appeared.

In the centre of the pitch, Brooke and Danica were conversing. Matt focussed his attention on that, rather than the impending rollocking that Ray was going to give Eggs. Across the field, under the arc of the dugout shelter, a familiar figure in a sub's tunic sank to the bench.

Five minutes later, Eggs ambled over, carrying less bonhomie than usual. 'Alright.'

Matt gestured towards the groundskeeper's hut. 'He tear you a new one?'

'Not really.'

'What excuse did you give?'

'Couldn't find my house key.'

'Is that accurate?'

Eggs looked offended. 'Course.'

'Is there a "but"?'

'No. Straight up. When I got back home, I realised I'd left my key... somewhere.'

Matt read between the lines. 'When you got back home *this morning*, I'm guessing.'

'Yeah. So?'

'After a night on the piss.'

'No.' Eggs shot him daggers.

'Ah. Club.'

'Nah.'

'Poker game? Torture dungeon? Visiting a sick uncle?'

'Torture dungeon? Gimp masks and all that? What do you take me for?'

Matt shrugged. 'Takes all sorts. And you're definitely *all sorts*, Ben.'

'Whatever. Anyway, I was in bed by midnight, as it goes.'

'Ah. Left your key in the pumpkin coach, did you?'

Eggs frowned. 'Dunno what that is. Point is, I got home, I'd left my key at the other place, and I didn't want to rock up here looking like something the cat dragged in. So I had to scarper over to get the key.'

'You're three hours late. Where was this other place? The *Moon*?'

Eggs shifted on his feet. 'Well, thing is, when I went back for the key, I got... held up.'

'By Dick Turpin, you mean?'

'Dunno who that is. Point is, I'm here now.'

Matt stroked his chin theatrically. 'The bigger point is why you're cagey about "the other place". And the holdup. Would Ray approve? By which I mean would he kick your backside all the way to Cow Corner and back? And I mean Cow Corner at The Oval.'

'Ray wouldn't give a toss. Dunno why *you* do.'

'Okay. So long as you haven't broken the law or anything idiotic like that.'

Eggs laughed. 'Hell no. I mean, if she was fifteen and not—' He stopped as if unceremoniously impaled on an incoming lance.

'Ah.' Matt nodded. 'The fairer sex.' He hoped to hell the woman in question wasn't currently opening the bowling for the Scorpions, or wishing she was. 'Thanks. That wasn't hard, was it?'

'S'pose not.'

'Great.' He sipped his tea. '"Fifteen and not..." what? Fifty?'

'Christ no. I'm not a bloody granny snatcher. Mid-forties, tops.'

Matt's mind, which had been going like a hamster on a wheel, came to a grinding halt. 'It's who I think it is, isn't it?'

Eggs grimaced. 'I only went to check she wasn't gonna sue me.'

'I'm assuming you're safe.'

'It went... well.' He leant in. 'They *know* stuff, these older birds.'

Matt patted Eggs' back. 'Maybe so, but next time, make sure Geraldine knows that a bonus round after breakfast could get you sacked.'

When the lad disappeared to catch up with his duties, Matt gave the mower a thorough clean, always keeping an eye on the game.

Brooke was having a mare. In the opening overs, her line and length were scattershot. In the middle spell, fielding at Long On, she dropped an absolute sitter of a catch. The visitors, the Western Fire, were building an impressive total.

Returning for her final two overs at the end of the game, Brooke put her faith in bowling slower balls to fox the lower order batters. Sadly, her technique was found wanting, and she conceded 20 runs.

As the team left the field at the end of their innings, her shoulders were bowed. Matt recognised that look. At the dugout, there were supportive high-fives and a hug from Eden, which buoyed him. Even if the girls' longtime friendship wasn't fully repaired, they were bonding as teammates.

During the innings break, Matt and Eggs rolled and repainted the wicket, then Ray sent them off to repair holes and tangles in the practice nets.

Atop the roller two hours later, sipping his fourth mug of tea, Matt's attention moved between the action and the scoreboard. The Scorpions had their backs to the wall. They were 228 for 9 with three overs to go and 19 runs needed. This was a tough ask for the final two batters, Brooke and Jade.

Jade was easily the more accomplished with the blade, and had reached 16 when Brooke came in. Matt knew that the best tactics were for Brooke to play for her teammate, getting Jade on strike whenever possible.

So, on the last ball of the 47th over, with Brooke batting, she had to ensure she was at the same end for the next over. The safe option was to defend the delivery for 0. A single run was okay, but it would strand Jade at the wrong end.

Brooke made a good connection with the ball, thumping it towards Square Leg.

'Yes!' she called, accelerating hard.

The batters passed. She saw the fielder fumble, tapped her bat in the crease, turned, and headed for home, a vital 2 that would accomplish all goals.

It was the wrong decision.

Matt's hands went to his head as the fielder arrowed the ball towards the stumps. Brooke was barely halfway down the strip.

'Come on,' he willed through gritted teeth.

The keeper caught the ball. Brooke was four yards out. Three. Two.

The keeper swept off the bails. Brooke dived.

'Fuck,' Matt spat.

Brooke came to rest in a tangle of limbs and dust. The Western Fire mobbed the fielder and the keeper. Brooke lay there, distraught.

"The Western Fire win by two wickets," announced the PA.

Over the last two years, Matt had become invested in the team and its success, not just on Eden's behalf. He felt part of the family. Now, his heart went out to Brooke. She'd tried her best but come up short—and he knew exactly what that felt like.

As the crowd drifted away, Matt helped Ray and Alan bring on the covers, then toured the pitch boundary, checking for issues.

Brooke trotted down the steps and went to the bench, where she picked up her med bag.

'Alright?' he said casually.

'What do *you* think?'

'Hard luck.'

Her jaw set hard. 'It wasn't about luck, but thanks.'

He held up a mollifying hand. 'Damned if you do, damned if you don't.'

'Whatever.' She rooted around in the bag, pulled out a couple of gummies and stuffed them into her mouth. She didn't offer him any.

His scalp prickled. 'Sorry.'

'Not your fault.'

'Oh. I get it.'

'What?'

He folded his arms. 'Your levels are off.'

She frowned. 'What the—?'

'You said that if you're too high, it can make you spiky.'

She looked him up and down, a sneer on her lips. 'Is that what it is?'

'I'm just saying—'

She nodded. 'Ah. Suddenly you're an expert on diabetes. And cricket.'

He took a step back. 'Only trying to help.'

'Well, it's not an insulin thing. It's a talent thing. You wouldn't understand.'

Bile gnawed at his throat. 'I *absolutely* understand what it's like for a player to have a bad game, lose their mojo. And what it's like to be in the line of fire.'

'Good for you.'

He shook his head. 'Is *this* the thanks I get for the other day?' He pointed towards the roller.

'Don't come over all heroic, Matt. There were other people in the stadium.'

'Fine. Whatever. I'll see you around.'

He turned on his heel and headed for the sanctuary of the hut.

Why do I bother? This isn't worth the heartache. I'm not cut out for this shit.

25th Over

In the dressing room, Eden watched as Brooke kept a lid on her disappointment and frustration. For all Eden's weaknesses in dealing with failure, her friend was occasionally prone to being a bear with a sore head.

Eden felt a tiny happiness that Brooke now knew what it was like to cost the Scorpions a game. It was kinship rather than schadenfreude—willing Brooke to fail, to feel that hurt, meant that Eden was hoping the team would lose the match. Whatever else happened, she would never wish that.

The difference between them was that, tomorrow morning, Brooke would be over it. She wouldn't wear the failure as an open wound. She'd move on. Expecting a tail-ender to save the game was a big ask. Brooke, like Eden, wasn't in the squad to score runs. She was there to take wickets. Unfortunately, Brooke had failed in that too.

The devil on Eden's shoulder jabbed its trident. "Maybe this means she'll lose her place and you'll get back in."

She told the devil to fuck off.

After the post-game wash-up with coach Susie, Eden went to the indoor school for half an hour to work on her batting, then headed to the car park. One of the remaining vehicles was Brooke's. Eden scanned the area, then dumped her gear in the boot and returned to the stadium.

She toured the offices, changing room and corridors, then went to the Members' Bar and looked out across the pitch. Away to her right, halfway down the stands, a lone figure sat hunched.

'Oh, Tweed,' she groaned.

In the early evening air, Eden navigated her way to Block 4 and traversed the steps down. Below, two figures were seated on the outfield mower. Both waved. She waved back.

Hands in her tracksuit pockets, Eden stood at Brooke's shoulder. 'I'd have run the 2.'

Brooke glanced up without lifting her head. 'Would you, Ede? Honestly?'

This was a horrible thing to ask.

Why didn't you just say, "Thanks"?

No, she wouldn't have run the 2, especially as she wasn't as quick between the wickets as Brooke. But she'd have been out first ball anyway. Then there was the irony of scrutinising a decision that had caused ramifications.

That's the problem. Hindsight is 20/20, and decisions need to be made in a split-second.

What should she do? Criticise Brooke's gamble, or play the supportive friend—which was exactly who she was... or had been.

'I get why you did it.' She folded down the adjacent plastic seat.

'Yeah. Trying too hard to make up for bowling like shit.' Brooke kicked at a stone.

Eden laughed sadly. 'We've all been there.'

'Should have taken the single.'

'Life is full of "Should haves".'

'Well, the game, anyway. But no do-overs, right?'

'No.' Eden's chin dipped.

The silence pressed in on them.

'Would you do it again, Ede? What you did.'

Tell me you didn't just bring this up. I'm trying to let it go, put us back together.

Her mind spooled back two years. The first Final of the season, the early competition, a chance for silverware for the Scorpions against the Stars.

Eden had dropped two catches in the first innings and was without a wicket. She was desperate to contribute. The team had tried everything to dislodge the last two batters. Eden, shorn of belief in her ability, chose something no harder than deception and a flick of the wrist. If she'd known it would be one of the few things Brooke hadn't moved past, would she still have taken the nuclear option?

'I'm not sure,' she replied.

Brooke eyed her, the smile wistful and resigned. 'It won you the game, though. What I did today may or may not have been the wrong decision, but the difference is that we lost.'

'Don't compare them, Tweedie. We both know that the best result is to win *and* not have regrets. To remember the victory and not the emotional fallout. Trophies are built on points. Nobody cares or remembers who cried or threw a bat across the changing room.'

'I suppose.'

'We're only human.'

'Yeah. But... I pissed off one of the groundsmen. We had words.'

'Which one? The old one, the young one, or the fit one?'

Brooke bit her lip. 'The... fit one.'

'Hmm. Pretty sure I know who that is.'

'I think I... spoiled things.'

Eden swallowed down a pang of jealousy. 'Is there something to spoil?'

'A friendship, definitely. And almost losing those is not much fun.'

'No. But he'll understand. He's had a dry run at... the ups and downs.'

'He's never seen me fuck up before. Didn't expect Medusa.'

'I'm sure you weren't that,' Eden said.

Brooke leant back, looked at the sky, then peered across the pitch. 'Does it bother you that I care about hurting his feelings?'

'You don't have a heart of stone. None of us want to hurt each other.'

'That's fair.'

It seemed that Brooke, like Eden, and possibly Matt, was working out how they could all share the stadium, even the whole of Maidstone, without treading on toes.

Of course, the easy answer would be for Eden to take him back. Assuming he'd have her. That would be fine—except she'd only be doing it to stop Brooke dating him. A pre-emptive strike. Hardly a valid reason.

Brooke appeared only interested in Matt for how he looked. That was risky. Relationships don't end because someone wakes up ugly one morning. They end because of an emotional disconnect, an incompatibility.

Eden hadn't stopped fancying the guy, but at a moment of crisis he'd let himself—and her—down. Today, Matt had said or done something wrong. Eden was disappointed. He should know that when you've had a bad game, it's best to steer clear, let the player regain their emotional compass.

The devil appeared on Eden's shoulder and whispered in her ear. Had today's spat kiboshed Matt and Brooke's chances of romance? Would he sense that a hiccup so early in their friendship was a bellwether? Eden's winter crash had proven that Scorpions have a sting in their tail. Would he back off, saving them all from snipes and difficult atmospheres?

'I just want to have a good season, Ede,' Brooke said.

'I know,' she affirmed.

'And I'm... pleased we're on the mend.'

'Me too.'

The girl fixed a direct gaze. '*Would* you have run the 2?'

Eden's shoulders fell. 'No. It wasn't there.'

Brooke nodded slowly. 'Live and learn, eh?'

'One player can't single-handedly win a match, but one can lose it.'

'Oh, I knew that. I wanted to win it, that's all.'

Eden shrugged. 'Same. Losing sucks. Games, men, friends.'

Brooke smiled, the first since breakfast. 'I'm glad I came here, babe.'

'Same. How long's your contract?'

'A year.' Brooke grinned. 'But I did promise to move out of yours as soon as I found a place.'

'I'd settle for some *actual* rent money.'

Brooke grimaced. 'Shit. Buy you a drink as well?'

'You mean so you can drown your sorrows after bowling like... well, I did in the Final?' Eden winked.

'I was worse today. I got clubbed for twenty.'

'*Two* overs, babe. You smacked me for seventeen off *one*. So I win the "Who's more shit?" prize.'

Brooke laughed. 'Alright. But... drinks anyway?'

'And karaoke. Then, maybe when your resistance is down, I'll take you to the tattoo place.' She rubbed her hands in mock evil glee.

Brooke's smile vanished. 'Oh no. Me and pain are not friends.'

'You can't *not* get the Scorpion branding.' She pressed a finger against the girl's thigh. 'Tssss.'

Brooke playfully batted Eden's hand away. 'Maybe let's wait and see if Susie decides to loan me out for the rest of the season.'

That would be a shame.

No, truly.

Although it would solve a lot of issues...

Eden brushed the invisible demon off her shoulder, then she and Brooke headed off.

26th Over

Matt and Ray watched the girls leave the terrace and enter the pavilion. They exchanged a glance.

'Never doubted it,' Ray said.

'A problem shared is a problem halved.'

'Certainly a *shared* problem,' Ray added sagely. His subtext was that the women had something else in common—they could be tricky to handle.

Today had shown that perhaps Brooke wasn't the unflappable superstar he'd expected. If he'd thought she'd be easier to date, the day's events suggested he might have similar issues coping with the travails of her career.

Or is it me? Am I too unforgiving? Expecting a smooth wicket that plays perfectly, not realising that a ball can keep low, or rear up, or hit a crack, making it unplayable.

If he scoured the world for the perfect girl to chase, to date, even to marry, that was a fool's errand.

In the morning, Matt hit the gym.

After reps on the leg press and bench press, he did a 5k run, then lifted weights for five minutes. As he was having a breather, taking on fluids, and considering what to do next, someone walked up.

'Hey.'

He jolted. Whilst this was a person he could reasonably expect to see here, the timing wasn't ideal.

'Hey,' he replied.

'Look, I'm sorry.'

He set the bottle of water at his feet. 'It's fine.'

Brooke gestured to the bench. He shuffled along. She sat. 'No. It's not fine. I was shitty to you. Undeserved. Bad day at the office. No excuse for that attitude.'

'We're all allowed days like that.'

'I suppose. But not to take it out on friends.' She frowned. 'We *are* still friends?'

'Yeah. I've had enough of falling out with people, well, players... well, one player... at the club.' He ran a hand over his damp forehead.

'Me too. And... sorry if I had any part in that. I don't like seeing Ede unhappy. And she caused you pain too.'

He shrugged. 'Hers was worse.'

'And a perfect storm. Yesterday was nothing. Me trying to make amends. A bad decision. And now you're probably thinking I'm as likely to go off on one as she is. Which may be true. I don't know. I hope some online troll doesn't fuck up my mental health like they did to hers.'

'The slings and arrows of outrageous fortune.'

She smiled. 'Something like that, yeah.' Her eyes widened. 'And get you! First, piano, now Shakespeare. What next?'

'Juggling?' He nudged her.

'Please don't. That's about all I have.'

'Oh, don't be modest. You have the odd good day with a cricket ball.'

She slapped his bare leg. 'Rat.'

'Sorry.'

'It's fine.' She pulled at her blonde ponytail. 'What I was saying is... don't *not* ask someone out because things fell apart before.'

Goosebumps swarmed down his arms. The subtext of her comment was in bold and underlined. 'I'll... bear it in mind.'

'Good. It's nice that you two are on speaking terms again.'

'Same with you. I've been regaled with stories of the dream team from years ago. What was it, a last-wicket stand of 32 to win against the top side?'

She looked at him askance. 'Hmm. Recent events prove that no team should rely on my batting to get them out of a hole.' She sighed heavily. 'Or not as much as they can rely on my bowling to put them in the hole in the first place.'

He laid a hand on hers. 'This doesn't sound like the Brooke Harris I know.'

'It'll pass. It always does. It's like the saying goes, "Class is permanent. Form is temporary".'

'They knew that when they brought you in.'

'And I'm sure they still know it about Ede,' she added.

'If she can get back in the side,' he breathed.

'That's never in anyone's control. Unless you want to spike Rojo's cocktail one night.'

'You could have done that yesterday.' Matt had seen Brooke's Insta post. A handful of the players had gone out for drinks and karaoke.

She laughed. 'Wanting to play is one thing. Sabotage? Hmm. I love Ede, but I love my career more.'

'Ditto,' he mumbled.

'What?'

'Nothing. I mean... if I was that bothered about being a distraction on the boundary, being a wasp in her head that meant she couldn't get her mojo back, I would have left. Plenty of other grounds in the area.' He met her eye. 'But... and keep it under your hat, I was hanging on for a promotion, and... I might get it.'

She gripped his hand. 'That's great.'

'Of course, I'll still have to work with Eggs, so it's not all good news.'

She chuckled. 'He's pretty harmless... right?'

'Yeah. Actually, he's starting to pull his socks up. Probably thought it was a bit of easy summer money, get a tan, watch a load of young women in sports gear run around—'

'Hit on some of them.'

'You got off lightly. But I did tell him, when he arrived, that Eden was off-limits—'

'Oh, yeah?'

'Because she was still getting back on an even keel.'

'Had a bad breakup, that kind of thing?' Her brow arched.

He raised a palm. 'Okay, I did give him a potted history, but I didn't say, "Stay off my turf" or anything. I said to give her space. And you. Enough on your plate, what with a new team, settling in—'

'Escaping from a big hole in the ground.'

'And hoping your best mate *won't* spike your cocktail one night.' He grinned.

'Yeah. Irony that my best ever batting display was against *her*. I can sure pick my moments.'

He nodded. 'But you moved on. Like you will after that run-out. Like Eden will, about a lot of things. Time is the great healer, to be clichéd.'

'And you, Matt? Where's your head in all this?' She looked deep into his eyes.

'A lot happier recently.' An impish thought struck him. 'Plus, if I was *that* invested in winning Eden over, even stealing back her place on the squad, the easiest thing is to hide this.' He poked Brooke's insulin monitor.

Open-mouthed, she clutched her chest theatrically. 'I'm destroyed. Did our five minutes in the Dress Circle mean nothing to you?'

'Oh, I take *all* my dates there,' he joked.

She winced. 'Ouch. Must get pretty uncomfortable if things... develop.'

'Well, you're all pretty limber athletes, so I never had any complaints.'

His pulse pounded. She was flirting. But why was he reciprocating?

Because it's better than fighting.

She poked his bicep. 'They're a lot more accommodating than me. I'd want a Queen size feather bed, ensuite, and a bottle of champagne in an ice bucket.'

'I'll bear it in mind.'

She leant in closer. 'You do that,' she whispered.

'Brooke?' he murmured, spotting someone in his peripheral vision.

'Yeah?' she breathed, expectant, almost sultry.

'You know that bloke who kicked us off the equipment last week for time-wasting?'

27th Over

Eden's head wasn't sore, but her throat was. Karaoke with the team had been a great tonic after a frustrating game loss, and Brooke's spirits had certainly brightened.

It was after nine when she crawled from her bed, did the daily rolls and stretches, then went down for breakfast. Brooke wasn't around. She'd mentioned going to the gym, then to the stadium to work on her in-swinger.

Eden did some chores, showered, and was drying when she noticed the necklace on her dressing table.

What a conundrum. If I throw it away, it implies I hate Matt and refuse to admit that the gift meant anything. If I wear it, does that show I cherish it and the associated memories, or simply mean I've accepted it into my jewellery collection and the provenance is unimportant?

Alternatively, I can leave it here until the whole thing is a non-issue.

When will that be? Tomorrow? Next week? Next month? Next year?

The answer was obvious. It would happen when she no longer held Matt in her heart. At the moment, the only two things likely to catalyse that emotional flip would be if he was unmasked as a serial killer, or if he started dating Brooke.

One of those was morally unacceptable. The other was petty.

She slipped the chain round her neck. Ray had pointed out that he wasn't vengefully burning everything related to his marriage. Yes, he was moving out of the house he and Mum had owned for thirty years, but that was a practical decision. The engraved port decanter they'd received for a wedding present was still in good use.

Eden needed to be more Ray. Grow up. Chill out. Cross the rope.

She also had to get a wiggle on. There were more boxes to look through at his house.

How is it possible for two people to accumulate so much stuff? I hope that doesn't happen to me.

Of course, at this rate, marriage is unlikely anyway. Especially if I keep binning perfect candidates at the first sign of trouble.

Breathe. Move on.

She arrived at Dad's and rang the bell. There was no answer. Nothing on the second ring either, so she unlatched the side gate and headed to the rear garden.

It was a pretty safe guess, and there he was.

Unexpectedly, Matt was there too. Her breath caught.

They were standing by the old apple tree. Actually, it wasn't particularly old. It was the same age as her, which was no coincidence because Dad had planted it on the day after she was born. Apple trees symbolise love.

Dad was gesticulating at the tree as Matt looked on. He was probably recounting its life story. Had Matt heard it before? She didn't remember. They had spent time here, but no period was as momentous as this. The removals men were coming in a week, but they weren't taking the tree. Dad didn't want to risk uprooting it and replanting it at the new house, in case it didn't survive. That would be an inauspicious end to something connected to a daughter he loved as much now as the day she, and the tree, were born.

She remembered, as a girl, gleefully picking apples from the tree. Being lifted up to the higher branches. This was Dad's first Garden of Eden.

She was pretty sure he'd wanted a boy. Don't most dads? He'd always followed cricket, from the days of Botham et al., so probably accepted that he'd never get to take his kid to a match. However, when she took an interest in his memorabilia, then played knockout in the garden, he signed her up for an after-school cricket club. She was bitten by the bug, started going to games with Dad, then joined a local Under-11s team.

When he took Eden to the 2009 Ashes Test at Worcester, and she watched legendary fast bowler Katherine Brunt take 6 wickets, she knew that's what she wanted to do with her life.

She fingered the necklace charm.

At that moment, Dad looked round, then Matt. She hastily dropped the charm inside her shirt.

The men walked over.

'Alright, father? Enjoying "the Garden of Eden" before it becomes someone's "the garden"?'

Ray patted Matt's shoulder. 'Did you have to put up with this kind of backchat?'

'I took your daughter as I found her.'

Eden tensed.

Please, Dad, don't say, "Until you lost her."

'He also had to take *you* as he found you, Dad.'

Ray eyed Matt. 'See what I mean?'

'Yeah.'

Ray pointed at her. 'I think you've had plenty of practice saying those words. Son.'

'Eden *has* to wear the trousers, Ray. Otherwise, the spectators would get a show every time she ran up to bowl.'

'And what about poor Ben? He wouldn't know *where* to look.'

'Oh, he'd know exactly where,' she said.

'He's harmless,' Matt suggested. 'Actually, he's not the rubbish hire I first thought.'

'Careful. Remember who hired him,' Ray cautioned.

'Yes, boss,' Matt said cheekily.

Ray tutted. 'You two are as bad as each other.'

Eden raised a hand. 'No. I'm worse. But that's due to a terrible upbringing.'

Ray shook his head. 'I give up. Come on in, Matt. Take that painting away and leave me in peace to throttle my daughter.'

They went inside. Ray brewed up in the kitchen while Eden helped Matt take the picture off the wall in the living room.

'Brave, teasing the boss like that,' she remarked.

'Especially now.'

She frowned. 'Why?'

He glanced toward the kitchen. 'Well, Alan's retiring, and someone needs to fill those shoes.'

She cupped his arm, a reflexive gesture of support and care. 'Matt, that's great.'

'Nothing's fixed.' He explored her face. 'And I hope you didn't... say anything to Ray.'

'Like what?'

'Have a word, curry favour.'

Her hand fell away. 'Why would I?'

He sighed. 'I don't know, Edie.' He shook his head. 'Sorry. I just... want this on merit. I don't want help. I'd settle for your forgiveness. Respect. Friendship.'

'You *have* all those.'

He looked down. 'Thanks.'

Her chest filled. 'I know I need to get over myself. I'm trying. Be nice if you forgave me too.'

'I have. It was stress. I was in the wrong place at the wrong time.'

She sank onto the sofa arm. 'You did your best.'

'But it wasn't good enough.'

She patted the cushion beside her. He sat. The uncomfortable silence was broken by a phone ringing in the kitchen. Dad's mobile. He answered.

She eyed Matt's toned frame. 'A locked door needs a key. You didn't have it, that's all.'

He looked up. 'You could have lent it to me.'

'I didn't have it either, mate. Still don't. Still can't figure it out.'

'Brooke's probably better to help with that.' A wry smile appeared. 'Seems like you all have bad days.'

Her stomach knotted. She wanted him to realise that, if he *was* considering chasing Brooke, she might not be the easy ride he hoped for. As Dad had said, Matt was never going to find an "artificial grass" relationship... not if he was hell-bent on dating another athlete. However, Eden did want smooth waters between them. No reason Matt and Brooke couldn't be mates. She couldn't be *that* controlling.

'Did you two patch it up? Maybe I should have warned you that she wears her heart on her sleeve when she's batting.'

He frowned. 'I don't understand. Neither of you are top order. Why so precious about getting out?'

'We did this already, Matt.' She smiled. 'It's not all about getting out. Part of the game. It's how it happens. Tweedie was pissed off with her error of judgement. Getting beaten by a good ball, that's fair enough. Bad umpiring decision? Hard to take. Stupid mistake? A lot of self-reflection, I can tell you.'

He nodded. 'Hmm.'

'So? *Are* you two okay?'

'Yeah. Thanks for asking.'

She shrugged. 'Falling out with each other is *so* last season.'

He glanced around the room. 'New starts for us all.'

'True.'

'I wish this hadn't happened, Ray needing to move. What I mean is... I wish your mum had been more supportive.'

She picked at a nail. 'Sometimes I wish I *had* taken her advice. Stuck with the nine to five.'

He thumbed at the kitchen. 'Don't let Ray hear you say that. Better yet, stop saying it, thinking it. Accountancy will be there next year, in five years, ten. It can wait. You hit rock bottom because you *care* about this life, Edie. About doing your best. If I don't get promotion, am I going to jack in the job? Hell no.' A smile crept across his face. 'But maybe I'll wish I'd asked you to give Ray the Puss In Boots eyes.'

'You don't need it, mate. Dad would be mad not to appoint you. I'll keep everything crossed. You deserve it. For putting up with me, if nothing else.' She grinned.

'Thanks. But I promise not to call it the Garden of Eden.' He winked.

She squeezed his hand. 'You're the best.'

28th Over

At home, Matt hung the painting on the living room wall, rustled up dinner, then settled down in front of the TV.

As the minutes passed, he found himself repeatedly glancing at the picture. Partially, he was getting used to a new thing in the room. Sometimes, he was picking out the details. Then came a realisation that he was cohabiting with an object which connected him to the Palmers—not only Ray and Liz, but Eden too. The painting was entwined with the marriage, now defunct, and its offspring... with whom his relationship was a memory.

Odd that he'd chosen to live with something that reminded him of her. Or perhaps not? She'd worn the necklace, and that had more significance than Ray's painting did.

What did it mean? Maybe that they were grownups and didn't want to throw the baby out with the bathwater. Yet why had they given up on love after one fight?

Unarguably, Eden had done the dumping, and if there was to be a reconciliation, a second chance, it needed to come from her.

But did he want that? If it fell apart again, it would likely be worse, and they truly would be enemies. The atmosphere at the stadium would be unbearable. One of them would *have* to leave. And that felt like too high a price to pay.

Besides, what had changed? He was no different, no less caring and supportive as a person—but no more so, either. Yes, he was wiser, but was he any more perfect, more dateable?

The jury was out.

On the other hand, was Eden more self-aware, more together, less prone to buffeting by the mental and emotional forces that inhabited the sport? Had she grown happier, more confident, more resilient? Was she, crucially, *over* what had happened?

Up for debate.

What she needed was game time, good performances, and a reconnection with Brooke. Those were much harder to engineer than the simple act of buying the girl you love a necklace... or hanging a painting in your house.

Even if the painting was Brueghel's "The Garden Of Eden".

The following day, Matt was at the stadium, as was the team. As the pitch was being mown and prepared, the players were using the indoor training school.

Early afternoon, a few of the players headed away to other engagements. Eden was taking a coaching session with Lily and her teammates. Matt stumbled upon Brooke in the pavilion. She appeared pensive.

He perched on an adjacent chair. 'Hey. Everything okay?'

'Yeah. You?'

She laid her phone down. She'd been browsing the webpage of a tattoo parlour.

'You don't want to go to that one,' he remarked.

'Why not?'

'Mate of mine went last year. Got an infection.'

Her eyes widened. 'Okay, thanks.'

'You want a recommendation?'

She pulled a face. 'Not really. Sorry, I mean, yes, that would be great.'

He frowned. 'Which is it?'

She sighed, glancing around. 'I kind of... feel obliged to go, you know?'

'Ah. The team branding.' He poked his bicep. 'Tssss.'

She laughed. 'That's what Ede said.'

'I see. It's peer pressure.'

'No,' she hissed. 'It's fine. Only needs to be a little tattoo, right?'

'Your choice. Eden's is about an inch long.'

She played with her watch. 'I bet it hurt.'

'Before my time. But I'm pretty sure they *all* hurt.'

'You don't have any experience, then?'

'Me? No. Anyway, if you don't want to get inked, don't. I can't believe *every* player has one.'

'Twelve do.' She looked sheepish. 'They've been so welcoming, such a great bunch of girls.'

'Then get the tattoo.'

'I do want to.'

The penny dropped. 'You're not *scared*, are you?' he teased.

'Me? No. I'm an elite athlete. My *life* is pain.'

'So...?'

She grimaced. 'I was hoping to go with Ede. You know, for moral support.'

'And to cover your mouth when you scream in agony?'

She shoved him, then looked up with timid, slightly coquettish eyes. 'Maybe a bit.'

He checked his watch. 'You were going today, weren't you? Get it done before you change your mind.'

'I forgot that Ede has coaching.'

'I would offer to come along, but my record in helping women through painful experiences is iffy at best.'

She searched his face. 'I promise not to be as challenging… or dismissive.'

Nerves prickled his neck. 'Will she… mind?'

Brooke tutted. 'It's a tattoo parlour, not a bridal suite. Come on, Matt, you can't be tiptoeing around forever. You're allowed to *hang out* with people. Even me, her archenemy.'

'But you aren't that,' he pointed out.

She poked his chest. 'Exactly.'

As they sat in the tattoo parlour, he noted Brooke guardedly assess the visual onslaught provided by the walls, the equipment, and the tattooist's lower arms.

He never expected someone like her—or Eden, or any of the players—to be fearful of something. When you've had thousands of balls hurled or hit at you, felt pressure to perform, what's an hour of localised needling?

Where was she going to have the tattoo? Hopefully not somewhere intimate, because that would be awkward… though the prospect of a glimpse of her backside or upper thigh had his pulse racing.

Brooke chose her calf. Eden's was on her right hip.

Seven months since I've seen that. No, nearer eight now. Might not see either of these creatures ever again.

She beckoned him. 'Sit with me?'

'Sure.'

He grabbed a spare seat, she raised her leg onto the stool, and the tattooist readied himself. Brooke's jaw tensed.

He leant close, not wanting to embarrass her, and lowered his voice. 'You *live* with a needle inside you. What's another one for a few minutes?'

She raised an eyebrow. 'Hardly the same.'

'See what I mean about being a useless support mechanism?'

She took his hand. 'That's crap. You're here. And, while that makes me a useless, scared little girl, it also makes you a legend.' She squeezed. 'Thanks.'

He squeezed back. 'Anything for a friend.'

'Okay,' said the tattooist. 'I'm starting now.'

Brooke swallowed hard. 'Fine,' she peeped.

Then she interlaced her fingers with Matt's and pulled his hand into her midriff. The machine buzzed.

She screwed up her eyes. 'Talk to me,' she said through gritted teeth.

He was about to foolishly, uselessly, ask for a topic when her hand jolted against the initial pain, pulling their hands towards her belly button. He hoped she wouldn't move any closer to her groin, yet his heart pattered.

'So... er... Why "Tweed"?'

Her expression was half side-eye, half gratitude. 'It's hardly rocket science. When Ede and I met, she asked whether I had any Scottish heritage. Don't know why. Maybe because her mum did. Anyway, I said no, I didn't think so, but she mentioned that stuff called Harris tweed. The fabric, you know?'

'Ah. I think I can join the dots from there.'

She eyed her calf, digging her short nails into him. 'So. Next question. *Please*.'

'Um... what's the worst pain you've ever experienced?'

'Easy. Tore my Achilles a few years ago. Actually, being laid up was worse. Like Ede just found out.' She fell sober for a moment, then winced. 'Sheesh.' She gritted her teeth in discomfort. 'What's *your* worst pain?'

He cast his mind back. 'Not really a physical pain. Does that count?'

'Of course.'

'Honestly?'

'Your secret's safe with me.' She lifted his hand and kissed it.

His nerve endings fizzed. 'Losing Eden.'

Her face fell. 'I can... understand that.'

'You were really close too. I mean, are.'

'Yeah.' She held his gaze for aeons. 'Are you... still in love with her?'

An indescribable sensation permeated his body. He pondered. Brooke didn't press him. Instead, she looked at her calf, her fingers stroking his hand.

'You would tell her to look forward, not back, right? Let go of a bad episode and move on. Don't dwell on mistakes.'

'Sure.'

'So... *I* need to move towards what I *might* have, not what I've lost.'

'That's sounds... healthy,' she said.

'Feels like it.'

She licked her lips. 'So... about moving on, trying again. Anyone in mind?'

'Maybe,' he said, stroking her hand with his thumb.

Half an hour later, the Scorpion design was complete. They agreed it was great, definitely worth the pain.

Then something unexpected happened. Brooke asked the guy for another tattoo—two interlinked letters.

Matt shot her a question.

She shrugged. 'Sometimes you just know that two people have an unbreakable bond.'

Afterwards, they walked to the car park. Both had driven across from the stadium.

He blipped the remote of his ageing Fiesta. Nothing happened. 'Bloody thing.'

'Change the battery?' Brooke suggested.

'Can't be arsed. Changing the car soon. Hopefully. Seeing one this weekend. Not far from your game, actually.'

'You should come along. I fancy our chances of a win.' She grinned. 'Assuming I'm not needed to bat.'

He jabbed her arm. 'I thought you were a person who moved on from mistakes.'

'I am. This is all assuming I'm picked to play. But... why don't we all ride up together? You reckon we can survive a car share?'

He waggled his head. 'I don't want to cramp your style.'

'Yeah. Actually, we don't tend to mix with the manual workers. Bit below our station.'

Wide-eyed, he shoved her. 'I hope the tats *really* hurt.'

She poked out her tongue. He reciprocated.

She fell calm, reflective. 'Hey, thanks for *literally* holding my hand through this. It was a good decision.'

'No problem. And no, I won't tell.'

She pulled him into a hug. 'You're the best,' she whispered, pecking his cheek.

Dopamine coursed through him. Guilt was hard on its heel.

'Thanks,' he said. Then, desperate to change the subject, he added, 'Now remember to look after your new pet Scorpion.'

She saluted. 'Will do. I'm good at medical routines.' She patted her insulin pump.

'Most of the time.'

She angled her head. 'My white knight. Two times now.'

That was perhaps over-egging the pudding, but undeniably he'd successfully helped Brooke twice, having failed Eden once. Perhaps dating her *was* worth a try?

29th Over

Eden watched Lily run up to bowl. The delivery seamed beautifully, passing the bat of the teenager at the wickets.

Eden clapped twice. 'Nice one, Lily.'

The batter collected the ball from where it nestled in the black netting, tossed it back with her gloved hand, then took guard. Lily walked back to the start of her run-up as another girl delivered another ball down the wicket. It was short and wide, so the batter flayed it through where Cover would be.

'Lovely stroke,' Eden called to the batter.

Lily ran in. The ball hit a perfect length, angled in, outfoxed the batter, and clattered into the sprung stumps. The girl punched the air.

'Beautiful nip-backer,' Eden said, offering a high-five.

Lily slapped. 'Thanks, coach.' Her chest heaved.

'Take a minute. Have a drink.'

'Will do.'

Eden watched her protégé go to the refreshment table situated on the edge of the small rural pitch. Across the grass, a group of players was doing fielding practice. A pair of red kites wheeled in the calm May air. Below them, the ground rang with thwacks, shouts and chatter.

Eden breathed deeply.

Oh, to return to such heady days of innocence.

In the rutted car park beside the pavilion, a few mums chatted. Perched on the back of a chair, his feet on the seat, was Lily's young suitor.

Eden recalled the numerous times over the last two seasons when she'd secretly hoped she'd be allocated a fielding position near the groundsman's hut. It was hard to make out Matt's features from across the pitch, and sometimes it took mammoth self-control to focus on the game and not imagine what would come afterwards. Dinner with him, laughing with him, lying with him, moving in rhythm together.

'What's up?' Lily said.

Eden jolted. 'Sorry.'

'You okay?'

'Of course. So… did Toby ask you out yet?'

The girl folded her arms, all sass. 'Did Matt ask *you* out yet?'

Eden's eyes flared. 'How is that your business?'

'How is my love life *your* business?'

The words "love life" from such a young mouth made Eden splutter a laugh. 'I suppose it isn't. Only looking out for you.'

Lily's nose wrinkled. 'Hmm. Sounded like fishing to me.'

'Water cooler chatter,' Eden said defensively.

'How about coaching me?'

'How about a bit of gossip from my favourite bowler?'

'Are you, like, trying to live vicariously through me?' Lily said.

Eden's mouth hung open. She tried to deflect. 'Good word, Lil. A-star in English for you.'

'You literally are, aren't you?' Lily wasn't fazed.

'Nothing of the sort.'

'But he hasn't asked you back?'

Eden's stupefaction didn't wane. 'Why would he?'

'Because he knows he didn't support you like he should have.'

'Lily, you're very sweet, but I don't want to rake over that shi—' She cut herself off.

'"Shitshow", coach. I'm fifteen. *Effing* shitshow.'

'All the same—' Eden began.

'So that's a "No".'

'You *are* an inquisitive mademoiselle today.'

'I earned it. "Beautiful nip-backer", you said.'

'I did. All the same—'

'So that's a "No".'

Eden sighed heavily, the breath mixed with sadness. 'I think he would rather date Brooke.'

'Why?'

'Because she's a lovely girl.' Which was true. A person only needed a few hours with Brooke Harris to discover that she was a nice, dedicated, caring, outgoing, steely, attractive young woman.

'So are you, Eden.'

'Thanks. But I also have *form*.'

Lily scoffed. She tapped her wrist. 'What happened to "focus" and "breathe"?'

'I do. And I'll never forget that you gave me that bracelet. But it can't erase history. Or does it have some magical power that you didn't train me on?'

'What're you like? You do remember the Final? All hundred overs?'

'I mean, I've tried to lock it away in a little cabinet in here,' Eden tapped the side of her head. 'Which is a healthy thing to do.'

'Doesn't sound like it. You took two for twenty-three—'.

Eden guffawed. 'I so did not. I took two for forty.'

'Two for twenty-three off nine overs. And that one-handed diving catch at Point. Come on, twenty-three off nine? That's, like, tight as a duck's—'

Eden raised a palm. 'Okay. But who gives a shit about those nine overs? It was the last one that cost us the game.'

'You mean the lesson here is to only remember the failures?'

'Hell no.'

Lily nodded. 'Exactly. So you and Matt *weren't* good?'

Eden was thrown by the change of direction... which was nothing of the sort. She cursed the girl's sharp mind.

'Yes, we were.'

'And without that bad spell, you two would have carried on.'

Eden put a maternal arm around Lily's shoulder. 'Yes. But you're describing *every* relationship, Lil. You'll learn that. Things are fine until they end. Peace persists until war breaks out.'

Lily laughed. 'You weren't at *war*. It was like... an earthquake, right? It's scary for a bit, then people rebuild. They *know* shit like that can happen. But do they jack it in and move to Belgium or Leeds or whatever?'

Eden frowned. 'Are you saying that Matt dating Brooke is the equivalent of him throwing in the towel and moving to Belgium? Tweedie is more like... Cannes.'

'I'm not sure about *that*, but are you just gonna let him?'

'I think *someone* needs to get back to the nets.'

Lily removed Eden's arm from around her shoulder. 'Coach, I know I'm only a *teenager*, but can't you just, like, ask him back?

Either that or let him go. You're torturing *both* of you. And me, a bit, as it happens.'

Eden's mouth worked soundlessly.

Lily pointed at the nets. 'Let's go then.'

Eden restrained her departure. 'Oh no you don't, Miss. What about you and Toby?'

'Er... I'm... like, waiting for the right moment.'

'Well, don't wait forever. If I was in your place, and a hottie like Toby was on the scene, I'd snap him up before someone else did.'

Lily nudged her. 'Ooh, looking for a toy boy, are you?'

'That's not what I mean, and you know it.'

'Yeah. You mean I should date him to block another girl?'

'No, not that either.' Eden exhaled fake exasperation. 'Date him because you *want* to.'

The words reverberated around her head like an echo chamber.

When Eden arrived home, Brooke was replacing the insulin cartridge in her pump.

'You okay, hon?' she asked.

'Sure. Why?'

'Nothing. Worried I'd missed a ping.' She pulled out her phone, ready to check the monitoring app.

'No, you're good. But thanks.'

Eden sat beside Brooke on the sofa. 'All part of the deal.'

Brooke fell sober. 'You're too good to me, Ede.'

Debateable. Certainly she'd behaved far from good, kind, *professional* lately. 'Not really.'

'I do... feel guilty that I kind of swept in and stole your spot.' Brooke's grimace was small, apologetic, friendly.

Eden laughed. 'You didn't. I lost it because of my form, and because I stupidly busted my finger. Anyway, you were always going to be ahead of me in Susie's choices. Your figures last season were brilliant.'

'I know it hurt, the Final and everything.'

Her insides caroused, happiness and sadness entwined. Regret and affection. 'We're *mates*, Tweedie. Yes, we were on different sides, and what happened was shit, and my fault, but now we're *okay*. I certainly don't deserve you being worried about me not getting game time, especially after how I behaved. You *know* this is the most individual team sport. I can only play my game...' A wicked smile appeared. 'And maybe hope for another sinkhole to open up on you again.'

Brooke grinned, slapping Eden's hand. Then she picked at a fingernail. 'Actually, one crack *has* appeared. Dad's not well. I've asked Susie for a couple of days' personal time.'

Eden's shoulders fell. 'Oh hon, that's awful.'

'Shit happens. So I miss a game? It's a long season.'

'Yeah. I took a few days off when the divorce hit Dad hard.' She chuckled sadly. 'At least he had the sense not to smack a wall in frustration.'

Brooke patted Eden's leg. 'You need to stop beating yourself up for lapses in judgment. Wounds heal.'

'You know how to say the right thing, Tweed.'

'I'm hardly perfect.' She tapped the sensor on her arm. 'In fact, I'm going to be a little bit broken forever.'

This wasn't news to Eden, yet it still hit hard. What she'd been through was nothing compared to Brooke's life challenge. More than that, Eden was in control of her future.

If being apart from Matt was that painful, she could do something about it.

If.

30th Over

At work the next day, Matt's thoughts repeatedly drifted back to the tattoo parlour. Three things played on his mind—seeing a new side to Brooke, the kiss, and the second tattoo.

They all pointed in the same direction—towards opportunity and away from fear. Still, he wanted a sign from Eden that she'd be comfortable with him dating Brooke. In some ways, he wished their breakup had been more acrimonious, more final. It would be easier if there were no residual friendship, no concern about hurting feelings, but he couldn't turn off his affection. After all, it wasn't the *real* Eden that had broken up with him.

Soon after he got home, Brooke texted.

His spirits dropped. She was going away for a couple of days, needing to take personal time, so she'd miss the game at Southampton. That put a spanner in the works for the planned three-way bonding session.

He stared at his phone. There was nothing to be done about her absence, only a question of whether to still offer Eden a lift, or if he should even go. However, Ray had approved the time off, and Matt really wanted to visit the second-hand car dealer. Could he travel all that way and keep Eden in the dark? Besides, he'd volunteered to act as chauffeur, so why back out now?

Taking a deep breath—which was ridiculous nerves—he texted Eden. This would be a litmus test of their relationship. Chatting for five minutes at the stadium wasn't the same as the enforced proximity of a two-hour car ride.

Eden took an eternity to reply, during which time he cooked dinner.

His phone pinged.

She asked whether the car had a current MOT and had been valeted this year. He confirmed yes to both. She requested no rap music on the stereo. He agreed. She told him to pick her up at 6 a.m. He set the alarm for an early start.

Cricket—so rock 'n roll.

Eden slid her kit bag onto his back seat, hopped in the passenger seat, belted up, then crossed herself.

'Hilarious,' he said.

'Actually, you're probably safer than Tweed. She's always playing with her bloody hair.'

He started the car, pulled down the vanity mirror, and inspected his carefully gelled mop.

'You're not funny, Matthew Alderson.'

He closed the mirror. 'You used to love how much I made you laugh.'

'That was then.' She pointed ahead. 'Let's go, driver.'

He tapped his forehead. 'Yes, Miss.'

She jabbed his shoulder. 'Don't be a dick.'

'I think the boat has sailed on that. Six months ago.'

She sighed. 'Is this what I signed up for? One hundred miles of dissecting our breakup?'

'At least we're speaking... finally.'

She eyed him for a long time. 'Matt?'

'Yeah?'

'Not now, okay? I need to get myself in the zone.'

'Sure. I know that games have been like rocking horse shit for you.'

She shrugged, then adjusted how the strap cut across her chest. For a microsecond, he took in the view—a familiar one whose appeal had never dimmed. Unfortunately, the microsecond coincided with her glance across. He lasered his attention on the road ahead.

'Sow the wind, reap the whirlwind,' she replied. 'But Brooke's loss is my gain. So I need to have a good one today.'

'I'll be rooting for you.'

'What happened to visiting this dealership?'

'I'm doing that at two o'clock. Why, do you not want a cheerleader?'

She reached across the seat bolster, as if to pat his thigh, but retracted her hand. 'Of course I do, mate.'

'Thanks. Anyway, you do your Zen thing. I'll stop for a takeout coffee in an hour, okay?'

She beamed. 'Thank you... driver.'

He tugged a fake forelock. 'Pleasure, Miss.'

They arrived at the ground in good time, and he dropped her at the players' gate. Even at eight-thirty, the weather was glorious.

Matt parked the car, then circumnavigated the pitch, searching for the Head Groundsman. He and Eden had travelled to every ground during the last two seasons, and he'd spoken to colleagues at each one—as well as cheering on his girlfriend.

How different things were today, underscored by the discovery that the veteran Head Groundsman had retired due to ill health. Still, his crew had prepared a great wicket, and as Matt chatted to the lads, he watched Eden's warmup and bowling practice. She was in good form.

He took a seat on the terrace and settled in for the first innings. The Scorpions were batting, so he hoped not to see Eden on the pitch, as this would mean that, in a 20-over game, the Tornado had ripped through the visitors and 9 PALMER would need to bat.

She looked so out of place in pads and helmet. Much better, more graceful, with ball in hand. When she batted, the concentration meant her tongue was half poked out.

Focussed. Determined. Adorable. Endearing.

Today, she mostly stayed out of sight in the pavilion. Probably chatting to teammates, getting fuel on board for her bowling spell.

At one-thirty, he headed off to view the car. The timing wasn't ideal, as he missed the end of the Scorpions' innings and the start of their fielding spell. However, the news was all good. The dealer knocked £500 off the asking price, and Matt shook on it. He'd come back next week to trade-in the old car and drive away with a spanking new—well, four-year-old—replacement.

He returned to the stadium to find that Eden had taken two wickets. His heart filled with pride. Would that feeling ever die, pleasure her success? He hoped not.

As he hadn't brought a hat, and the sun was in his face, he moved to the opposite side of the ground. Coincidentally—or was it instinct?—this was near Eden's habitual fielding position.

Half an hour later, the home side was struggling at 98 for 5 in reply to the Scorpions' 187 for 4. Risk-taking and big hitting were needed, which was good news for the bowlers. With guile, they could tempt the batters into making mistakes.

In an overs break, Eden spotted him a few yards away.

He raised a pair of fingers, mouthing, 'Two!'

She blew on her fingernails and rubbed them on her shirt—a familiar gesture in response to his appreciation from the sidelines, an echo of better times. His brain remembered the better times... as did his hands, which curled into a heart shape.

Shit!

He snapped his hands down.

Eden's eyes flared briefly, then she swatted a hand, as if to say, "Forget it, easy mistake".

Yet he felt a fool, accidentally declaring affection. His stupid mind, his ridiculous vestigial feelings for her.

He sprang up and paced, desperate to shake off the embarrassment. He had to focus on something real, something to believe in. He counted the Scorpions like he was counting sheep—except he was trying to be hyper-awake and dispel the daydream.

Bry, Fi, Kat, Bakes, Dani, Roddy, Hawks, Mac, Ede...

Oh shiiit!

Then he wasn't looking at any of the fielders. The whip-crack sound drew his attention to the batter, willow high above her head... and the ball, much higher.

Heading in his direction.

It was a 6, beyond doubt. The crowd knew it, and their voices told the story.

Matt had lived this situation once before. It was etched in his memory.

He tracked the arc of the ball, half stepping, half stumbling towards the hoarding which separated the pitch from the front row of seats.

The sun peeked behind his shades. He shook it off, disoriented, spied the ball ten yards above him, stuck out his hands—in the way Eden had once coached him—then lunged.

The ball smacked into his grasp, momentum pulling him down and left. He clung on fiercely, determined to manfully seal the catch, keen for fifteen seconds of pointless fame. He toppled forwards, bracing at the last second as he hit the ground hands first, then elbow, then waist. Breath burst from his lungs.

The crowd cheered.

He levered himself upright, raised the ball aloft, then tossed it to Eden, who was a few feet away. Pain stabbed into his left wrist. He cradled the arm into his waist, gritting his teeth.

Eden lobbed the ball back to wicketkeeper Izzy, then came over, putting a hand on his shoulder. 'You okay, Matt?'

'Yeah, just banged my hand.'

'You landed badly.' She raised an eyebrow. 'Don't give up the day job.'

'And don't get balled out for first-aiding a spectator. I'll be fine.'

She reached for his left hand. 'Show me.'

She gently probed his wrist with her fingers. It felt sore.

He sought her face. 'Prognosis?'

'Go and see Mads. You know Mads, right? Tell her I sent you.'

'I can't use the team physio!'

'You bloody well will do, after that stunt. Go on. I've got a game to play.'

His resistance evaporated. 'You're the best, Edie.'

'Yeah. I am.' She thumbed at the pavilion. 'And no clapping when we win.'

He fired a fake salute. 'Yes, Miss.'
She eye-rolled. 'It's a good job I lo— *Like* you.'

31st Over

Eden jogged back to her position. In her peripheral vision, Matt headed to the pavilion.

Was that a stunt, mate? A ridiculous show of alpha cockiness? Very unlike you. You wouldn't be trying to impress me, flirt with me, win me back through heroic gestures?

But the heart shape? That's more like the guy I know. Knew.

She dismissed it. Worrying and speculating about romance had to wait. There was a match to be won.

With four overs to go, victory was almost certain, but Eden couldn't let her concentration slip. She and Rojo were bowling the last four overs in tandem, as the Scorpions tried to get the remaining batters out.

Eden collected the ball from captain Dani, adjusted the field, and walked to her mark.

What should I open with? How about... this?

She took a precise grip of the ball, inhaled deeply, and set off. Into her stride, accelerating, right arm coming through, the ball delivered deep into the crease, right on line, past the batter's feet, and catapulted middle stump down the strip.

Eden leapt, arms aloft. A perfect yorker, first delivery of her death spell. Did it come any better than that?

She was mobbed, high-fives and hugs all round. The batter trudged off, shaking her head.

The subs ran on, passing drink bottles around. Eden sought out her friend, keen for words of mutual support... but of course, Brooke wasn't there.

Her disappointment spoke volumes. She glanced toward the pavilion. Matt was standing, watching. He raised his arm. It looked like a thumbs-up.

She took the ball and walked back to the start of her run up.

Now, don't showboat with a ridiculous display of athleticism and power. I'm not trying to win him back by showing that I'm a half-decent bowler.

She focussed on the new batter.

Last thing she'll expect is another yorker. But am I good enough to nail two in a row?

Let's find out.

An hour later, after the congratulations, the debrief, the ice bath, and a few selfies and signatures with fans, Eden met Matt in the bar.

'How's the wrist?'

'It's not broken. Maddy says it's sprained.' He frowned. 'But this isn't about me. You had a great game, Edie. Really happy for you.'

She cupped his arm. 'Thanks. Hat-trick would have been nice, but I mustn't get greedy.'

'I thought you had her LBW, but then, I'm not the umpire.'

'No, and you should probably skip work tomorrow. Go easy, okay? I'll tell Dad you've had a mishap.'

Matt shook his head. 'I'll tell him. My fault for trying heroics.'

'Well, ten out of ten for the catch, but three for the landing.'

'Thanks. So... shall we?' He pointed. 'Your carriage awaits.'

She gestured. 'Lead on, Jeeves.'

In the car, they buckled up, he started the engine, then shifted the gear-lever into reverse.

'Fuck,' he muttered.

'What?' she asked. Then the penny dropped. 'Didn't think this through, did you?'

He looked across sheepishly, gingerly moving his wrist. 'Not really.'

'Want me to drive?'

'You're not insured on this crate. But I'll be okay,' he insisted. 'It's mostly motorway.'

Her stomach skipped. 'Look, I'll change gear for you, okay?'

A laugh sputtered from him. 'What?'

'We tag-teamed on the piano enough times. You think I can't move a lever when you put your foot down?' She tapped her chest. 'I *nailed* those yorkers today. Me. Miss Can't-Bowl-For-Toffee.'

He scrutinised her face, mulling her suggestion. 'Okay.'

'I'll try not to bugger up your gearbox.'

'Thanks.'

'...Mister Can't-Catch-For-Toffee.' She grinned.

'You want to walk home?'

'You want a Chinese burn?'

He tapped the gearstick. 'First gear, please.'

Ten minutes later, they were cruising up the M27, heading for home. Every gearchange had gone smoothly. The dance, the symbiosis, warmed her heart.

'You know what's funny?' she asked.

'That bit when Del Boy falls through the gap in the bar?'

She fake punched his arm. 'Remember the first time you tried to catch a 6?'

'Hard to forget.'

She recalled the day, the inflection point that turned their acquaintance into friendship and then, speedily, romance. When he'd caught the ball and tossed it back to her, she'd fumbled it because she wasn't concentrating. She was distracted by this Adonis.

'Feels like yesterday,' she said wistfully.

'A lot has happened.'

'Most of it good.'

'Most of it,' he agreed. 'Hey, thanks for sending me to Maddy. It's not up to you to look after me. Not anymore.'

'Care is mutual, Matt. Was and still is.'

'Hmm.'

He fell silent. The tyres click-clacked over the cat's eyes as they changed lanes.

'What?' she asked, concerned.

'I did a poor job of caring for you.'

Her shoulders fell. 'No, you didn't. You gave it everything.' She looked out of the side window. 'But I was a bitch. Sorry.'

'It's okay, Edie. Bad timing, that's all. Everything at once. It was horrible even being me. God knows what it was like for you.' He sighed. 'Just showed I'm not cut out for this.'

'"This"? Love?'

'No. The athlete life.'

'Oh, don't talk like that. It was a blip. And I'm me. Please don't judge everyone against that yardstick. Take people as they come. Look at Tweedie. We're not exactly peas in a pod.'

'She has her moments too.'

'We all do. Perils of the life. Plus, we're only human. But Brooke is a lovely person, truly.'

He glanced across. 'You both are.'

That brought a smile. 'Thanks. But I'm probably a better cricketer than girlfriend.'

'Nobody's perfect.'

They arrived at her house at six-fifteen. Matt opened the back door, ready to haul her bag out, but she didn't let him risk worsening his hand sprain. Still, the gesture was lovely.

He leant on the driver's door. 'Played today, Edie.'

'Thanks. It was... nice to have you along. And the lift.'

'No problem. Thanks for being my gearshift partner.'

She shrugged. 'Better than crawling up the M3 in first gear.'

He chuckled. 'Definitely.'

'And... I'm glad you and I are out of first gear too.'

'Think we were in reverse for a long time.'

'That's fair.'

He indicated the house. 'Go and have a good soak. See you whenever.'

'Definitely.' Then she pulled him into a clench. His smell tickled her nostrils, spiking her hormones. 'Take it easy with that hand. The Garden of Eden needs its keepers to be in top form.'

His arms loosely encircled her. 'I will.'

An hour later, after a bath and a meal, the landline rang. Few people had the number. The caller was Mrs Harris, Brooke's mum.

Eden was immediately on the back foot, worried. Had something happened to Tweedie? Eden's pulse raced. She whipped out her mobile, frantically swiping to the diabetes app. Had she missed a vital notification?

Nothing so alarming. Mrs Harris was curious why Brooke wasn't in the team. She was a huge supporter of her daughter, coming to games whenever possible or watching the livestream. Brooke wasn't even on the bench. What had happened?

Eden sank onto the sofa. This didn't make sense. Wasn't Brooke back home, a mercy dash to help care for her ill father?

No. Her dad was right as rain. She hadn't turned up or been in contact.

What the fuck are you doing, Tweed?

And are you okay?

At eight-thirty, Eden heard the front door open. It was blessed relief, as she'd been stewing over Brooke's apparent deception... accompanied by a large glass of wine.

Brooke breezed into the living room and dropped her holdall on the floor. 'Hi Ede. Great game today.' She moved in for a hug.

Eden stepped back.

Brooke frowned. 'What's up?'

'Your mum rang.'

'And?' Then her face fell. 'Oh. Shit.'

'Want to explain?' Eden folded her arms.

'Not really.'

'Well, good. Glad I was worried about you,' she sniffed.

Brooke flopped onto the sofa. 'I took a couple of days, that's all.'

'Why? And why lie about your dad? Why the smokescreen? What's the big secret? Is it England? Is that it?'

Brooke laughed. 'No. God, no.' She massaged her face. 'I just thought you could use a game.'

'What?' she whispered.

'I wanted to give you a shot. Help... rotate the squad.'

Eden sunk to the chair. 'What the *fuck*, Tweed?'

'So you *aren't* happy,' Brooke snipped.

'Of course I'm bloody well not happy! You can't skip matches for me. Or lie about it, not to me, and *definitely* not to Susie.' She shook her head, mind whirling.

'Did you tell Susie how you broke your finger?' Brooke shot a cutting look.

'That is *not* the same!'

Brooke sneered. 'You don't get to take the moral high ground and lecture me.'

'I'm looking out for you. And your reputation.'

'Me too, Ede. *And* trying to give you a break.'

Eden raised a palm. 'I don't want to be on the team out of *generosity*. I want it because I earned it, because I'm in good form. We're supposed to *support* each other.'

Brooke stood, throwing up her arms. 'What do you think *this* is?'

'Guilt,' she sneered.

Brooke's nose wrinkled. 'About coming here and taking your place, or what happened last season?'

'You tell me.'

'I have *no* reason to feel guilty for either of those. You don't give two shits about that Mankad.'

'Actually, I do,' Eden blurted. A shiver went down her spine, as if she'd walked over a grave. Had she really said that aloud?

Brooke's eyes were wide. 'Wow, there's a thing,' she murmured.

'We're not talking about me, Tweed. This is about what *you* did. Why the hell are you jeopardising your England selection? Taking a random two-day break to give your mate a leg-up.' Eden stood. 'I'm a big girl. I did alright here before you arrived. I can make my own bloody way.'

Brooke sneered. 'Doesn't seem like that lately.'

'Get someone to threaten to slice *you* open and see how you cope with the sleepless nights and depression and a useless boyfriend.'

'Useless? He bent over backwards for you! He's an absolute catch, and you treated him like shit.'

Eden moved into her friend's personal space. 'Is that so? Then you can fucking have him. I hope you'll be very happy, but don't expect me to carry your bouquet.'

Brooke's jaw hardened. 'Not a chance in hell.'

'You send me an invitation and I'll burn it.'

'I wouldn't waste a postage stamp on you,' Brooke spat. She swept up her bag. 'I can't stay here tonight.'

'Good.'

Brooke strode into the hallway. 'I was only trying to do the right thing.'

'Well, you screwed up.'

Brooke spun on her heel. 'Then I know how Matt feels.'

Shaking with rage, filling with sadness, Eden followed on as Brooke opened the front door. 'Going to his house, I suppose?'

'None of your fucking business. I don't have to excuse myself to *you*.' Brooke slammed the door.

Eden collapsed to the carpet and sobbed.

32nd Over

Matt swung his legs down from the sofa. Who was ringing the doorbell at this time of night? Amazon wasn't due.

In the hall, he switched on the porch light. A girly squeak emerged from outside.

He tugged the door open.

'Brooke?' Immediately, his pulse raced. Had something bad happened to Eden? Surely Ray would have rung.

'Hey.' Her voice was small, cheeks puffy. Over her shoulder was a carry bag.

'What's up?'

'We... Ede and I... had a fight.'

He beckoned her inside. 'Come on. This is a sweet tea emergency.'

Her forlorn face creased into appreciation. 'Thanks.'

Into the living room, he gestured toward the sofa. Her bag slid to the floor with a thud. Only now did he see that she'd been crying. It spoke volumes about her and Eden's underlying friendship that a spat could bring Brooke to tears—and she couldn't brush it off. She needed succour, a friend.

Actually, Brooke looked like she needed a hug. So he pulled her into a supportive embrace. She drew him tight, squeezing as if in frustration. He hugged back, and her head lay on his shoulder.

'Did she kick you out?' he asked.

'No. I just needed to get out of there before one of us said something worse.'

'I thought you two were mended.'

'Me too.' She eased away from him. 'But I fucked up.'

'Welcome to my world,' he chuckled sadly.

'Exactly. I could have rung Fi and bitched to her, but you have recent experience of Ede's... moods.' She shrugged. 'So, sorry. This is who I've come crying to.'

He glanced at the door. 'Let's hope she doesn't have the same idea.'

Brooke winced. 'Would she? I mean... are you two okay now?'

'Seems like it.' His shoulders stiffened. 'Especially after today. Did you see the livestream?'

She grinned. 'You mean some idiot in the crowd taking a diving catch and having to go to the physio? Yeah, I saw that.' Her smile thinned. 'And Ede looking after him.'

'First on the scene,' he said defensively.

Yet why be coy? He didn't have to apologise for his relationship with Eden, whatever its status. Certainly not for her running to his aid, like the compassionate soul she was.

Was it because he didn't want Brooke to think that Eden was competing for his affections? Did he want to reassure her that he was *available*?

One thing was certain. He wouldn't use the circumstance—Brooke's emotional state—to initiate a romance.

She needed an arm around her, physically and emotionally, but that arm would not be sliding down to her waist, or allowing its hand to wander onto her chest.

She explained what had happened, factually and without sniping. His insides knotted.

What a conundrum. Whose side to take? The girl who'd done nothing wrong except overreact to a kind gesture, or the one who'd made an error of judgement but chosen him, out of the entire world, to pour her heart out to?

It wasn't as if things weren't already tough. Life was like walking a tightrope between two irresistible opportunities—to regain something wonderful with Eden, or try with Brooke. Of course, either choice risked one or more other relationships. But that was tomorrow's problem. Today's was how to help Brooke through her woes.

'Well?' she asked finally.

'I know you were trying to do the right thing.' He stared into his tea. 'Seems like we're both unable to figure Eden out. Perhaps she's fundamentally impossible.'

Brooke shook her head vigorously, earrings dancing. 'No. She's the best person. We always got through any arguments.'

'Then you'll get through this. You didn't do anything wrong to her.'

'I lied.'

'But you couldn't say that you were stepping back to give her a chance? She'd have hated that.'

'She still did.' Brooke thumped her leg. 'I'm trying everything to help, to get back to where we were, and it's thrown in my face. Why is she not *over* this?'

'Because she hasn't made peace with screwing up in the Final. In the weeks afterwards, all she talked about was wishing she'd done it differently, tried any other tactic.' He met her eye. 'Be honest, how do you feel about tonight? Would you do it the same way again?'

She picked at a nail. 'I suppose not.'

'Then you can't be a bad person. I reckon if Edie had the time again, she wouldn't Mankad you.'

Brooke's face brightened. 'You know what? She basically just said that.'

Reflexively, he laid a hand on her leg. 'That's great. That's closer to "sorry" than she's ever been.'

'I need to apologise, don't I?'

He scratched his neck. 'I don't like being in the middle of this, taking sides.'

She cocked her head. 'Worried you'll offend me? You won't.'

Tension left him. 'Then I agree with Edie. Faking a family illness is not a great idea. And currying favour feels a bit patronising. I get your motives, but I think it was a mistake.' His head fell. 'We all have blind spots, take the wrong fork in the road.'

With a finger, she lifted his chin. 'Care to share?'

'You didn't come here for me.'

'No, but I was hoping for that tea.'

'Shit. Sorry. What a bad host. Gimme a minute.'

He went into the kitchen and put the kettle on.

Brooke leant on the door jamb. 'Want to share?'

It was hardly sensitive information, so, as he brewed their teas, he explained his part in the perfect storm. How the stag do in Las Vegas, and then the wedding in Scotland, had coincided with the worst of Eden's malaise. How, as Best Man, he couldn't duck out of these long-planned engagements. How he'd said it wouldn't make a difference to Eden's mental health because his presence and actions weren't lifting her anyway.

In fact, his absence wasn't as much of an issue as the argument that followed.

Now, standing here with someone who was regretting *her* actions, it was clear that he should have taken a different path. He'd made a bad choice—like Eden's decision to fly off the handle, kick him out, and smack the wall.

Brooke sighed. 'You can't undo the past, Matt. Apologise, yes, but that's not like waving a magic wand. And maybe you and Ede would have broken up anyway.'

'I suppose. All relationships have their rough patches. But you two are stronger than she and I were. You've been through a lot more.'

She sipped her tea. 'True.'

'The problem is I'm in the middle of that. The third wheel.'

She frowned. 'How?'

'If she finds out you came here, she'll... assume.'

'Assume what?'

'That something happened.'

She explored his eyes. 'Why would Ede assume that?'

His skin prickled. 'I think she has... preconceptions about you and me. Because we get along. Talk. Hang out.'

Brooke stepped closer. 'She... reckons we're involved?'

He swallowed. 'Or want to be.'

'Actually, she pretty much gave me the green light.'

'Really? That's not what I see.'

'What *do* you see, Matt?'

He put his mug down. 'I get the feeling she resents you.'

'That's hardly news. Especially tonight.'

'All the same, I don't want to tread on her toes, wind her up. Offend her.'

Brooke eased back and gently folded her arms. 'Why does that matter? You're a free agent. You don't have to get her *blessing*. Would you expect her to ask *your* permission to date anyone else? Be real, Matt. Move on.' She offered a sober smile. 'If you can't, then I'm not sure anyone else will ever be good enough for you.'

'It's not that. I'm worried what it would do to your friendship with Eden if you and I dated.'

'Friendships come and go, too, you know.'

He clasped her shoulder. 'But you're teammates. Do you want that bad blood? Especially when things are back on track?'

She took his hand down and held it. 'Honestly? Right now, I don't think she and I could fall out even more.'

'But you came here to save things from getting worse. Right?'

Her jaw hardened. 'I had to get out of Dodge, that's all. And I wanted someone who had context, who could tell me which of us is being the bitch. And yes, okay, full transparency, if I wanted a hug, which I did, you'd be my first choice. For a lot of reasons.'

'That's good... I suppose.'

She lifted his hand to her cheek. He stroked it with his thumb.

'Why are you tiptoeing around this?' she asked, low and warm.

'Because I fucked up before and didn't read the room. With her.'

She gazed into his eyes. 'Looks like you're not reading it right now.'

His chest was roiling. 'Brooke. *I* have to share this ground with Eden too, remember? If I piss her off, it might piss Ray off, and I'll get the boot.'

'There are other grounds. Why not leave?'

'So you want me to move away?' he asked in surprise and disbelief.

'No. But things you want have to be worked for.' She pushed into him. 'You do want me, don't you?'

His skull throbbed. What to do?

'I think... we're in a goldfish bowl. In an eddy in a goldfish bowl. On a tightrope across an eddy in a goldfish bowl. Juggling—'

She kissed him. Firm and brief. A statement. One that said, "Shut up" and "Here's something to help make your decision". His neck hairs stood on end. He moistened his lips, partly buying time to slow his pulse.

'Brooke?' he murmured.

'Yeah,' she breathed.

'Did you come here expecting... something?'

Her brow furrowed. 'Not *that*. I may be angry about tonight, but I'm not doing anything out of spite or revenge. Am I that kind of person?'

He brushed hair behind her ear. 'No. And this is the wrong time to be acting on impulse. For all of us.'

She eased back. 'Are you saying you *do* want to ask her permission to date?'

'I think...' He stared at the ceiling, desperate for a magical, perfect answer, a plan, a safe route across the tightrope. 'I think we can't rush into anything. Because... and I know this sounds like a stuck record... we risk setting the clock back six months if we have a fling that doesn't work out.'

'You don't think Ede would crow about that?'

'She'd be hurt. And neither of us wants that. Right? I *know* we're grownups, and can do what the hell we like, but we also worry about hurting people's feelings. And, being honest, if you *don't* care about Eden, your *best* friend, then we're a non-starter.'

She stroked his cheek. 'Actually, the impression she gave me was that *you* didn't care about her enough. Which *can't* be true. And I'd rather go slow, and find a man like that, than jump into bed with a dickhead.'

She sighed, her expression reflective. 'Before I slammed the door tonight, I said she was ridiculous to dump a guy like you. I want her to find the right person.' She met his eye. 'But what's done is done. And I'd like a shot with that guy, if he'll have me. So... Can we get a drink sometime? That's not too... inflammatory, is it?'

33rd Over

Eden's bedside clock read 02:38.

Falling asleep had been a challenge. It was a mercy that Brooke had walked out, preventing things from escalating. Still, the fight gnawed at her, a familiar self-examination of who'd been out of line. Yes, Tweedie's gesture was selfless, but it also felt like pity. Even if it wasn't explicitly *wrong*, the fake cover story was unacceptable.

Whatever Brooke had told the coaching staff, she had lied about her dad being ill. That's not a topic to trifle with. Not only had Matt lost his dad, Eden had also been through dark days worrying whether Ray was going to drink himself into the grave following the divorce.

A million things were buzzing around Eden's mind, but the distant sound of the front door closing at eleven thirty helped to quieten them.

She'd drifted off soon afterwards... until a demon came back.

It wasn't the first nightmare about a faceless man with a knife, nor the first time she'd woken in a cold sweat, but it had been three months since the last episode.

What had caused the relapse? Eden thought she'd put the matter behind her, regained positive mental health, but her stupid brain had other ideas.

Why? She felt safer and more content than last year. She'd had a great game, her form was improving, and things with Brooke and Matt were on the up.

The clock ticked to 02:39.

Did Brooke's actions feel like a knife in her back? That was ridiculous—her motives were good. If anything, Brooke had risked her own reputation more than she'd affected Eden's... and wasn't that what friendship and care meant?

She sighed. The truth, and its entwined conundrum, was responsible for the dream. She resented Brooke running to Matt. Even though she'd gracelessly said that Brooke could "have him", it was shock and anger talking. Her subconscious had other ideas. The green-eyed monster lived there.

And she hated that. But she also had to listen to it.

What did she truly want for herself, her friend, and her ex?

If she didn't decide soon, it was going to eat her alive.

She woke at 08:47, did the routine post-game recovery stretches, pulled on a robe and headed downstairs. Her neck prickled. Which way would this conversation go?

More than anything in the world, she didn't want to lose her friend. Without someone as dear as Matt to lean on, Tweedie was the next best thing, and if the stalker dream ever returned, a soothing hug was paramount. Brooke gave the *best* hugs.

Well, second best.

Every muscle tensed, Eden peered around the living room door. Brooke was on the sofa, legs curled underneath. Her gaze moved from the TV to the doorway and then to her landlady.

'Hey.' Her smile was tentative. 'You okay?'

In what way?

Chill. Don't start an argument.

'Yeah. Bednapped, that's all.'

'Why I asked. Not very *you*.'

Eden moved into the room. 'Tough night, y'know?'

'Yeah. Did I... wake you? Earlier?' She shook her head. 'I mean, before.'

Eden sat gingerly on the sofa. Her own sofa. 'No. Couldn't sleep.'

'Hmm. Am I... okay here? Should I have not come back?' Brooke's frown was deep.

'I expected you'd stay at Matt's.'

Now Brooke's eyes widened. 'You don't even know I went there.'

Eden sat up straighter. 'Did you?'

Brooke licked her lips. 'Yeah.'

'Then I definitely expected you'd stay.'

'That sounds like you reckon I'd jump into bed at the first chance.'

Eden folded her arms. 'Wouldn't you?'

'This is not *about* that. It's about us arguing. It's about you and me, Ede.'

'Because you lied.'

'Okay, yes, I did. But I tried to do the right thing.' She scoffed, shaking her head. 'Wish I hadn't bothered if it's going to backfire.'

Eden massaged her forehead and slumped back. Tears wanted to appear. 'I fucking hate this, Tweed. I *hate* fighting. My life was perfect and now it's shit.'

'It was shit *last year*, but it's better now. No? We're at least *speaking*, babe. You and Matt, too. And I only wanted to help. Truly.'

Eden put her head in her hands. 'I know. I am so ungrateful and awful. But you coming here is supposed to help your career, not hinder it.'

Brooke nodded slowly. 'I only wish it wasn't affecting yours.'

'I'm pretty good at doing that on my own. Going to pieces over one bad spell. Busting my hand. Busting my love life. Us.' She laughed, hollow. 'Mum said I should stick to a desk job. Less stress. But I thought I was stronger than that.'

Brooke reached out. 'And you are, Ede. One swallow doesn't make a summer.' She smiled. 'You know, last night I was cursing *my* Mum for being so dedicated to my career that she followed the livestream, worried about me, and rang here. If she'd been dismissive and distant, like your Mum, maybe all this wouldn't have happened.'

'You still would have lied. But I get your point. Maybe that's why I don't like being *handed* a place. I need to succeed on my own. So please, Tweed, don't do anything stupid, not on my account.'

Brooke slumped against the backrest and massaged her eyes. 'I'm sorry. You want me to move out?'

Eden shook her head vigorously. 'No.'

'Good. I'm pleased. I don't want to lose you.'

'Me either.'

Brooke nibbled her lip. 'Look... I didn't... stay over because of *you*. Matt and I agreed it was best that I didn't. He *would* have put me up. As a friend. Found a place. On the sofa, spare room. Then, it would only be about what you *thought*. And it seems you thought the worst.' Brooke's smile was sombre.

'The worst?'

'That's just it, Ede. Nobody wants to talk about this.'

She controlled her breathing. 'The prospect, the idea, of you seeing my ex.'

'It might not work out.'

Her shrug was small. 'Or it might.'

'Either way, we won't know until we try. And we do want to. Just a drink or something. Without sneaking around. Without lying, because I've done enough of that. And you don't deserve another painful spell just because I can't keep away from a guy I like and who, worse coincidence, you also liked.'

The last word rattled round Eden's skull.

Liked? Past tense? No. Inaccurate.

Like, definitely. More than like.

And there was the conundrum. In some ways, she didn't want Brooke to date Matt in case she dumped him and wrecked his appetite for love. She also feared him letting Brooke down as he'd let her down, and Brooke being hurt.

Hard when you care about both of them.

She moistened dry lips. 'So is this a... heads-up?'

Brooke sighed hard. 'Honestly, I don't know what the fuck it is. But if you tell me, now, to my face, that if he and I even have dinner together, you and I are done *forever*, then I'll have to re-evaluate my feelings.'

'But if I tell you that, then I'll have to take a good hard look in the mirror and accept that I've turned into this possessive, holier-than-thou witch.'

'And I don't believe you are.'

'You forget I stole your wicket two years ago.' Eden raised her brow. 'So I have form.'

'Yeah, well, don't give me the green light out of trying to make up for something else. You balled me out last night because you reckoned I skipped the match because of guilt. Which isn't true. And honestly, Matt isn't the only guy in the world. I'm not on some agenda, Ede.' A familiar, impish grin appeared. 'Sure, I'd love to get laid ASAP, but we all want a wicket in the first over, right?'

Eden laughed, a welcome release of tension. 'Based on yesterday's game, yeah, I can relate.'

Brooke took Eden's hand again. 'I want to do the right thing. For all of us.'

'So do I, Tweedie. So do I.'

34th Over

After Brooke left to go back to Eden's, Matt flip-flopped about whether sending her away was the best decision. It was like repatriating an asylum seeker back into a war zone.

Yet the friends would make up eventually, and what Brooke had on her side was a dose of humility, of objective reflection. He wished that Eden had done better last year, crossed the rope and put the game behind her. Recognised she'd made bad bowling decisions.

What she should have done was stay off social media. Of course people were going to be unhappy at her performance, but none would ever be as disappointed as she was. To harangue Eden implied that she didn't care, wasn't doing her best. Simply, she had a bad day. Everyone has those. Brooke had a bad day when she fibbed about her dad. Matt had a bad day when he steadfastly refused to skip a weekend away with the lads.

We're all human. Except perhaps Scotty441. He's pond scum.

He decided that encouraging Brooke to go home was for the best. The spare room wasn't spacious, but it was better than the sofa. However, it was adjacent to his room, which might have been too tempting—for either of them. Might she have asked him to "tuck her in" or asked for a goodnight hug—poor cover stories for another, sexier motive.

He recalled the kiss, enjoyed the memory, and wondered whether he should have kissed back. Would it have lit a fire they couldn't extinguish? Probably. But using her compromised emotional state to get her into the sack wasn't his style. It was better to kick the can down the road. What was to be gained by rushing into this? Nothing. What could be lost? Plenty.

It must be a lot easier if you don't have a moral compass. If I was a vengeful arsehole, I'd sleep with Brooke just to get back at Eden for dumping me.

But that was the pre-Christmas Matt. Now, his culpability for the breakup was obvious. And if the situation arose, he'd tell Eden. Sure, it wouldn't change things, but it might accelerate her emotional recovery. He wanted to get back—as a friend—the girl he knew.

The following morning, Matt reached the stadium at eight. The day's task was to prepare a new wicket for tomorrow's game.

Eggs was already on the mower, diligently taking care of the outfield. He gave Matt a thumbs-up. Matt waved back. Eggs made a drinking motion. Matt saluted.

Ray was in the groundsman's hut, waiting for the kettle to boil.

'Morning, Ray.'

'Morning, son.'

Matt tossed teabags into two mugs. 'Not long now.'

'The big van? Yeah.' Ray sighed. 'Funny old world.'

'Yeah. How?'

The man scratched his stubbled chin. 'Very real, isn't it? Moving on. Going to miss the old place. You get attached to things, don't you?'

Matt perched on a chair. 'True,' he reflected.

'Take that squeaky floorboard at the top of the stairs. It annoys the pants off me, but it's part of the house. Liz and I loved that place. It was perfect for us, from the wedding day, for little Edie growing up, to her having mates over. And the garden, and the tree.' He looked Matt straight. 'We're all a *bit* broken, son. I reckon my new place is perfect, but, pound to a penny, it won't be. There'll be something. And I'll get used to it.'

The kettle clicked. Matt poured the water into the mugs. 'You don't *have* to go.'

Ray waved a hand. 'It's a new start, simple as that. The big work is up here.' He tapped the side of his head. 'And I leant on Edie for long enough. She left her other club to come back here for me, you know that?'

'I did, boss. But we all need someone by our side in the tough days.'

Ray prised open the biscuit tin. 'And you were there for my daughter, and she's grateful, even if it didn't work out how it was supposed to.'

Matt stirred two sugars into Eggs' mug. 'Fine margins, I think. Neither of us was our best selves for a while there.'

'But you know it, and that's good. Anyway, enough agony aunt. How's the picture look?'

Matt visualised the painting. 'Good. Really good. Gives the place a touch of class, which is hardly me.'

Ray laughed. 'Class doesn't matter.' He tapped Matt's chest. 'It's what's in here.'

Matt took the two mugs out to the pitch, and he and Eggs leant against the mower, sipping their tea. The stadium had an eerie silence about it. It wasn't unusual—empty days were much more common than crowd days—yet Matt felt uneasy. The calm after the storm? The calm before the storm?

'Matty?'

'Yeah?'

'What's a good present for a... lady?'

'Random.'

Eggs frowned. 'Why? You never buy Eden a present?'

'Tons. But did you never buy one?'

'Course. I got stuff for my sister and my folks. But this is different.'

'Can I get some clues? Buying for women requires thought. I couldn't, for instance, get Brooke the same as what I'd get Eden.'

Eggs' eyes widened. 'Buying Brooke presents?' A cheeky grin appeared. 'You smooth mover.'

Matt tutted. 'I was being hypothetical. I meant that things like chocolate and flowers aren't a panacea.'

Eggs looked bemused. 'One of those big Italian cake things?'

'That's a panettone. What I'm saying is you have to know the girl—'

'Lady.'

'And there's that word again. What happened to "bird"?'

Eggs' nose wrinkled. 'Geraldine's no bird.'

'Ah.' Matt processed everything. 'Are you *dating*?' he asked with incredulity.

'We're not *not* dating.'

Matt passed on that. 'Is it her birthday? The two-week anniversary of you falling into her clutches? Is it to celebrate her getting into the Guinness Book of World Records for the greatest collection of sex toys?'

Eggs thumped him. 'I'm asking for serious advice, mate.'

'Okay. If you want to make a good impression, give her something she'll treasure.' He was reminded of Eden's necklace. 'Assuming this isn't just a bit of fun for you. A summer of fooling around, drinking tea and watching girls.'

Eggs scowled. 'Piss off. And no, Geraldine and I aren't doing some April to September thing or whatever. I'm getting her a present, aren't I?'

Matt exhaled. So much to unpack. 'Don't buy lingerie. Or flowers. Make it *personal*. What does she like? Use that. Or if she's into experiences and not trinkets, organise a trip somewhere.'

Eggs nodded. 'Yeah. Right. So what did you get for Brooke?'

'Me? Uh, well, nothing yet.'

Eggs leant in. 'But you want to. Is she into… what did you say… experiences, or trinkets?'

Matt's mouth moved silently. 'Um… not sure. It's early days.'

That was fair. He and Brooke were only at the "attraction" stage. He knew little about her. Maybe that would change after they went for a drink.

And it was only a drink. Not even advertised as a "date", let alone anything more. True, Brooke was more flirty and flighty than Eden, but he didn't want a one-night stand, a revenge hookup, or something shallow.

Was Brooke's appeal more than skin deep? Time would tell.

35th Over

For the first time in too long, Eden was at peace with the world.

Relatively.

It was game day. She and Brooke were both playing, and they were friends again. Sure, she'd had to sacrifice any hope of getting back together with Matt, but you have to play the percentages.

Don't run a 2 that's not there. Don't bowl an over of slow balls when the first two go to the boundary. Don't hope your ex-boyfriend will suddenly forgive you when he'd rather make eyes at someone else.

Brooke *hadn't* come to the Scorpions with the intent of stealing Eden's bowling slot and her boyfriend. Eden merely hadn't been up to the task of holding onto either of them. Now, she had her squad place back.

One out of two would have to suffice.

In the changing room, Susie gathered everyone together for the pep talk, then the players collected their gear and headed out into the May morning sunshine. Eden shared a word with a few friends from the visiting side, the Northern Storm, then the teams took opposite sides of the pitch for the warm-up session.

She, Brooke and Rose, along with bowling coach Jonno, went to the practice wicket. Nearby, Matt and Eggs were attending to a faulty sprinkler. Matt waved. She waved back.

Dad and Alan were on the match wicket. As usual, Dad didn't acknowledge her. It was a professional understanding—everyone knew they were family, but on match days they were at work. Any chat would keep until after the game.

As the men strolled off, deep in conversation, Eden and the other four bowlers gathered their equipment and returned it to the bench area. Eden took a moment to survey the stands, watching people choose their seats. One of the squad subs handed her a water bottle, and she took a long, slow drink. In the middle of the pitch, Dad lined up the roller for a final pass over the wicket.

Bless you. I know what you're thinking. Make the Garden of Eden as perfect as can be.

At least I get to play on it today.

Ray steered the machine down one half of the strip, then took a wide circle, lined up, and headed back up the wicket. He was precious about doing this last step himself. Matt never got a look in—though that might change when the promotion arrived.

She glanced towards the groundsman's hut, where Matt and Eggs were chatting.

The roller continued past the batting crease. Dad was leaning forward, probably checking his line.

It trundled on. And on.

Eden frowned. Why wasn't he turning towards the hut?

The vehicle was halfway to the boundary. Dad was hunched over the wheel. Motionless.

Fear seized her. Then realisation.

She screamed. She ran.

Matt stopped listening to Eggs. He knew that scream. He located the source. Eden was pelting across the pitch. Not a bowling run-up. Full tilt.

He saw her destination.

'Oh, fuck.' His chest tightened.

He dropped his mug and ran, plotting an intercept course.

'Call the paramedic!' he yelled over his shoulder.

A hundred yards ahead, the roller crashed through the digital advertising hoardings.

Eden was shrieking. Matt's heart shattered. In his peripheral vision, Brooke was running, two medics close behind.

The roller, with Ray a lifeless sack of potatoes aboard, slammed into the railings and came to a dead stop. Matt zeroed in on Eden, converging diagonally, and brought her to an equally abrupt halt. They were twenty yards from the roller.

Her red eyes were saucers. She shoved him.

'No, Eden,' he rapped

'Get out of my fucking way!' She grappled with his shirt.

He wrapped both arms around her. 'Stay away. *Please.*'

'Get *off* me.' She writhed like a snake.

'You don't want to go there,' he insisted.

'It's my fucking Dad!' she bawled.

'I know. And believe me—'

She kneed him in the groin. 'Stay *out* of this.'

Matt went down like a ninepin. He took pride in his gym work, but when an elite athlete crushes your wedding veg with a hammer blow, it smarts.

He watched, prone, as Eden brushed the two medics aside and scrambled onto the roller.

You are impossible, Edie. I do everything in my power to protect your mental health, and this is what I get for it.

I watched my father die, and I don't want you to go through that.

He closed his eyes in pain and anguish, and begged the universe to save her from trauma.

'Are you okay?' came a voice.

He opened his eyes.

Brooke crouched. 'Matt?'

'I'll be fine,' he groaned, clutching his groin. 'Look after Edie.'

Another face peered down. 'Mate?'

'Kill switch on the roller. Now.'

'Yup.' Eggs vanished.

'Sure?' Brooke's forehead was lined in sympathy.

'Yeah. Just stay with her. *Please.*'

'Will do.' She jogged away.

Matt lay back and looked at the sky. A tear dripped onto the grass.

Please be okay, boss. Please be okay, Edie.

Eden was hyperventilating. She knew this. Stopping it was a different matter. Someone had pulled her off Dad. Sensibly, she hadn't tried to kick their balls into the East Stand.

Danica had marshalled her a few yards away, gently turning her back. 'You don't need to watch. It won't help.'

'But—'

'He's breathing,' the medic called.

Not as fast as me.

That was an awful thing to think.

Danica gripped Eden's shaking hand. The stadium PA was blaring something. Not far away, her ex-boyfriend was being helped up, his face etched in pain.

You always hurt the ones you love.

Another player ran up. 'Ede?'

'Tweed,' she replied through half sobs.

'Have you got her?' Danica asked Brooke.

'Yeah. Go back to the girls.'

Danica jogged away. Paramedics trotted down the steps from the concourse to the pitchside.

Brooke put her arm on Eden's shoulder. 'He'll be fine.'

You can't say that. It's an empty promise.

'Yeah,' she murmured, breath hitching.

'Maybe this will be the wake-up call.'

'What?'

Brooke shrugged. 'He was unfit. Overweight. You know that. Is he still drinking?'

Eden backed off, quivering. 'You've got some nerve. Lying about your own dad, and now badmouthing mine.' She arrowed a finger at Ray's helpless form. 'He's on a gurney and you're questioning his lifestyle choices?'

'Look, Ede—' She reached out.

'No. Go away. Play the game.'

Brooke raised a calming hand. 'I'll come to the hospital.'

'You bloody well won't. Stop trying to help, Tweed. It's not working.' Tears dribbled down her cheeks. 'Go and bowl. You're good at that.'

Brooke's face cycled through myriad expressions, then her shoulders fell. 'Fine. But I'll be thinking about you. You can't stop me doing *that*.'

Eden wiped her eyes. 'Okay.'

Brooke looked her up and down, seemingly at an impasse.

Please, Tweed. Read the room. I don't want a slanging match. Not now. Not when we're fixed.

'Go well,' she murmured, a non-inflammatory full stop to the encounter.

Brooke licked her lips. 'I'll try.' Then she backed away, turned, and broke into a jog.

Eden watched Dad's stretcher being carried up to a waiting ambulance.

I have to go. I can't stay here. Definitely can't play. Cricket's just a game. Family is more important. Love is more important.

Across the ground, the teams were warming up. The start time had been delayed, but the game had to go ahead. Whilst everyone at the ground loved Ray, they knew he wouldn't want any fuss.

Eden was allowed to fuss. And cry. And go to the hospital. And sit by his bed all night. Alone. Because Brooke had annoyed her, and she'd poleaxed the next best person who could have helped.

However, the next best person was walking up.

Not for the first time, Matt felt for Brooke. She'd rankled Eden. Another time of emotional distress, and Eden was being a cactus. A cactus with a powerful kneecap.

Should he have left her alone? If she wanted to potentially watch her father breathe his last, that was *her* choice. Who the hell did Matt think he was?

Someone who cherished her, never stopped caring about her. It wasn't the *real* Eden Palmer who'd kneed him in the wedding tackle. It hadn't been the real Eden Palmer who'd given him his marching orders last November. It was another girl, one consumed by anger at the world for the pain it was inflicting.

Offering friendship and support now was possibly a waste, certainly a gamble. It didn't matter how deeply he cared, or how much he empathised, he could still do or say the wrong thing.

But he *couldn't* let Eden go to the hospital alone. This time, he wasn't risking a relationship, so things couldn't get worse between them. He'd spent months wishing Eden would forget a bad experience, recognise her many positive attributes, and regain her form. Now, *he* had to take that medicine.

With a deep breath, but wishing for ibuprofen, he went to Eden. Her chest was heaving—she was barely holding it together.

'I'll drive you,' he said softly.

She took her attention off the ambulance. 'No, it's fine.'

He cupped her elbow. 'Eden. I'm doing this.'

'I can drive a *car*.'

'Yes. But then you'll be at the hospital alone, and that's not happening.'

'Honestly, Matt, I'm a big girl.'

He took her shoulders and slowly rotated her to face him. Her cheeks were puffy, ponytail loose and dishevelled.

He tapped his chin. 'Hit me here this time. Full pace delivery. Lay me out, Edie. If not, I'm driving you to the hospital.'

Her lip trembled. 'Okay.'

Matt spoke to the paramedic, who said the prognosis was good. Ray had suffered a cardiac arrest, but was conscious and needed tests and observation.

Eggs ran up. Matt told him what was happening and said that Alan and the lads could easily cope without him. Eggs gave Eden his best wishes. She replied with a small smile.

Matt took her hand and led her up the steps to the concourse.

A girl ran up. 'Coach, coach. Is he okay?'

Eden shakily patted the girl's shoulder. 'For now, Lily, yes.'

Lily took Eden's hand in both hers and squeezed it. 'Be strong.' She tugged at the beaded bracelet. 'Remember. Focus. Breathe.'

Eden nodded. 'I will.'

The girl embraced her. 'I'll cheer extra loud. I'll text you the score.'

Another nervous smile. 'Thanks. We should go.' She looked at Matt. 'Right?'

He waved ahead. 'Yes, Miss.'

The smile broadened. She led him to the pavilion, collected her phone, then they hustled to the car park and jumped into his car. Without fuss, he headed quickly but legally for the hospital.

'Thanks, Matt,' she said.

'No problem.'

'After what I just did?'

He wanted to say that a boot in the nuts would heal much faster than the pain of the breakup, but bit his tongue.

'Because nobody should be alone at a time like this.' He changed gear.

Her hand rested on his. 'I don't deserve your friendship.'

'Things happen. We all make mistakes.'

She glanced at his groin. 'Sorry. Does it hurt?'

'This isn't about me.'

'You want someone to look at it while we're there?'

He shook his head. 'That would mean leaving you alone for a bit, or dropping trou with you in the room. And neither of those works.'

She flapped a hand. 'Aw, I've seen it all already. Plenty of times.' She winked.

Despite his cheeks colouring, this was a huge step up in mood for her. Was this what Eden needed to help her get through the next few hours? Distraction, playfulness?

He coughed. 'Shall we focus on Ray's heart and not my balls?'

'Yeah.'

36th Over

Eden let the conversation end there. She was too numb to navigate everything without pissing off Matt. Even a stab at humour was risky. It would be self-sabotaging to refuse his help. She'd done that once before and regretted it. Yet it said much about Matt's character that he was prepared to forgive her, even run to her aid again.

She toyed with the bracelet, wishing for a third prompt too. "Be kind."

Try that, Edie. Be kind to Matt, because he's being kind to you. Don't blame him for today, because it's nobody's fault except the universe's.

She sniffed.

And you, Dad.

A single sob escaped her.

'Hey. Don't cry,' Matt said softly.

'I wasn't... I'm not...' She burst into tears.

By the time she'd composed herself, gathered the ranging thoughts, they'd arrived at the hospital car park. Not wanting to look like a grieving widow, she wiped her eyes on her long-sleeved shirt, breathed and focused, as Lily's gift reminded her, and got out of the car.

Matt indicated the route to A&E, then matched her pace as she walked. 'If you want my hand, it's here.'

She clamped her fingers around it. 'Thank you.'

'Shall I do the talking?'

'Yes, please.'

So much for the mentally, emotionally and physically resilient elite athlete...

Deep breath. Sometimes it's okay not to be okay. Like when you or your father's life is in danger. Being weak is okay. Being cruel is not.

Matt spoke to a receptionist, and they were directed to a Waiting Area. With a hand between her shoulder blades, he guided them to two chairs. She sat.

'Water?' he asked.

She looked up into his gorgeous, sympathetic eyes. 'Thanks.'

He went to the water dispenser, but there were no cups left.

'Back in a sec.' He beetled away.

She pulled out her phone and checked WhatsApp. Lily, Susie, club secretary Debs, and two of the team subs had all sent well wishes.

Then another ping arrived... from Dad's mobile. Her spirits leapt.

"Hi Eden. This is Ben. I'm using Ray's mobile as it was here in the hut. Alan and I send our best. Tell Ray and Matt not to worry, I haven't burned the stadium down yet! BTW Brooke took a wicket in her second over. 17-1. Go Scorpions!"

Her lips perked. Then they fell. She shook her head.

I'm not doing this shit again. I'm not letting something terrible ruin my friendships. The ink's barely dry on the ceasefire with Tweedie and I pulled a gun. Only place I'm shooting is my foot.

She swiped to the chat with Brooke. The most recent message was from 07:11 that morning. Brooke had spent an age in the bathroom—*very* her—and they needed to leave.

Eden had sent, "Taxi for Harris. Outside. E."

She tapped the box.

"Sorry for snapping. You're right. Dad wasn't in great shape. If he gets through this, I'm reading him the riot act. Sorry. Go well. Looks like you already are :-)"

Brooke wouldn't pick up the message until the innings break, but Eden had no idea how long they'd be at the hospital. Hopefully a long time... because a quick visit implied an outcome she didn't dare consider.

She leant back in the blue plastic chair and stared at the stained false ceiling.

Don't die, Dad. I'm not ready. I haven't made you as proud as I want, as a cricketer or a daughter.

I will try harder.

Matt bypassed the next water station and went to the café. It had undergone a makeover since he was here last time, drinking multiple mediocre coffees on many visits. He and Mum had been marking time, waiting for the end to come. Arguably, that was easier than now, when the outcome was anyone's guess. Was Ray on life support, having tests, or in surgery? Or... worse, and they simply hadn't been told yet?

He tapped his foot impatiently. The customer at the till was ordering six different beverages. Matt was desperate for Eden not to be alone when a doctor brought news.

Finally, he dumped the bottle of water on the counter, ordered an oat milk latte and a white Americano, tapped his card on the reader, and waited.

He was gripped by a desire to donate blood. Ridiculous, really, as it would hardly make the difference between life and death for Ray—the hospital had bottles of the stuff—and it would mean leaving Eden alone again.

Manfully tolerating the two scorching cups in his hands, the water bottle a teetering bulge in his jeans pocket, he hustled back to the waiting area.

He sat heavily beside her. 'Any news?'

'No.'

His shoulders relaxed. The water bottle, squeezed like a vice now that he'd created a lap, sagged from his pocket and slapped onto the floor.

Eden raised an eyebrow.

'Bottled water with added floor germs?' he asked, wincing.

'Exactly how I like it.'

'Try the coffee. It's hotter than the sun.' He passed her the cup.

She switched hands and blew on the first one. 'Too kind.'

'The barista creates sinkholes in her spare time.'

She prised off the lid. 'Is this what I think it is?'

'One and a half sugars, right?'

She inspected his eyes. 'In a Large.'

'This *is* a Large.'

'It's a very medium-y Large.' Her pupils glistened with a familiar impishness.

'I'll get straight on to the Secretary of State for Health.'

'If you would.'

'Can I do it after...' He circled a finger. '...this?'

'Sure.' Then she frowned, looking past him.

He turned.

A nurse, maybe mid-forties, smiled. 'Miss Palmer?'

Eden sat up straighter. 'Yes?'

'Just to let you know that your father is in surgery.'

Eden grabbed Matt's hand. He squeezed hard.

'Right,' she replied.

'It's a routine operation to clear a blocked artery. I can take you through to the cardiac ward waiting area.' The nurse gestured. Her enamel badge read, "Kathryn".

Eden looked across at Matt.

'We get to carry our nuclear cups a bit further,' he remarked.

Eden eye-rolled. 'Please excuse him,' she said to the nurse.

He shrugged. 'Or don't, Kathryn. I'm a real pain in the arse.'

Eden glanced down. 'Or family jewels, actually.'

'I think that was you, Edie.'

'I stand corrected.' Her eyes twinkled.

'Shall we both stand? And walk?'

'Yes, let's.'

The nurse led them down three corridors to the Jenner Ward and indicated the seating area.

'Thanks, Kathryn,' Eden said.

'You're welcome. Sorry you had to miss the match.'

Eden frowned, then remembered her attire. She hadn't changed out of her match kit—red shirt and black trousers. On the back was her squad number and her name.

'Oh, thanks. But circumstances, y'know?'

Kathryn nodded sympathetically. 'I think Mr Palmer will be fine. Back out there, pitchside, sitting on that old camp chair, watching you play.'

Matt nudged Eden gently. 'Seems your cover is blown.'

She jabbed him in the ribs, then eyed the nurse. 'Sorry for him. Again.'

'At least you have someone. Many people don't.' Kathryn looked around. 'And whilst I'd love to sit and chat about cricket, it's frowned upon by the charge nurse.'

'Cricket, or chatting?' Matt joked. 'Oh, and sorry for me. Again again.'

Eden cleared her throat. 'Maybe on your break, Kathryn.'

'Do you do… autographs?'

Matt's spirits lifted. There was nothing better than seeing his girlfriend—

No, ex-girlfriend.

—get recognition and appreciation. She worked so hard, ran the gauntlet of drawbacks, yet was always the same down-to-earth person. It was why girls like Lily looked up to her. Eden Palmer was a magnificent woman, athlete, human being.

'Of course,' she replied. 'Come and find me later.'

Kathryn beamed. 'Thank you. Ruth, that's my eldest, is a big fan. Of you and the team.'

'Oh, thank you. I'll try to get you a pair of tickets for a game.'

She touched Eden's arm. 'Ruthie would love that. Anyway, I should get on. I'll bring you news when I get it. May be a couple of hours.'

'Thanks,' Matt said.

This was a pleasant conversation with a nice lady, but equally, the coffee cup was making his palm feel like cinders.

37th Over

Eden chose two seats in the corner.

Emotions crashed over her. Dad in surgery. Being recognised—though the kit was a big giveaway. Having another fan. The well-wishes. Wondering how Tweedie and the team were getting on. Matt being flawless. Yes, he made her eye-roll, but she loved that. He didn't take himself too seriously. And he knew *exactly* when to hold her hand, when to assume control. He was judging things perfectly.

She looked across. He flashed a sober, "Well, here we are then", expression.

Without thinking, she clasped his toned thigh. 'Thank you.'

'Honestly, Edie, I don't need thanks. Anyone would do this. Not just if it was their boss in trouble, or because a friend was in need. Because it's the right thing to do.'

'And because you've walked in my shoes.'

'It wouldn't make a difference. Maybe if I wasn't the guy on point back there at the stadium. If it was a training day, you'd have brought Brooke or Phoebe. You know, someone you're actually close with.' He winked.

'Are we… that far apart?' She swallowed down disappointment. 'Did I break us that badly?'

'Not so much that I wouldn't come here. Clearly.' He shrugged.

'Like you said, it was you or nobody.'

'I'm the least worst option.'

'Yeah.' A playful smile broke. 'And I didn't want to hurt your feelings.'

'Too kind. Anyway, I got you here, I got you boiling and over-sugared coffee, and I found you a new fan.' Eyes twinkling, he thumbed at the corridor. 'So I'll sod off, yeah?'

She grabbed a fistful of his shirt. 'Please don't.'

He kissed her knuckles. The feel of his lips made her pulse race. 'No chance. How about a nice artisan croissant, hand-baked by a machine in a factory in Milton Keynes?'

'Can you find me one that's left over from yesterday? Or a ham and cheese toastie with almost no ham and only a sprinkling of cheese?'

He stood. 'I'll try. If I had Izzy's wicketkeeping gloves, I'd get us another coffee.'

She sipped her hot brew. 'Nah. Dad'll be out in a couple of hours, and this one will still be drinkable.'

'You're such a lightweight.' He drained his cup.

'I always said you had an asbestos throat.'

'And that was one of the nicest things.'

He was joking, but the sentiment resonated. 'Was I that awful?' she murmured.

He rubbed her shoulder. 'No. You were fucking incredible, Eden Palmer. And you still are. But I wasn't.'

She shook her head. 'I'm not sure *anyone* could have pulled me out of that funk, Matt. And if Dad doesn't come back out of that room, I don't know how I'll cope.'

'I'll be there for you. If you want me.'

She nodded. 'I really do. Especially as I screwed it up with Brooke.'

'I'm not sure you have. She'll understand. It was the heat of the moment. Stress. Emotion.'

'Like kicking you in the nads.'

'It's already forgotten.'

'Still, you put up with a lot of shit.'

'I made you break your hand.'

Tears pooled behind her eyes. 'No, I did that. Actually... I think I did everything.' Her head fell.

A finger rested on her chin and lifted it. 'You didn't.'

And she remembered why she'd loved him. In fact, she'd never stopped.

Matt lowered his hand. Alarm bells were clanging. There was a time and a place for these conversations—in fact, this *exact* conversation—but they didn't pair well with her demeanour. It seemed like she regretted the breakup and, whilst that should have made his mood rocket, they were in the middle of a head-scrambling, life or death situation. Making decisions at emotional times was a recipe for disaster.

Just as he'd ushered Brooke out of the house that night, he wouldn't do anything today to raise the stakes. Yes, Eden could lean on him, but he wouldn't let her go gooey, because it would be a flash in the pan. What if the worst happened, and Kathryn came back with an ashen face while he and Eden were romantically reconnecting?

He could see the outcome in 3-D. The following day, amidst her crushing grief, she'd berate him for coming on to her in the waiting room, heartlessly oblivious as Ray breathed his last. She'd extrapolate and project and assume, maybe even slam her foot into the wall and break a toe. And they would be finished. Not friends. Not on speaking terms. Nothing.

And that would be an awful waste. Because they had something special and, right now, vital. They had regained almost everything they'd lost. The final mile—a fondness bordering on true love—was not for today. Or tomorrow. Or possibly ever.

You'd have to be a real piece of shit to drive your ex-girlfriend to the hospital in the hope that, by putting a supportive arm around her, she'd show her gratitude later on. At home. In the bedroom. Matt merely wanted her, and Ray, to be okay. And he really believed he could make a difference this time.

Her lips pursed. 'Maybe. Maybe not.'

'Let's park that.' He pointed over his shoulder. 'I should get to the café. I'd hate for them to run out of yesterday's pastries.'

She tutted. 'You're an idiot sometimes.'

He doffed a fake cap. 'Yes, Miss.'

'I'm going for a wee.'

'Thanks for the heads-up.'

She batted him on the arm.

He rubbed the impact site. 'I'll get this seen to as well.'

She indicated his groin. 'And that. Find a nice nurse to take your trousers down.'

He fluttered a hand. 'They'll be queuing up.'

She smiled, shook her head, and looked around for the Ladies. He pointed at a sign down the side corridor. She gave a thumbs-up. He headed off.

Across the concourse stood a small bookshop, an ideal store in a place where people often spend a lot of time waiting or recuperating. Eden wasn't much of a reader, besides her accountancy textbooks, but he wanted something bitesize and humorous to lift her spirits. Perhaps a collection of cricket commentary bloopers or a comedic cat book. She'd often said she'd like a cat, but the regular absences from home made it impossible. If they lived together, it would have been feasible, but the breakup had put paid to that.

He trawled the shelves, avoiding the mass market titles and ghostwritten celebrity trash, hoping for a gem.

Five minutes later, he'd found two. "From Catnip to Cupid" was a pocketbook that promised to help the reader use their pet cat to help secure a successful date. "Tess & The Ashes Catastrophe" was a kids' cricket adventure for the younger reader, but Matt liked the joke value of buying it and felt sure Eden knew someone suitable to pass it on to.

In the café, he picked up another latte—one sugar this time, a pasta salad and a cinnamon bun for her, a sandwich and rocky road for him, and a tea—because the coffee was too bitter for his tastes.

He carried the wares back to the cardiac waiting area. Eden was engrossed in her phone.

She looked up. 'Are we settling in for the night?'

He sat. 'I bloody hope not.' He passed her the coffee, which was double-cupped.

He's trying to prevent hand injury this time. For both of us.

She set it on the small table beside her. 'That'll be drinkable in a couple of hours.'

'I asked them to make it not too hot.'

'Very kind, Jeeves.' She winked.

'Wait 'til you see the rest.' He passed her a cinnamon bun.

'My favourite.'

'The Milton Keynes factory does special orders.'

He drew out a salad, along with a napkin and a wooden spork.

'You're on a roll, Matthew.'

'Hold that thought.' He gave her a small paper bag.

She eyed him curiously. 'Should I be worried?'

'You know me, fifty per cent chance of misreading the room.'

Her shoulders dipped. 'Don't say that. You are *smashing* this.'

The last wisps of mental fog evaporated. It was becoming clear how much the breakup had affected him, how it had knocked his confidence, left him with a tainted view of her. Regret had never loomed so large in her soul.

He pointed. 'Don't keep me in suspense.'

She jolted from introspection. 'Sorry.'

She opened the bag and peered in.

Books? I don't recall him ever buying me books. The necklace, yes. And other touching gifts.

She pulled the first book out, noted the genre, and shot him a query.

'Not insinuating your reading age,' he said.

'Hmm.' She read the back cover blurb, then thumbed through the pages. 'Lily has a younger brother.'

'I know.'

Her brows arched. 'How?'

'You mentioned it.'

'So you had him in mind?'

'No. I had *you* in mind. Adults read kids' books, you know. But, yeah, pass it on to someone.'

She tapped the book against her chin. 'How old do you think Ruth is? The nurse's daughter.'

'Don't know. Ten? But I get where you're going.'

'Well, let's see. Anyway, maybe the other book is one I can keep.' She grinned.

'It's definitely not for Ruth. Maybe Lily, though.'

She reached into the bag. 'Now I'm worried. Mostly why you're buying presents for other people.'

'If they'd sold whisky, I'd have got Ray a Get Well Soon present. Notwithstanding the irony. Besides, I probably peaked with the cinnamon bun anyway, so...'

She rapped his thigh. 'You.'

'Yeah. Sorry for me.'

She gave an exaggerated eye-roll. 'Come on, then. Let the dog see the rabbit.'

The book immediately piqued her curiosity. Such a sweet gift, but so many questions...

'Matt?'

'Mmm?'

'You know I don't have a cat?'

'Yeah.'

'And to have one, I need someone else in the house. Ideally, a boyfriend.'

'Yeah. We discussed this.'

'Then, if I already have a cat, and a boyfriend, why do I need my cat to help me find a boyfriend?' Her lips pursed cheekily.

His cheeks reddened. 'Ah.' His pupils circled. 'Maybe... you could get one now. With Brooke there.'

She folded her arms. 'And if she's allergic to cats?'

Matt slumped back. 'Okay. Badly considered gift.' He grimaced. 'But I'm sure the cinnamon bun's nice.'

She laughed. 'Tweedie's not allergic to cats. And it's a lovely gift.' She squeezed his leg. 'Because I'd love a boyfriend. Especially one who knows what I like.'

He took her hand. 'You'll find him, Edie. I guarantee it.'

38th Over

Matt picked up his tea. 'Did anyone stop by while I was gone? For updates or selfies?'

She put the books away. 'No. It may be a while.'

'Hmm. Wish I'd brought something to do.'

'Yeah. I'm a terrible conversationalist.'

His throat constricted. 'I didn't—'

She nudged him. 'Kidding. I was trying to sign in to the Wi-Fi and watch the livestream. But the signal's terrible.'

'Use 5G.'

She picked up her phone. 'One bar.'

'I have four bars. Different network. Want to watch on mine?'

'Can we?'

'There's always conversation. I could tell you about Eggs sleeping with a woman twice his age.'

Eden's mouth formed an O. 'What?' She shook her head. 'Why am I surprised?'

'I was. But sometimes you get the wrong impression about people.'

She frowned. 'Her or him?'

'Both, I suppose. But if it stops Eggs hitting on you or Brooke... or any of the players, that's a result.'

'Definitely. I should find this woman and slip her a few quid to keep dating him. Then, when Tweed and I get a cat in the house, our hunt for a man will be much easier!'

He covered his eyes. This topic was getting harder to push aside. He hoped Brooke wasn't actively looking for another man, because he thought she'd already found one...

But he couldn't say that. He couldn't sit beside a woman he cared for deeply, supporting her, buying her gifts, and burning through his data allowance, and say how he fancied her best friend. He might have misjudged things last year, but this was hardly rocket science.

Best to lead Eden away from the matter. 'What would you call it, this cat?'

She nibbled the cinnamon bun. 'Ray.' A grin appeared. 'Perfect. If the selfish git dies on me this afternoon, I'll still have a Ray in my life. If he doesn't, I get to make endless jokes at his expense. You know, going into the changing room and telling the girls that Ray has shat on the living room carpet again.'

He guffawed. 'You're a cruel woman, Edie.'

'Your crushed bollocks prove that.'

He deliberately cupped his groin. 'It's definitely the last intervention *I* stage.'

She rested a hand on his shoulder. 'I get why you did it. In my best interests. To stop me from being emotionally scarred.'

He met her gaze. 'I've already seen you struggle. This time it was preventable. But it wasn't my decision to make. You're your own person. I don't have any hold over you. Just... trying to do my best.'

Her eyes fell sad. 'I know.'

'Hmm.'

Silence cut into them. He felt on a precipice. Blood roared in his ears. To break the tension, he sipped his drink. She did likewise.

Quickly. Think of a topic. Not the cat. Not the heart attack. Not the—

'I forgive you,' she said.

He frowned. 'For what?'

'Going on the stag do. You deserved a break from me. I was being impossible.'

'You were... grieving. You were living in the shadow of death. Yours. You'd lost all hope of being worthy of the shirt. You were... probably a lot like Ray was when he and Liz split.'

'I caused that.'

'What?' His mind whorled.

She angled her body towards him. He sensed floodgates opening. He set his cup down.

'If I'd given up cricket, followed the proper career, like Mum wanted, it wouldn't have driven a wedge between them.'

'But... he wanted you to carry on. You were always going to disappoint *one* of them. Right?'

She shrugged limply. 'Dad would have understood. He wouldn't have dug his heels in. If I'd been happy to go, we could have made it work in Dubai, no problem. Even if he didn't get a job. Mum was on six figures. But the two against one didn't work.' Her head drooped. 'I may have... said some things. Said she never cared about my career. Overreacted. Like I did with you.'

He tentatively put a hand on her leg. 'I said the wrong thing. Red rag—' He cut himself off.

'To a bull. Which I was. In a china shop. And you and I got broken.'

The air was lit by an alarm, shaking them from the tender moment.

His palm lifted from her leg, causing a cool spot. Had he felt guilty about the gesture? There was no need. It was supportive, and genuine, and caring... and she wanted it to continue.

Matt tried to identify the source of the noise. It couldn't be related to Dad because he was a few corridors away, maybe even on another floor. She pushed that out of her mind, the image of him on an operating table. His chest cut open. The mask on his face. The blood.

A shiver racked her. Then a wave of sorrow hit. A noise escaped her throat.

Matt looked across. 'Edie?'

She searched his eyes, hers wide in fear. 'I... did this too. I put him in here.'

He took her hands in his lap. 'What are you talking about?' he asked gently.

She gripped his fingers. 'If they hadn't split up, Dad wouldn't have let himself go. Drunk too much, ate crappy food, spoiled his liver and hardened his arteries.' She sobbed. 'I put him in the fucking hospital, Matt.'

'Hey, hey.' He stroked her hand.

She sniffled. 'I should have done accountancy. I went to pieces in the Final. I can't handle the pressure. I dumped someone I care about. I fell out with my best friend. I wish I hadn't done this job.

Maybe played for fun.' She wiped tears from her cheeks. 'I thought I could do this. And now look.'

He shuffled closer and pulled her head into his shoulder. 'I don't agree. You're only human. It's okay to fail. It's okay to not be okay.'

She absorbed those words, their truth and the consequences. He'd implied that she *could* be a cricketer, *should* be one. Which didn't sound like the voice in her skull, the one replaying that fateful night.

She'd said something like,

'I don't think I can do this anymore.'

'Maybe you're right,' he'd replied, kind of. 'Accountancy is a lot easier.'

'So you're telling me to give up on my dream?'

'I didn't say that. I just want the best for you, Edie.'

'And the best thing is to let me feel like shit?'

'No. It's awful seeing you like this.'

'I don't care what it's like for you! It's hard enough dealing with myself.'

'Ah. So you don't care about my feelings, and here I am trying my best to care about yours, to fix you.'

'I don't need fixing! I am fine how I am.'

'Fine? You're a fucking nightmare, more like. I can't do this.'

'Sounds perfect. I hope for Christmas you get some fucking empathy and respect.'

'And I hope you get some perspective. It's only a cricket match.'

'How dare you! It's my life!'

'And look where it's brought you to.'

'Well, that can change, Matt. We're breaking up. Get the fuck out.'

She could still hear the door slam, feel her gut churning, visualise the primeval scream that ripped from her. Relive the instant she punched the wall in frustration, self-loathing and regret.

The lowest moment of her life.
Unless today pulled her lower.

39th Over

Matt saw something familiar in Eden's face, her deportment. She was wallowing.

Why? Ray's prognosis was good. The gifts had gone down well. He and Eden were getting on. They were at peace with each other, with what had happened. The blame game was over.

Or *that* blame game was. A new one had begun. She was spiralling into self-disgust, heaping everything onto her shoulders, which was ridiculous and unhelpful and harmful. And he wouldn't let it happen again.

But how to drag her out of the mire?

'Eden?' He cupped her face.

'Yeah?' she whispered.

'What can I do? How can I help?'

She looked deeply into his eyes. 'I... don't know.' Then her brow tightened. 'Yes. I do. I need a hug.'

He smiled. 'I think I can manage that. Come here.'

The chairs made closeness impossible, so he stood, drawing her up, and opened his arms. She pressed in, arms locked around his waist. He cupped her shoulder blade and back, and pulled her into a bear hug.

Contentment flooded every inch of him. She laid her head into his neck. He lifted a hand, stroked the back of her head, then kissed her hair. It smelled of memories, of better times.

He closed his eyes and let time disappear.

Holding Matt, feeling safe in his arms, would never grow old. Why, in a flash of madness, has she jettisoned this?

But it was moot, irreversible. She could only enjoy the moment, be soothed by his care, metaphorically talked down from the ledge.

She held there, processing the past and present. Something became clear. She'd reached a place of calm that never happened during the winter. Why? What had changed?

It hit her.

Wow. Was it that simple?

'Matt?'

'Hmm?'

'I know why it didn't work last time.'

He eased her away. 'Why?'

She got lost in his face. 'You *suggested* stuff, told me it would be okay. Asked me how I was, which was always low. What I needed was for you to ask how you could *help*. Asked, "What can I do?". That's all anyone needs when they're hurting.'

His eyes grew sad. 'Oh.'

She waggled his arm. 'No. It's *good*. You marched me off the pitch, determined to help me through Dad's emergency. And you *have*. You were right, Matt. I shouldn't be alone here. It took a kick in the bollocks, but you were right.'

A smile broke. 'Good. And... no pain, no gain.'

Her gaze dipped. 'Are you sure there's no lasting injury *down there*? Want to drop trou for Kathryn?' Her eyebrows danced.

'Not especially. But if she has a younger, more *available* colleague...'

'Cheating on Tweedie already? She won't be happy.' Eden's own words were like nails down a blackboard.

Matt looked away. 'I thought we were okay about this.'

She took a deep breath, then patted this arm. 'Sorry. We are. Didn't mean to spoil the moment.'

He nodded slowly. 'Okay.' He released their embrace. 'We should... find something to pass the time. Not that hugging isn't lovely, but... you know.'

'Yeah. Reopening old wounds is a bad idea.'

His brow arched. 'Although, we *are* in a hospital. Ideal place to get the wounds repaired.'

She pondered the play on words. 'Actually, I reckon we've done pretty well at repairing them ourselves.'

'Yeah. We have.'

She forced out a heavy breath, a full stop to the last few minutes. Then she waggled her limbs. 'I'm going to find Kathryn, see if there's any update.'

'Good idea. I'm going for a wee.'

She grinned. 'Thanks for the heads-up.'

He batted her arm.

Kathryn wasn't able to provide definitive news, but Dad's surgery was progressing well. Eden returned to the waiting area and pulled out her phone.

Lily had texted, asking if she was okay. Eden said that Dad was in good hands, and so was she, because Matt was there. Lily replied with heart and hug emojis.

Then Eden opened YouTube and tried to access the livestream of the Scorpions game, but one bar of 5G wasn't having any of it.

She tutted.

'Everything okay?' Matt sat beside her.

'Yeah. Was hoping to catch up on the game.'

He pulled out his phone. 'Let's try mine.'

She shuffled closer, so their shoulders were touching, and he held the phone in his lap. The livestream buffered, then settled down. The Northern Storm were 155 for 7 after 38 overs, which was a brilliant bowling performance by the Scorpions. Eden clenched her fist in support. Matt nodded appreciatively.

She angled her head. 'You're really getting into this, aren't you?'

'Why would I not? The Scorpions are a great unit. I always wanted *you* to succeed. That never changed. But, yeah, you made a fan of me.'

'I'll sign an autograph if you ask nicely.' She nudged him.

'I'll settle for your friendship.'

She stroked his knee. 'You have it. And hopefully it stays that way.'

'Me too.' He clasped her hand.

On the phone screen, Brooke began a new over. Her figures came up in tiny font.

Eden peered closer. 'My God, she's on fire.'

Matt raised the phone and noted the 4 for 24. 'Yeah.'

'I'm pleased she joined the squad.'

Matt shot her a query.

'Truly,' she added. 'I am.' Her chest filled with pride and an almost sisterly affection. 'It will work out, Matt. We can *all* get along.'

Something else jostled for space in her head. Belief. Determination.

She eyed her bracelet.

I can do this. I didn't give up on cricket. I took a fall, then had a reset, and started again. Maybe, just maybe, I can do the same with Matt.

'Yeah. We really can,' he echoed.

Letting her smile linger, she concentrated on the match. Danica, sensing the opposition were on the ropes, was using her best bowlers in an attempt to wrap up the innings. Normally, Brooke—and Eden—would be saved until the end of the innings, but not today. This meant Brooke was on her final six balls.

'Come on, Tweed,' she whispered, urging her bestie to complete a 5-wicket haul.

Matt chuckled.

'What?' she asked.

'Remember when you got that hat-trick last... July? And we sat up in bed that night and watched the livestream replay?' He shook his head, amused. 'We both knew the ending, but I was so nervous you'd take the last LBW.' He laughed. 'What an idiot.'

She laughed too. 'I was, a bit. Couldn't believe I'd had such a bloody good day.'

'The night was alright as well.'

She suppressed a flush of embarrassment. Why was he mentioning a fondly remembered night of passion? Because he felt comfortable? Was it that they'd let go of the resentment and could reminisce like wiser, reflective souls?

A longing stirred within her. She licked her lips, tilted her head towards his. 'Hmm.'

'Sorry. Crass comment.'

'No. It's fine, honestly.' She swallowed down the awkwardness, the almost-but-not-quite. 'We did have good nights. And days.'

He toyed with his stubbled chin. 'Lots of them. But in hindsight...' He sighed.

She tapped his thigh. 'What?'

'We rushed it. I skipped the part where I learned who you were, what made you tick.' He gave a resigned shrug. 'Where the weaknesses were. Whether I could cope with an unhappy Eden. It was all... sex and banter.'

'Only at the start, though.'

His smile was sober. 'Perhaps we were never strong enough to weather storms like what happened.'

'Maybe.' Her heart pounded. 'And... what about now?'

His gaze moved around her face, explored her eyes, then landed on her lips.

The envelope of silence and expectation was broken by footsteps.

'Miss Palmer? Your father is awake.'

40th Over

Matt looked up. The nurse's expression was upbeat, friendly.

'Really?' Eden asked, shaking in excitement.

'I'll take you through,' Kathryn said.

Matt pocketed his phone, Eden grabbed the paper bag of kooky gifts, and they followed along. The electricity charging his frame subsided. He'd worried that Eden would kiss him.

Worried, or hoped?

Worried, because a reckless, spur-of-the-moment act would surely have been followed by regret, a retraction, or worse. The kiss itself wouldn't be unpleasant—he always relished kissing Eden—but it wouldn't have been real, meant, or informative. Better not to kiss, not to have false hope. He didn't need the head-fuck. Today was absolutely the wrong day to rekindle their relationship, or even hope for it to reignite. There was something much more important. In the battle of life and death, life had won.

The evidence was half propped up in bed, wires sprouting from his arm, tubes emerging from his nostrils.

Matt had imagined she'd run to Ray, fling her arms around him like a six-year-old. Instead, the reality hit like a hammer. Eden stopped dead.

'I'm here,' Matt whispered, rubbing her shoulder.

'Daughter of mine,' Ray said huskily.

She stepped closer. 'Dad.' Her chest was heaving.

'You skipping matches?' Ray asked.

'You trying to bulldoze the West Stand?'

Matt beamed. Kathryn was frowning.

'It's okay,' he mouthed.

'Did you bring the old man any chocolates?' Ray said.

'He'll get a clip round the ear for nearly dying,' Eden replied.

'I'd settle for a hug,' Ray replied in an uncharacteristic lapse of manliness.

Eden glanced at Kathryn, who nodded approval, so Eden went to the bed, pecked Ray's forehead, and gave him a long embrace.

'You had us all worried.'

Ray patted her hand. 'Call it payback for what you put me through last winter.'

'So we're quits? Please?'

'I'll do my best.'

Eden glanced at Matt. 'My biscuit spy will make sure that gut of yours isn't over-exerted. Things are going to change, Dad. But I'll let you keep the bottle of whisky.'

'Ah. The fun police are here already. I'm barely off the table and you're setting rules.'

Kathryn stepped forwards. 'All for your own good, Mr Palmer. But yes, we will be giving you a pamphlet about diet and exercise for good cardiac health.'

'And I'll be checking the waste bin, Dad, so no cheating.'

Ray eyed Matt. 'Was she like this to you too?'

'Eden wants you well, boss. As do we all.' He shook the man's hand. 'Take it easy. The boys and I will keep the... Garden of Eden just perfect.'

Ray didn't release his grip. 'Thanks, son. Have you been taking care of my girl?'

'I've done my best.'

'Cheers. I hope they didn't call off the match, or anything stupid like that,' Ray grumbled.

'No chance,' she replied. 'It's not like anyone gives two shits about some old geezer who mows the grass. Girls gotta play cricket.'

Ray looked at the nurse. 'Could you give me some really strong drugs? Knock me out for a couple of days so I haven't got to listen to this cruelty?'

'I'll see what I can do,' Kathryn said.

Seeing that the father-daughter banter was all present and correct, Matt cupped Eden's arm. 'I'll give you some space, okay? Want anything from the café?'

'You can go home. I'll be okay from here.'

'Sure?'

She guided him to the door, leaning in close. 'Honestly, I'm fine. I'm sure Alan and Eggs could use you.'

'Just don't want to desert, y'know?'

She stroked his bicep. 'I'm calm. Dad's fine. And you've been... exemplary today, babe.' She pecked his cheek. 'Bowled an absolute pearler. Thank you.'

He moistened his dry throat. 'No problem. You'll get a cab home?'

She nodded. 'As soon as the old git falls asleep, I'm out of here.'

'I heard that, daughter,' Ray called.

She sniggered. 'See you soon, Matt. Tell Tweedie and the girls that we're all okay.'

He patted her waist. 'Will do.' Then he waved towards the bed. 'Got to go, boss. Work to do. Apparently, some drunk driver tried to trash your favourite roller.'

Ray raised an index finger in farewell.

Matt held in a laugh, winked at Eden, waved thanks to Kathryn, and left.

As Matt drove back to the stadium, his hand came to his cheek. The kiss wasn't an inflammatory one. Quite the opposite—it had cemented their bond and given him an unequivocal seal of approval.

Nevertheless, that made him a little sad. If only he'd done as well last time, they wouldn't have endured this hiatus of estrangement. Maybe they'd still be an item.

But it was pointless to mull over the 'what ifs'. Experience was a teacher, and today's journey through adversity had been plain sailing. It felt like the good old days, the blackened pages of history ripped out. Eden had gone from spikily harbouring a grudge to enlightened, apologetic and self-critical. If that made her a rounder, nicer person for the *next* man she dated, he'd be even luckier than Matt had been.

One thing was for sure—the next man wouldn't be him. The moment had passed. The almost-kiss in the waiting area had been ripe for a romantic reunion, an opportunity for Eden to ask him back... but she hadn't.

From one perspective, this was good—she'd become better at drawing a line under things and moving on. Hopefully, she'd take that attitude into her gameplay.

On the flip side, he couldn't deny disappointment. If she'd asked, he would have said yes.

Instead, he needed to focus on the future and its possibilities, not the past and its consequences. He and Eden had mended their friendship, and besides, Brooke *had* already asked the dating question.

Unfortunately, tonight's romantic dinner was the wrong thing to do. He hoped Brooke would understand.

At the stadium, the match was entering its final phase. Matt went to the groundsman's hut and caught up with the staff.

While Eggs disappeared to brew up, Alan updated Matt. Apparently, Eggs had risen to the occasion, working diligently to repair the roller, ready for the innings interval. During the drinks break, Brooke had asked if there was any news from the hospital, and the lad had relayed Matt's text message saying that Ray was on the mend.

Matt was fast having to reevaluate Eggs. Had something as simple as buying a knackered van—and inadvertently using it as a magnet for blousy cougars—matured him?

Stranger things had happened.

Matt pulled up a seat, recounted the highlights of the hospital trip, and made a mental inventory of tasks for the following day.

Ten minutes later, the Scorpions' last batter was out, ending the game in defeat for the home side. As the teams vacated the pitch, Matt and Eggs brought the covers on, then he headed to the pavilion.

Players were signing bats and posing for selfies. Among the fans was Lily, who hustled over.

'Matt, what's happened? Is Eden okay? Is Ray okay?'

'They're both fine. Ray's had a scare, but he'll mend.'

'And Eden?' Lily glanced around. 'Was she okay with you going along?'

'Because of us falling out before? Yes. But that wouldn't matter. She needed my help.'

'Did she, like, *ask* you to go to the hospital?'

'No. But I went anyway. Eden realised she needed someone to hold her hand through the situation.'

'*Did* you literally hold her hand?' Lily asked suggestively.

Matt chuckled. 'Yes, Lily. For support. And stop stirring.'

'I don't *need* to stir. It's obvious.'

He frowned. 'What's obvious?'

'Eden's still in love with you.' She grinned.

His eyes widened. 'What? That's... I... Look—'

'But she is, though.'

He folded his arms. 'How do you reckon that?'

Lily shrugged. 'A girl knows.'

His laugh was a reflex. 'Lily, you're *fifteen*.'

She held up an index finger. 'Sixteen next month. And a girl. One who knows. Us cricketers do. We know about each other.'

He nodded mockingly. 'Is that so?'

Brooke appeared in his peripheral vision, so he bypassed that topic and said he'd pass on Lily's regards to Ray and Eden. The girl hustled away to grab more autographs.

Brooke pulled Matt into a clench. 'How're you doing?'

'Is this about my wedding tackle?'

She let go, frowning. 'Sorry? Oh, right. Haha. No.' She leant in. 'But do you want me to check for bruises?'

'Why is everyone obsessed with *my* welfare? I'm the one who's least in pain.'

Her smile vanished. 'Yeah. How's Ede?'

'She's okay. They both are. But I wish you two hadn't fallen out.'

'You did too. At least she didn't knee me in the *playing area*.'

'Stress can cause people to react in funny ways. But we made up.' He searched her eyes. 'I hope you two will sort it out.'

Brooke rubbed his arm. 'She texted to apologise. And I'm relieved that Ray is alright. That would have destroyed Ede.' She checked around. 'Look, I said I'd take her gear home. Can you give me a hand to the car?'

'Sure.'

'Back in five.'

Matt hung around, chatting to players, while Brooke got changed. Then she passed him Eden's huge shoulder bag—which he was familiar with carrying—said farewells to her teammates, and they moseyed out to the car park.

She blipped the remote, loaded the bags, then leant on the car. 'So what time are you picking me up?'

His shoulders collapsed. 'The thing is—'

She shook her head. 'Great. You've got cold feet.'

'No. God, no.'

She glanced around. 'Sorry, did I miss something? We have a date booked.'

He moved closer. Brooke's tone hadn't hit confrontational, merely disappointment, but he didn't want an argument. Or another kick in the bollocks.

'I'm not sure that now is the best time to do this.'

She frowned. 'What does that mean? When *is* the right time?'

'Not when Eden needs people around her.'

'Ah. So this is suddenly about her, not me.'

He cupped her arm. 'I think she would appreciate you being there, in the house, distracting her from Ray's situation.'

Brooke's jaw tensed. 'Meaning you *are* putting her welfare above mine? Above us?'

'Don't you think it's important? You're her best friend.' He gestured around. 'All of this, navigating a path for the three of us, is about trying to protect your friendship. You and Ede have been closer for a *lot* longer than you and I have. You've got a lot more to lose. And I don't want her pissed off and abandoned, not now.'

Her eyes narrowed. 'Because you're still in love with her.'

He threw up his hands. 'What *is* it with this? Can't I *try* to do the right thing? And you too? Remember that her dad is *actually* ill.'

Brooke stepped back, sneering. 'Nice shot, Matt.'

His heart thundered. He was on the verge of screwing this up before it had even started... unless she was the one inflaming things?

He spoke quietly. 'Look, it's just a drink. Plenty of days for that. And what did we say about not rushing? This is a reschedule, not a cancellation. I promise.'

She considered that. 'Okay.'

He checked around, then tugged her waist inwards and planted a mollifying kiss on her cheek. 'Next week, okay?'

'Hope so. Have to check my diary for other stuff. I'll let you know.'

'Cool. Talk to you soon.'

41st Over

Eden perched on the bed and took Ray's hand. 'You really gave me a scare.'

He glanced at the door. 'Ah. You can go all mushy now you don't have to put on a front for the audience.'

She eased a fingernail, *quite* gently, into his palm. 'I don't put on a front for Matt.' She chuckled sadly. 'He knows I'm not an ice queen. He's seen me at my worst.'

Ray licked his lips. It appeared laboured. 'Did you cry? Earlier, I mean.'

Her brow furrowed. 'No. I was in shock. I gave Brooke a balling out, and kicked Matt in the nuts, but no tears, no.'

'Why were you such an angry little sausage, daughter?'

'Sausage?'

'Go easy on me. I've just had life-saving surgery.'

She waved a hand. 'Forget it.'

'I will. Did he? Forgive you for rearranging his tackle, I mean?'

'Matt? Yeah. Like I said, he's had worse.'

Ray fiddled with his blanket. 'Yet he sticks with you. He's a diamond, that boy.'

Eden reflected on the past few hours. 'He is. I don't... or didn't... deserve him.'

'Maybe. Maybe not.'

Eden saw a familiar look in her father's eyes. 'Ah. Is this a subtle way of suggesting we get back together? A dying wish I can't deny you?'

'I'd better not be fucking dying. I already came close enough.'

'Honestly, they say you're okay.'

He grimaced. 'But it's a warning, yeah? Less pies and beer.'

'"Fewer",' she corrected.

'Fewer pies, less beer. Right.'

She winked. 'Right.'

'Edie, I'm not telling you what to do with your life. That was your mum's job. But you always had my blessing to date Matt, and after today, doubly so.'

Her heart fluttered. 'But he has to want me too.'

'I believe that's how it works, yes.'

'I see they didn't insert a missing funny bone when you were under the knife.'

He pointed to the corridor. 'No, but maybe *you* ought to go in there, get the rod out of your ass.'

'We're in England. It's "backside". Oh, and fuck off.'

Ray raised his other wrist, which held the cannula. 'Bit difficult. And you only swear when you know I'm right.'

'Here's a secret. I swear a fuck of a lot more than you think.'

'I doubt it.'

Eden shook her head, amused, as ever, by his wit and insight. 'So even though I missed a game for you, sat here drinking scalding coffee, I still owe you a reconciliation with Matt, is that it?'

He laid a hand on her knee. 'I can't *force* you to love someone. But I can point out that Brooke is your best friend.'

Dad's clearly not up to speed.

'We're okay, all of us. There's been a lot of forgiving, even forgetting.' Her head fell. 'But I can't repair you and mum.'

Ray groaned, sorrowful rather than in pain. 'That wasn't your doing. We'd had a few niggles, differences of opinion. Sometimes people's paths diverge. I wanted to stay too, remember. Mum and I never saw eye-to-eye about your future.'

'But that *does* make it my fault.'

'No, love. Mum did rather put her career ahead of spending time with you. She didn't want to be a kept woman, and nor did she want to scrape along on a groundsman's wage. She was, is, bloody good at her job.' He met Eden's eye. 'It's *okay* to be driven by something. In fact, it's laudable. But you have a smart head on those shoulders. You never lived in the clouds. You know you can't be an athlete forever. Your mum worried that you'd settle down, have kids, and never get to use that accountancy brain.'

She laughed. 'Oh, the irony. Further from settling down than I've ever been.'

He shook his head. 'No. That was November time. You're getting closer again.'

She folded her arms. 'You don't do subtlety, do you?'

'Having a coronary in front of a stadium crowd, smashing a few grand's worth of gear, and trying to drive up the terrace steps, isn't particularly subtle.'

She leant over and kissed his forehead. 'Don't ever change, Dad.'

'Apart from the *fewer* pies and *less* beer lifestyle.'

'Yes, apart from that. It would be an awful shame if you weren't able to walk me down the aisle to Matt, wouldn't it?' She winked.

Then a technicolour image popped into her mind and she was flooded with warmth.

'Do as you wish, daughter dear. History shows that you'll find your way, make your peace with a situation... eventually.'

She shot a look. 'Is that another dig? Are you banking on me not berating a sick man?'

'Do the math, as they say. You're good at that.'

'I'm not too shabby with a cricket ball either. On a good day.'

'And I'm pretty sharp with a roller. On a normal day.'

She angled her head. 'Seems like we both have the odd mare on a cricket pitch.'

'Well, I'll try to stop my medical emergencies if you'll learn to bowl better at the death.'

'Not sure "death" is an appropriate word, father dear.'

'Sorry, daughter dear. What I meant was,' he tapped her wrist, 'Focus and breathe, whether it's the final ball or the first.'

She ran a fingertip over the bracelet. 'Or any day, I suppose.'

'That would be an idea, yes.'

'Sounds a lot like *you* should have bought me this, rather than Lily.'

'But I've always believed in you, Edie. Known you. More as a girl than a cricketer. I'm only a guy who cuts the grass.'

She beamed. 'When not causing a spectacle.'

He raised a finger. 'Go easy on the patient. Don't want me to have a relapse, do you?'

'Never.'

A forlorn smile appeared. 'Do you have somewhere to be? Or will you sit with me a while?'

'I'd love to.'

Eden pulled the vinyl chair to the foot of the bed and sat down. Ray put his head back and closed his eyes, as if thinking. Beside him, the monitor's squiggly line scribed its up-down pattern.

Eden set her phone on silent, closed her eyes and calmed her breathing.

Everything's fine.

She was woken by a tap on her shoulder. Nurse Kathryn smiled. Eden got her bearings and checked the wall clock. She'd dozed for an hour. Dad was motionless, but the digital display cycled through his heartbeat.

'Are you okay, Miss Palmer?'

She stretched. 'Eden, please. I'm fine. Is it time for his checkup?'

Kathryn shook her head. 'No, but I wanted to poke my head in, as I'm going off shift.'

'Oh, thanks. I might go *off shift* myself. Need to decompress.' She gestured at her attire. 'Change into something less comfortable.' She stood. 'I won't wake him. I'm sure he needs a lot of rest.'

Kathryn nodded. 'Yes. We'll keep him in for a couple of days, monitor everything. Standard protocol, nothing to worry about. Visiting hours are eight til eight. A maximum of two people, so if you and your boyfriend come back tomorrow, I'll be around.'

Eden opened her mouth but let the nurse's assumption slide. Inside, her stomach caroused.

A few minutes later, as she was in a cab home, that pang evolved into a flashback, the sense of a lost opportunity. The fleeting instant in the waiting area when she thought he'd kiss her, because that would have been the icing on the cake.

Arriving home, she realised that her keys were in the pocket of her civvies, which were in the Aurora Stadium's changing room.

Bollocks.

She rang the bell, hoping her housemate was back, thus saving another cab ride. The door opened and Brooke's smile was immediate.

She hauled Eden into a hug. 'Oh, babe. I'm so sorry for what I said about your dad. How is he?'

Eden squeezed back. 'He's okay. They didn't give him a personality transplant, but you can't have everything. And I'm sorry too. I was out of order.'

They broke off. 'You were in trauma. I was trying to help.'

Eden ushered her into the living room. 'I know. Same with Matt. Except you didn't get smacked around.'

Brooke winced. 'Yeah. But he seems to have forgiven you.'

'You spoke?'

'He came back to the ground, updated everyone.' She pointed. 'Helped me with your gear.'

Eden's heart filled. 'Oh, Tweed, thanks. I'll drop him a text.'

Brooke rubbed Eden's shoulder. 'I *would* have skipped the match, you know that?'

'Yeah. But you have to hold up the bowling unit's end.' A hand came to her mouth. 'Shit. I forgot all about the game. How did you get on? Eggs said you skittled one of the openers, then we saw you get three more.' Girlish excitement gripped her. '*Please* tell me you got a fifer.'

Brooke shook her head. 'Sorry, hon. But I would have felt bad, having a brilliant day when you were going through all that.'

'Honestly, you can't worry about me. That's *my* job. Actually, something I'm working at, trying to shut out the bad shit and focus on my game. Move on.'

Brooke clasped Eden's arm. 'Not this. You can't pretend everything's magically okay. You need to take personal time.'

She sank onto the sofa. 'Thanks. But I can't. Dad won't want that. He's seen me spend enough time stewing. And he'd hate for me to skip games. He's in good hands.' She clenched a fist. 'I *have* to get back on the horse. The drama is over. Besides, now the England girls have gone, I can't weaken the squad any further.'

Cheer broke on Brooke's face. 'I'm glad, Ede. You're back again. This is what I'd hoped for, that we could be the dream team, roll back the years.'

Eden laughed. 'Roll back the years? What are we, forty?!'

Brooke whacked her leg. 'You know what I mean.'

Eden did. They truly were teammates again, not rivals. Not competing at work, certainly, but in matters of love? That was harder to call.

42nd Over

Matt was at the stadium by seven the next morning. He needed to step up for a few days—technically he was temporarily doing the Assistant role as Alan had been de facto elevated to interim Head, and Matt was the second longest-standing member of the team. Also, he wanted to allow time for a long lunch hour trip to the hospital. Eden might struggle to visit Ray, as she had sponsor promo engagements.

Brooke texted, giving her diary details, and they agreed to go for a drink after the next game, which was an away match at her former team, the Central Stars.

At the hospital, Kathryn was on duty, and gave him an update—Ray was doing fine. Matt picked up lunch in the café and took it to Ray's room.

He took a seat. 'Hey, boss. Sorry I didn't bring you chocolates or flowers. Or pies and beer.'

'Edie *will* be pleased. How is she?'

'Good. Not spoken to her today. But you can message her now.' He pulled Ray's phone from his pocket. Collecting it from the hut before the ambulance departed would have been helpful, but hindsight is 20/20.

Ray took it, then clasped Matt's wrist. 'Matthew?'

He swallowed nervously. 'Yeah?'

'I'm giving you the Assistant role. Long wait until Alan leaves at the end of the season, but I can't keep you on tenterhooks for months. Not after... all this.'

Matt fashioned a handshake. Inside, fireworks detonated. 'Thank you, Ray. I'll try not to disappoint.'

'You won't. All the same, don't mess your life up to visit me, or worry about taking a break when I'm not at work. You're not a shirker. You're a good man.'

'Thanks.'

Ray's stubbled face broke into a grin. 'You won't be saying that in a minute.'

Matt frowned. 'Why?'

'You remember it's the Conference next week?'

'Ah.'

'I don't want to miss it, but I can't push things. Not with Edie, not with the NHS. And an Assistant should be prepared to step in when the boss is indisposed, right?'

'I'll go, of course I will. Even though you said I'm still Tea Boy until October.' Matt winked.

Ray pointed at the coffee cup. 'Then you're doing a shit job where I'm concerned.'

Matt indicated the Call button by the bed. 'Have someone prettier than me bring you one.'

Ray glanced at the door. 'Kathryn?'

Matt's mouth hung open. 'You... old...'

Ray shrugged. 'I think it's the uniform. Or that she's divorced.'

'And has ten years on you.'

Ray angled his head. 'Is this lessons in love from the guy who struck out with my daughter?'

'Circumstance caused that. Or I like to tell myself so.'

'That's a fair assessment. But we're none of us perfect.' The man pensively sipped from a water cup. 'We lasted a long time, me and Liz. Sometimes I regret that an argument about career priorities caused the end.'

Matt chuckled sadly. 'Same here.'

Ray looked up. 'Edie says she blames herself for causing the divorce.'

'Said that to me too. All rubbish, of course.'

'True. But at least she's... reflecting. Shame she couldn't count to ten at the time. Bit impetuous, my daughter.'

'A kick in the nuts says so.'

'She told me it was a knee,' Ray replied.

'Elite athlete's knee, elite athlete's boot, same difference.'

'But she apologised?'

'Oh, yeah,' Matt said. 'And it was a heat of the moment thing.'

'She needs to use that bracelet more often. Maybe get a tattoo of it.'

'Well, there's no way *I'm* suggesting that.' He covered his groin. 'Twice would be silly.'

Ray beamed. 'I should do it. You know, play the "Poorly Dad" card.'

'I bet she'd see through it in a second.'

'True. She's a smart cookie. Smarter than some.' Ray's smile vanished. 'I spent the last six months telling her to get over... it. The match, that dickhead online, you and her...' He sighed. 'Wish I'd taken my own medicine five years ago. Stopped wallowing. Moved on. Then maybe I wouldn't be in this bed.'

'Don't be hard on yourself, boss. But take the medicine *now*. Draw a line. New start.'

Ray chuckled sadly. 'Fewer pies, less beer.' Then a sober expression. 'But a new house. Good way to draw a line.'

'Definitely.'

Ray jolted. 'Oh, shit.'

'What?'

'Tomorrow's the removal day.'

Matt grimaced. 'Ah. Not sure you're quite fit for that.'

Ray shook his head. 'Have to call it off.'

'Why? Eden said you were using a removal company.'

'I am. And half the stuff's already gone. But someone's got to pack the last bits, empty the fridge, do the keys—'

Matt stood. 'And someone will.'

Someone with a couple of helpers, thought Matt as he drove back to the ground.

After work, and a chat with Alan and Eggs, he retrieved Ray's coat, containing the house keys, from the groundskeeper's hut. He hadn't mentioned the promotion, but needed to share the news with someone.

At Eden's house, she answered the door, radiant as ever, notwithstanding the baggy t-shirt and joggers. 'Hey.'

'Hey. How was the day?'

She led him through. Brooke was on the sofa. 'Media stuff, y'know?'

'Not really, but I guess it doesn't have the same endorphin hit as knocking out middle stump.'

'Very true. How's Dad?'

'Almost back to his old self. It'll take more than a coronary to kill his wit.'

Eden clicked her fingers. 'Damn. I'll have to think up something else.'

'Well, on the off chance you're *not* joking, can you wait until the winter?'

She frowned. 'Why the winter?'

'Because if he pops his clogs after October, I'll automatically become top dog.'

Eden's mouth opened and closed. Her eyes became saucers. 'You mean...?'

He puffed out his chest. 'Yep. Meet the new Assistant Groundsman... elect.'

Letting out a squeal, she pulled him into a hug and landed a smacker of a kiss on his cheek. 'That's brilliant!'

He tensed against the unexpected emotional onslaught, nice though it was. 'Thanks.'

Across the room, a tic of embarrassment passed over Brooke's face. Self-conscious, he eased Eden away. Inside his head, a voice said that if they were still together, her congratulations would be more fulsome and probably horizontal.

As Eden sat, still smiling, a tinge of redness coloured her cheeks.

The awkward atmosphere was quickly cut. Brooke, doubtless for support, but possibly also out of jealousy, sidled over and gave him a hug.

'Well done, Matt.' Her lips brushed his cheek.

He didn't dare meet Eden's eye. 'Thanks. I just hope it wasn't a... sympathy appointment.'

'He's probably still high on morphine,' Eden commented.

Now he looked at her. She winked.

'One thing is for certain,' Matt said. 'The removal guys are booked for tomorrow, and I'm not sure Kathryn will discharge Ray, however many bats you two sign for her daughter.'

Eden's eyes widened. 'Shit. Is it that soon already?'

'Time flies when you're a busy pro.'

She worried her lip. 'We can't reschedule. Jade and Phoebe are dying to move in.'

Matt nodded. 'Yeah. That's why I called in. Eggs and I can spare the time. But we could use some help.'

He arrived at Ray's soon-to-be former home at nine o'clock the following morning. Eden and Brooke were in the living room, packing boxes. The removal firm had taken surplus items the previous week, leaving only a bed, sofa, TV, and the basics for Ray to live on. This two-step process avoided the emotional "big bang" of clearing out the family home in a crazy weekend.

When Eden went upstairs to pack her dad's remaining clothes into a few suitcases, Matt and Brooke manhandled the TV into its box.

'Are we still on for Thursday?' she asked.

He rested a hand on the box. 'Something's come up. A legitimate something. I need to take Ray's place at a conference.'

Her mouth snapped open, as if to berate him, then her shoulders fell. 'Okay.'

'I have to show willing, Brooke. It's only a couple of days. We'll keep... won't we?'

'I suppose. Where is it?'

'The Conference? A venue in Sussex. Nice place.' He didn't mention that he'd stayed there with Eden.

She sighed. 'Okay. So have a good time, I suppose.'

'Thanks. And we *will* reschedule. A much-needed drink, given everything that's gone on.'

She smiled. 'Too right. Just when things were settling down, too.'

He tapped the TV. 'Look on the positive side. A few weeks ago, I could imagine you and Edie trying to smash this thing over each other's heads.'

'Yeah. We're almost ourselves again. And you had a lot to do with that.'

'Time is the healer. And perspective.' He gestured around. 'I hope this is a reboot for Ray too.'

The doorbell rang.

Eggs had arrived with the van, which they'd use to take the smaller boxes, leaving the removal men to move the furniture.

As they loaded, Eggs' attitude was courteous and measured. Matt didn't once catch the guy ogling Brooke's backside. Either it was a new maturity, or he was content with Geraldine's backside, or possibly both.

The removal men arrived and set to work. Brooke volunteered to stay and monitor them while Matt and Eden went on to the new house. Eggs followed behind.

It was Matt's first time at Ray's downsized but more modern property. As Eden opened the door, he was hit by an odd, downbeat sensation.

Eden paused. 'You okay?'

'Yeah. Just a silly... Nothing.'

She rubbed his shoulder. 'Weird for me too. That old house is all I ever knew, and I can't help thinking if things were different...' She shook her head.

He patted her waist. 'We did this already. None of this is your fault. Come on, Edie, get a grip. That's not you anymore.' They walked through the hallway into the lounge. 'And you helped him choose a good place.'

A smirk appeared. 'How did you know I had a hand in this?'

'Because it's not a depressing cop-out, a bachelor's three-room pad. You stopped him from feeling sorry for himself, turning his back on love, on a second chance.' Matt shrugged. 'That's my psychoanalysis, anyway.'

She nodded. 'Pretty damn accurate, Matthew.'

'None of us should be once bitten, twice shy.' He pointed to the kitchen. 'Or starved of biscuits for much longer.'

As they were brewing up, Eggs arrived, so all shared a cuppa and digestives, then they unloaded the van and let Eggs leave—he was eager to get back to the stadium.

Soon after, Brooke arrived. All three took the suitcases upstairs. Mercifully, Ray's bedroom wasn't an embarrassing mess.

Brooke spotted something on the bedside table.

She lifted up the framed picture. 'Was this last year, Ede?'

Eden snorted. 'You think I was in a fit state for any public appearances last October? That was the year before.'

Matt peered over her shoulder. The professional photo, taken at the end of season awards ceremony, showed a happy couple, dressed to the nines, arms around each other's waist.

'You look amazing, babe,' Brooke commented.

'I scrub up okay,' Eden replied. 'So does he.'

'Hollywood couple,' she murmured.

'A long way from that,' Matt said. 'Feels like a lifetime ago.'

'Did you win anything?' Brooke asked.

'It was... Most Wickets Taken.' Eden coughed. 'The less said about the Strike Rate, the better.'

Brooke nudged her. 'Well, you struck lucky *that* night.'

Matt wondered whether she meant the trophy in Eden's cabinet, or the one in the photograph. Probably the latter.

43rd Over

With the removal completed, Eden took the old keys to the estate agent, ready for Jade and Phoebe to pick them up the following day.

At the petrol station, she bought a New Home card for the girls, and another one for Dad. From there, she went to the hospital, caught up with the old reprobate, and handed back the new keys.

She wanted to ask why he kept that particular photo beside his bed. There were plenty more of her—looking less glamorous, but still. Was it merely a snapshot of a happy time in her life, when both career and personal journeys were on an upward trajectory?

Hopefully, by this autumn she'd have regained the lost momentum. In her cricket, that seemed likely, but in love? Not so much. She'd never reach that level of comfort and togetherness with someone new, especially in four months.

What would *this* October's photo show? Would she have a man on her arm? Would Brooke? And would either of them be Matt?

The following morning, she and Brooke drove to the stadium for a training session. After the gym and the skills session, Susie led a team briefing about the following day's away game at the Central Stars. Brooke contributed heavily to the analysis of their opponents, as she had years of experience playing in the team that, tomorrow, she'd be hoping to defeat.

Eden's stomach had begun to skip. This was the first meeting of the two teams since September. The stakes felt higher than ever—but this time, things were different. She had her bestie by her side, not facing her from 22 yards away.

And she was damned if she'd fall apart. That Eden Palmer was a weaker, snider person, who she hoped never to see again.

At four o'clock, she and Brooke loaded the car and set off for Worcester. This was the first overnight of the season, and they were rooming together.

Barely a mile from home, Eden's pulse spiked. 'Did you bring all your supplies?'

'Chill, babe. I'm fine.' She patted her abdomen. 'New cartridge, spare cartridge, full battery. Honestly, this isn't my first rodeo.' She glanced across. 'But thanks.'

Eden exhaled. 'Sorry. Got caught up in what-ifs. How're you doing? Inside?'

'I've crossed the rope, Ede. I don't love them any less, but do I want to win? Hell yes. Not as much as you, but that's understandable.'

'I'm... glad you're here. God knows how I'd be if you were still a Star.'

'Honestly? I think you'd get me out first ball. Because that's the new you. I truly believe that. In fact, I'll bet you a tenner you get a fifer tomorrow.'

Eden laughed. 'Doubt it. Remind me about you. Three *weeks*, isn't it?'

'That LBW was marginal, to be honest. And the second one? She *gave* that away.'

'Hmm. *Excusing* your brilliance, Tweedie?'

Brooke slapped Eden's arm. 'Stop stirring. Does this mean you won't take the bet?'

'Like I need *more* pressure!'

'Fair point. No wagers. Let's just get the win.'

A few minutes later, the conversation dried up, so Eden switched on the radio. Halfway up the M40, familiar opening chords blared from the speakers, and Eden glanced across.

Brooke's grin was wide. 'Remember this?'

Eden nodded. How many times, years ago, had they walked onto the pitch to this song? The Under-19s club "anthem" used to blare from the small ground's awful PA system but always got the blood pumping.

In seconds, the girls were singing along, jabbing their fists to the beat as if they were in a Marbella nightclub.

Life was good again.

An hour later, they checked into the team hotel. The guy behind the reception desk, all flowing locks and twinkling eyes, would have been a good find in that Spanish club, but a pre-game night wasn't about excess and wish fulfilment.

Instead, Eden and Brooke located room 235, selected their beds by rote—Brooke always on the left—and flopped down. The working day was already 12 hours old.

Brooke sighed heavily.

'What?' Eden asked.

'I miss this. I don't want another two years of ships passing in the night. Even... ships avoiding each other.'

She picked at the duvet cover. 'Me either.'

Brooke's pupils flickered in thought.

'What?' Eden prompted, worried.

Brooke pinched her lip. 'Confession time.'

Eden's shoulders pushed back, tightening. 'What?'

'It's nothing, really. A silly impulse.' Brooke lifted her left foot onto the bed and pulled up her trouser leg. 'You know I got this?'

Eden eyed the small scorpion. 'Yeah. And?'

Brooke pulled up the other hem. 'Well... I got a two-fer.'

Eden's mouth hung open. 'God, babe,' she whispered, her heart melting.

'This is why falling out hurts. Not as much as half an hour of stinging needle, but still.'

With a fingertip, Eden traced the entwined letters E and B on her friend's calf. 'Wow, fuck, do I feel bad for everything.'

Brooke clasped Eden's hand. 'Needle in me beats a knife in you any day.'

Eden swallowed hard. 'No shit.'

'So please let's not do anything which means I have to endure more pain by getting this removed.'

Eden squeezed her friend's fingers. 'Deal.'

Brooke let go, then sat cross-legged, facing Eden. 'Remember Tom Wilkie?'

'Is this a "long hair" thing?'

'Downstairs reminded me, that's all. But, yeah. And Apollo.'

'I can't believe you dated a guy called Apollo. Was he *actually* a surfer dude?'

'He did surf. And do... other things.' Brooke grinned wickedly. 'Less keen on the man-bun, better when he wore it down. Still prefer Tom, though.'

Eden propped herself up on one elbow. 'For the hair or the... other things?'

Brooke shook her head. 'I don't want to rub salt.'

'Water under the bridge. You won him fair and square.'

Brooke frowned. 'Won? You make it sound like a raffle. Or a competition.'

'We both bought tickets.'

'You were never sore about that... were you?'

'No. Truly. I'm okay with fair and square, best girl wins.' Eden sat up. Moisture gathered at the corners of her eyes.

'Ede?' Brooke asked softly.

'I'm sorry, Tweedie. I'm sorry for the Mankad. I started all this, pushing us apart. Then I was so stubborn, so fucking determined *not* to take the easy way out... again... in the Cup, but I failed to let my talent do the talking.' A tear dripped onto the duvet cover.

Brooked moved close. 'I wasn't trying to punish you. We've had friendly rivalry for *years*.'

Eden nodded hard. 'I think I was subconsciously trying to prove to Mum that I *can* be successful, but I'm not sure she cares anymore.'

Brooke wiped at Eden's tears. 'You have to play for *yourself,* not for anyone else. Liz isn't *spiteful*. I met her many times, remember? She wanted the best for you. Same as Ray.'

Eden sniffled. 'I suppose I should be grateful for the space to be who I am and do what I want, not feel her disappointment every time I went round for dinner.'

'Yeah. And you *will* still follow her preferred career eventually? You can't give up your head for numbers.'

This was the sixty-four thousand dollar question. 'I... Maybe. But I do enjoy coaching.'

'And I'm jealous that you have *two* options when you stop playing. I have none.'

'Then *you* should coach. Christ, you're good enough.' Eden stopped short of saying "Better than me" in case it sparked an argument. That was the last thing she wanted. They were at a tipping point. Apology done. Slate wiped. Boundary rope crossed. Friends again. As it should have been, months ago.

Brooke picked at a nail. 'You know... I did think perhaps...'

'What?'

'Remember at the outreach, that girl Sophie?'

Eden dredged her memory. 'The kid with Type 1?'

'That's her. She came to the game this week. When you were,' Brooke grimaced, 'at the hospital.'

'Tweed, you don't need to be on eggshells, okay? So what about Sophie?'

'I don't know. I thought maybe... if her parents wanted extracurricular help, I'd do a few hours pro bono.'

Eden brightened, inside and out. She patted Brooke's leg. 'That's great. From little acorns and all that. Even helping one girl makes a difference. Until the cricket world properly catches up to equality, and schools start taking it seriously. Go for it. Definitely.'

Brooke gave a small shrug. 'I see how you and Lily have bonded. She idolises you.'

'Like young Grace does to Waitesy. Like I looked up to Katharine Brunt. It all starts somewhere. And you've got something I'll never have.'

Brooke frowned. 'What?'

She lifted the hem of Brooke's sweatshirt and tapped the diabetes monitor. 'You're a fucking inspiration. You can do a lot of good, be an ambassador or speak or *something*.'

Brooke's face creased. 'Oh God, babe. Don't set me off.'

Eden wiped her eyes. 'Sorry. But do it. Take it with both hands. Like you have at the club. If I was *half* as tough as you, last winter would have been water off a duck's back.'

'It was what it was, okay? Tomorrow's another day. And we win, or we lose, and we move on to the next game. And the next. And we try to be the best version of ourselves, on the pitch and off it.' She smiled. 'And, most importantly, those of us with uncooperative immune systems order Room Service before their friend gives them a lecture about not eating often enough.'

Eden laughed, a welcome full-stop to the conversation. 'And those of us who are *not* so afflicted will find which channel the highlights are on, and we can see how Rojo and Ellie and the girls got on against New Zealand.'

It was like old times as they sat up on their beds, dinner on their laps, cheering on friends and colleagues.

Then it was an early night, double alarms set, and fingers crossed that she could keep mind and body on the straight and narrow.

44th Over

After the task of bailing out his ex-girlfriend's father, Matt returned to the ground to check that everything on the job list was done. It was impossible not to assume the Assistant's responsibility in his *head*. Besides, someone had to cover for Ray.

Taking the man's place at the regional Grounds Management Conference wasn't Matt's ideal way to spend two days, but it was a timely litmus test of his ability to step up. Besides, it gave a welcome opportunity to get out of the emotional spotlight, to regroup and get a clearer head about what to do.

Unfortunately, the event was being held at Wharton Grange, a place with romantic significance. Still, a swanky paid-for getaway with a huge bed and great food? Putting on a shirt and tie was a small price to pay—and at least he didn't have to endure a long drive to a more distant venue.

That night at home, he rang Mum and told her about the promotion. She was thrilled.

As he lay down to sleep, basking in the positivity of the last couple of days, his thoughts turned to the picture in Ray's bedroom. Was there ever a stronger statement about how the man viewed his daughter's choice of beau?

Ex-beau.

Did it mean Ray still held out hope of a reconciliation, or was Matt imagining things? Could it purely be that Ray thought Eden looked lovely that evening, on a day when she'd also been acclaimed for her ability?

Matt couldn't deny her talent. Nor that she was the most gorgeous woman he'd ever met.

In the morning, he hit the gym early.

From there, he went to the hospital, knowing that Eden wouldn't have time to visit her father as the players had a full schedule, followed by a drive to Worcester.

In the room, Ray and Kathryn were laughing. Matt stood at the door, analysing the body language.

Is he flirting with her from his sickbed?

Although to be fair, Ray didn't look sick. The tubes had gone, but the fingertip heart sensor remained, its monitor cycling through a steady 129/77.

Ray gestured. 'Come in, son. Kath and I were comparing daughters. Sounds like she has a young Eden on her hands, and I don't know whether that's a good thing or a bad thing.'

'I'll tell her you said that,' Matt replied.

He brushed it off. 'Aw, she knows. Rather have a girl with a bit of vim than a shrinking violet.'

'I can see where she gets it from,' Kathryn remarked.

'Well, if you think the stubbornness is all from me, that shows you haven't met Liz. And we know who won *that* battle of wills, don't we, Matt?'

Not wanting to weigh in on this argument, he gave Ray the tea he'd bought at the café, then drew two biscuits from his pocket.

Ray wagged a finger. 'Edie'll have your guts if she finds out you've been giving me treats.' He stuck out a palm. 'Hand them over, then.'

Kathryn patted his other arm. 'You're a law unto yourself, Ray Palmer.'

'And you're an angel on Earth, my dear.'

She stood. 'Maybe, but with other mortals to minister to.'

Matt stayed for half an hour, catching the man up on work matters and taking notes about the conference, then he headed to the stadium.

During lunch, his phone pinged.

"So when's good for that drink?"

His sigh was drawn out, a battle between attraction and worry—worry that was possibly misplaced. He'd never explicitly asked Eden's permission to date Brooke, but neither was he required to. He and Brooke were free agents. Not only that, all three were at peace with each other, all hatchets buried.

So why the debate? Yes, it was a hard road to walk, but the easy route was to let the opportunity slip. What if he did, and regretted it? After all, he'd been vilified by Eden for suggesting she quit cricket and fall back on accountancy, just because of a perfect storm of bad circumstances. Why should he let a breakup with one cricketer stop him from trying with another? He couldn't run scared forever.

"When are you free?" he replied.

"I can only do Thursday."

He pictured the diary. It was Wednesday tomorrow, the first day of the two-day conference. Thursday night he'd be heading home, probably knackered.

The best thing, the easiest option, was to postpone. Again.

Unless...

They'd planned to go to a bar in Maidstone, maybe a meal if things went well. Wharton Grange was only an hour away. Swankier, better food, a wider choice of drinks. He'd be there anyway, so perhaps she could join him?

His skin prickled. Was it self-imposed mental torture to suggest the same hotel as he'd visited with Eden? Was it done out of hope for a similar outcome?

No. This was a date. An evening. *Not* a night. Besides, if Brooke's diary was that full, she'd want to be home for whatever Friday held.

He composed a suitable reply to her WhatsApp and hit Send.

The following morning, he was up at six. After a quick breakfast, he double-checked the roller case, pulled on a jacket and his smartest jeans, and grabbed the stack of business cards Ray had told him to take from his house.

Business cards. Matt had never considered that he'd be carrying business cards. True, these had Ray's name on them, but next year—or sooner—Matt would have his own.

Not even Eden had business cards. And she was an accountant.

Well, maybe not for a few years. She needs to keep being brilliant at cricket for a few more years.

The conference was an assault on the senses, a vertical learning curve. A day of handshakes, learning, slow Wi-Fi, weak coffee, and telling a great many people the reason for his presence in Ray's stead. There were lots of well wishes to pass on to the boss.

By the end of the day, besides being very comfortable in his skin, he was dead on his feet. Crazy that a day of networking and CPD was more exhausting than manual labour at the stadium.

He collected his case from the car and went to Reception to check in. He quoted his name and was given a keycard.

'Room 27, sir. Second floor. The lifts are to your right.'

A chuckle of disbelief left Matt's throat. The receptionist frowned. Matt smiled, waving away her concern. There was no point in asking if this was a practical joke, or if she was unaware of the concept of irony.

Was the universe sending him a sign, or laughing in his face?

It didn't matter. No point in getting sentimental—it would only risk more melancholy. A room was a room. He simply wanted a good night's sleep.

Still, it was unsettling to tap his card against the door reader and let himself in.

It's just a room. And they were happy memories.

He pulled off his jacket, unpacked his case, freshened up, then plugged in his phone charger. He flopped gratefully onto the vast bed, ordered Room Service, and switched the TV box to YouTube. He located the highlights package of the day's Scorpions vs Stars game, and pulled a beer from the minibar.

The squad selection indicated that the pitch was more suited to spinners than pace bowlers, so he didn't expect any fireworks from Eden, Brooke, or Phoebe. Still, he knew the match might present mental or emotional challenges for the girls, not counting the task of beating the table-topping side.

He devoured the burger and chips, watching a competent performance by the Scorpions, without drama or controversy. Eden and Brooke each took one wicket and scored single figures with the bat, but the team went down to a three-wicket loss. The seam bowling pair were good-natured, often conferring about tactics and, crucially, Eden's line and length remained consistent... if not spectacular.

So, to take the positives, whilst the Scorpions had lost to the Stars again, she hadn't contributed to the defeat. It wasn't the reversal of fortune that he, and all the players, had hoped for, but it was a marker of Eden's return to form.

Plus, in a coincidence of scheduling and the early-season knockout Cup's results, the teams would face each other again in five days' time. If today's game was important for league table position, the next was vital. It was the Scorpions' first chance of silverware this season. They had home advantage, a pitch better suited to a strong seam attack, and two girls whose friendship had been repaired with perfect timing.

Only one thing could derail the detente. Himself.

Tomorrow's drink date wasn't about the bedroom—this particular bedroom. It was about getting to know Brooke Harris as a *person*. He and Eden hadn't endured on sex alone. They'd lasted because of a bond. Equally, he hadn't fallen in love with Eden after their first night together. It had taken time, and would do with Brooke—assuming the ingredients were there.

But was this the right thing to do by Eden? Yes, she'd apparently given her blessing, but was it a test? Surely she wasn't that Machiavellian, especially after their heart-to-heart at the hospital? Unless that kiss was part of some warped grand plan, gaslighting him, messing with his mind? What had he done to deserve that? Nothing.

The kiss had been a reflexive action, an emotional outburst under difficult circumstances, any port in the storm. Eden wasn't interested in reigniting the romance, merely keen to smooth over the cracks in their friendship. Still, that was a great result. No tension in the air, no dancing around each other, logistically, socially or emotionally. Shame that it took Ray's near-death episode to catalyse his daughter into repairing old wounds.

No harm done, surely?

Unless, by meeting Brooke for a social—maybe romantic—evening, Matt busted those stitches apart.

45th Over

Eden slept well. Not "Slept well, considering", a familiar tale over the past six months.

That Thursday morning, yesterday's defeat was behind her. She had crossed the boundary rope, moved on. Of course, there were lessons to learn, ways to improve, things she could have done differently, disappointment—something the group always shared in such circumstances.

Nevertheless, there were tendrils of regret, but these were about wasted time—days, weeks, even months during which to bury the hatchet with Brooke.

Better late than never. And would it have changed the outcome of the Final? Would it have affected her performance, stopped the trolling, saved her relationship with Matt?

Who can tell? What's done is done. If I wanted him back, all I had to do was ask. Sure, he could say no—and he'd have just cause, because I treated him awfully.

At least I apologised for that too.

There was a lightness in her steps as she went down to the kitchen to make breakfast. A weight had been lifted. The joy of taking a wicket is fleeting, but the nourishment of friendships endures.

It was eight thirty, an indulgent lie-in, and with a two-day gap until the next training session, she and Brooke could afford to ease off a little.

The front door thudded shut. Brooke's idea of "easing off" was hitting the gym at seven o'clock rather than six.

'Morning.'

'Hey. Gym good?'

'Yeah. Dickhead on the next bench press saw me load one hundred, so he loaded one-ten, then couldn't shift it. Ha!'

Eden shook her head. 'Men. Coffee?'

'Rack it up. Just jumping in the shower.'

Ten minutes later, blonde hair towel-dried, Brooke reappeared in joggers and a tee.

She clasped the coffee mug gratefully. 'So, plans?'

'Better go and see the old sod. Matt says Dad's been getting friendly with the nurse. You know, Kathryn, the one I mentioned.'

Brooke eye-rolled. 'You said she was, like, late forties, tops. He'll give himself another coronary trying to keep pace with her.'

Eden nearly spluttered out her coffee. 'Get your mind out of the gutter, Tweed! He told me he courted Mum for six weeks before he plucked up the courage to even kiss her.'

'Hmm. Told you, yeah. Or maybe he's changed his spots. Stared death in the face and is thinking he shouldn't hang about, waiting to live his life.'

She flapped a hand. 'Matt's probably got the wrong idea. Even if he hasn't, Dad's allowed a second shot. We all are. But maybe I'll have a quiet word with Kathryn.'

'Warn her off?'

'I'm not interfering. "Love Lessons from Eden Palmer"? Yeah, great. So long as he's well, and happy, and ideally puts a lid on the "Garden of Eden" shtick once and for all, fine.'

'Aw, you love it really,' Brooke said.

'I indulge him. Which I ought to do until he's fighting fit. So, wanna come along?'

Brooke inspected her mug. 'No. I've got... other plans.'

'Ooh, cagey.'

Brooke glanced up. 'Going out. And no, it's not some bullshit about my dad. That was a bad call, given... circumstance.'

Eden swallowed hard. 'Yeah, well, we're in the forgive and forget club now, so let's not go there.'

'Agreed. Anyway, I need to get ready.' She drained the mug, flashed a smile, then trotted up the stairs.

Eden's nerves tingled.

I don't like this.

Is it an England training camp, and she's embarrassed to say that she's beaten me to the national squad? A big sponsorship deal? Did she look up Tom Wilkie on Facebook and they're having a let's-try-to-recapture-the-magic rendezvous?

Either way, she didn't care. She certainly couldn't be jealous or sniffy—Scratchy Eden had been laid to rest.

Instead she busied herself putting kit in the washing machine, making a grocery shopping list, and then got absorbed in scrolling Amazon, trying to find a moving-in gift for Dad.

Brooke leant against the living room door frame. 'I'm back late tonight. See you tomorrow.'

'Yeah. Have fun... whatever it is.'

Brooke nodded curtly. 'I hope so.'

'Got your meds?'

'Yeah.' Her posture softened. 'And thanks, babe.'

'No problem. Don't want *another* hospital visit, do I?'

'Definitely not.' She closed her eyes, rubbing her forehead.

Eden stood sharply. 'What's up?'

Brooke's arm flopped down, her expression pained. 'Look...'

Eden patted the sofa arm.

Brooke shook her head. 'No smoke and mirrors, Ede. Full disclosure. I'm going up to Bluewater, then on the way back I'm... Matt and I are having a drink. At that swanky hotel.'

Eden frowned. 'The conference?'

'Yeah. Kind of a... "get to know you" thing. So...' She shrugged. 'That's that.'

Eden's chest tightened. 'Okay.'

'Really?'

She couldn't tell Brooke not to go. That would be controlling and bitchy.

She met Brooke's eye *so* briefly. 'Yeah. Have a nice time.'

'I... hope so.'

'I know you will,' she murmured. 'See you tomorrow.'

Brooke studied her for a long time, then headed into the hall. Eden's shoulders slumped. She held her breath, awaiting the door's bang, holding back tears.

As in the Final last year, Eden was up against her friend. And, as then, she didn't want anything *bad* to happen to Brooke, for her to get injured and not be able to bat, or get a ball to the face guard and be taken off with a concussion. She didn't even want her to be emotionally hurt. She'd merely wanted someone else to take Brooke's wicket, thereby ending the match.

Now, she didn't want to deny her a chance with Matt. To intervene at this stage would be cruel and might re-ignite their spat. She *did* want Brooke to find love—just not with Matt. A short innings would be fine—a whirlwind few days or weeks—before she... *got out*. Then, perhaps, Eden would find the courage to ask him if he wanted to try again. In the last few days, she'd realised that punching the wall was not in frustration at *him*, but at herself for throwing him away.

There was a difference between moving on—putting a bad situation in the past, and regaining something inherently *right*. Being mates with Brooke was right, and nourishing, and uplifting. Getting back together with Matt would be the same... but impossible to achieve. At least, not without hurting Brooke.

She closed her eyes, repeating the mantra that he wasn't the only fish in the sea.

The front door still hadn't banged.

'I can't do this.'

Eden's eyes snapped open. 'What?'

Brooke shook her head. 'I can't do this.'

'Why not?'

'Because you're in love with him.'

'I... It's not about me.'

Brooke stepped closer. 'But you are, aren't you?'

'That doesn't matter. We broke up. And now *you're* in love with him.'

Brooke gingerly sat. 'I mean, I *fancy* him but...'

'But what?'

'I can't possibly be in *love* already. Only idiots talk like that.'

Eden forced a smile. 'I'm sure it'll happen. He's a wonderful guy. Truly.'

Brooke made a fist. 'This is impossible, Ede.'

'No, it isn't. I let him go. You have a shot, so *take* it.'

'You'll resent me. And I'll be sitting there, trying to have fun, knowing I'm hurting you. Because you *are* still in love with him.

Do me the courtesy of admitting it. Please. As besties. So I know what I'm getting myself into. So I know the stakes.'

Eden reached for Brooke's hand. 'Go, okay. *Please*. We drew the line under arguments. Under guilt. Wallowing over mistakes. Time to move on.'

Brooke gripped hard. 'That's the thing, hon. I don't think Matt *has* moved on. I see how he is around you. At the ground, during the house move. I bet, if I was a fly on the wall in the hospital, I'd see it there.'

'You're the one he's been flirting with, Tweedie. I've seen it.'

'Okay, can't deny it. And is it nice? Yes. In different circumstances. Circumstances in which he's not still holding you in his heart.'

'You can't know that.'

Brooke nodded. 'Agreed. But I know *you*, Ede. I have for ten years. And you regret the breakup as much as you do the Mankad, or blowing me off for six months because you thought I was conducting a one-woman batting vendetta. And without those two things, maybe you and Matt would still be together. Which you want.' She locked her gaze. 'Don't you?'

Eden's brain pushed at the inside of her skull. 'I'm *not* ruining your plans, Tweed. I can't risk it. You want this, don't you?'

'I do. And it's only a *drink*.'

Eden's brow raised. 'But...?'

'But you want it *more*. And not just a drink, a date. You want another shot. Right?'

Yes. Yes, I do. With every fibre of my being.

She jammed fists into her eyeballs. 'What the *fuck* do we do?'

Brooke's arm came around Eden's shoulders. 'Clone him? Alternate weekends?'

A laugh burst from her. Brooke was grinning.

'A throuple?' Eden suggested without a shred of seriousness. Jokes were the only answer because the situation was unfixable.

Brooke flopped against the backrest. Eden clasped her shaking hands together. This was worse than trying to hold onto a game when the opposition needed 1 run to win off two overs.

'Here's the thing,' Brooke said. 'I know what I want. I know what you want. We just have to find out what Matt wants.'

'How?'

'I have an idea.'

46th Over

Day two of the conference was less of a blur, but it was still a distraction from the nervous excitement of the evening's dinner date with Brooke.

His phone was on Airplane mode for most of the time—he didn't want the social faux pas of a loud ping during a seminar—but when he checked notifications during the afternoon coffee break, Brooke had messaged.

"Hope you've had a good day. I have a feeling you'll have more fun tonight!"

His heart pounded. A Herculean effort would be needed to keep the date out of the bedroom.

When the day's events drew to a close at five o'clock, he was ready to flop on the bed and snooze for an hour. Brooke was due at six thirty. Time to shower, shave, and congratulate himself on making the brilliant plan of staying on an extra night.

At Room 27, he held the keycard against the lock and eased open the heavy door. Just inside the room was the ensuite, and from behind its closed door came the sound of a shower running. His neck hairs prickled.

What?!

Isn't it obvious? Brooke's never backward about coming forward. But this? She must have blagged a spare key from Reception, spinning a yarn about being "Mr Alderson's girlfriend".

Clearly, she wasn't going to take no for an answer.

He locked the main door, pulled off his lanyard and put it on the desk. In the corner, a bottle of champagne lay in an ice bucket. The bedsheets were turned down, and on top of them lay a set of black lingerie. His loins stirred.

Was she planning to greet him dressed like that, and he'd spoiled it by arriving early? Never mind—she'd now be the one getting a surprise.

Pausing to check that the shower was still hissing, he stripped naked and padded to the bathroom door. He gently depressed the handle. It gave. Electricity crackled through his limbs.

The walk-in shower was at the far end of the tiled room, its wide glass partition smeared with droplets and steam. Beyond them stood a blurry vision, her back to him.

I can't creep up on her. She'll get a shock, scream, lose her footing, go arse over tit and crack her head open. Not an ideal start to the evening. I've already done the A&E thing, and that was a whole lot of no fun. Not forgetting that my behaviour last year caused a different cricketer to get injured.

He moved closer. Steam warmed his face.

'Hey,' he offered, essaying his best sexy voice.

She turned. He stepped to the edge of the tiled shower tray.

'Holy shit!' Instinctively, his hands shot to his groin—which, given the circumstance, the bather, and many months of intimacy, was utterly ridiculous.

She wiped water from her face. 'Surprise?'

'I... But...'

'Were you planning to take a shower?'

'Yeah... But not with... I mean...' His mind whorled.

She slicked back her hair. 'This was a gamble.'

'I just...'

'Matt. One question, okay? Are you *disappointed* that it's me and not Brooke?'

He searched his mind and heart for a millisecond. His attention settled on the one thing she wore—the necklace. 'No. Hell no.'

Her frame relaxed. 'Good.'

'You're all I've ever wanted, Eden.'

She glanced down. 'And still do, it seems.'

Well, can you blame me? I mean, look at you. You're perfect.

He stepped into the shower. 'Well, can you blame me? I mean, look at you. You're perfect.'

Her beautiful lips formed a smile. 'You too.' She took his hand, stepped back, and they were enveloped by the warm water.

'But all of this? How did...? Why...?'

'Come here and I'll explain.'

He let her pull him close, resting a hand on her hip as she pressed her lips to his.

Lately, he'd believed that his memories of their relationship—everything before the final few days—were seen through rose-tinted spectacles. He'd almost convinced himself that the breakup was fine because, on reflection, they'd never been utterly together and in love. He wanted to believe that losing her was okay because she wasn't as beautiful, sexy, smart, tough, funny and adorable as he'd once believed.

Now, he knew that was complete bullshit. The kiss was ambrosia. Like waking from a nightmare. Endorphins consumed him. He kissed with unrestrained desire and relief.

A lifetime later, she broke off.

'What about this explanation, then?' He stroked her backside.

Her gaze explored his eyes. 'Brooke subbed me in.'

'That's *it*?'

'That's the short version.'

'And the long version?'

Her fingers skipped across his chest. 'Later. Let's get clean. Then let's get dirty.'

Something niggled at the back of his mind. 'Edie?'

'Yes, darling?'

'What *is* this? An apology? Desperation? A fling?'

She stroked his face, attention never leaving his eyes. 'This is "I want you back". *If* you can put up with me. *If* I'm worth a second chance.'

He ran a fingertip across her wet lips. 'I'm the one who should be asking for a second chance.'

She shook her head gently. 'It's only *us* that needs another shot. And I want to start now. Immediately. This very second.'

'I'd like that.'

She pressed her cheek to his. 'No more apologies, Matt. No looking back. Only forwards.'

He pulled her into a lovers' embrace. 'Agreed.'

'Good.'

'Then... let's play.'

47th Over

Eden woke in Matt's embrace. A toned arm was draped across her midriff, their bodies half spooned. It was like coming home.

She listened to him breathe, inhaled his musk, inspected every inch of his forearm and hand, reacquainting herself with the details of the man she loved... and had never truly stopped loving. Then she replayed every nuance of the evening and night—the rhythm of their bodies, his face in unbridled laughter, the feel of his lips on every inch of her.

Across the room, in the half-dark, a small patch of light winked on, held, then dimmed. A notification, maybe a text.

Her skin goosepimpled.

Tweedie?

Guilt spiked through her. Fifteen hours in Matt's company and she hadn't spared a thought for Brooke, who'd stood aside to give her a shot at happiness. Eden hadn't stopped having fun to check in on the girl, see how she was coping with passing up the guy she wanted.

True, Eden wasn't planning on giving a running commentary, or even a thumbs-up emoji to indicate that the secret switch of romantic partner had gone down well—and he *had* gone down well—but she should have been in touch.

But no. Phone on silent while she looked after number one.

She eyed the device. Retrieving it meant moving, and waking Matt. And it was only...

What time is it?

No bedside clock. No room clock. And her sports watch was *juuust* out of reach.

She inched her shoulders leftward, trying to keep her torso steady. Her hand slid across the bedside table, towards the strap, and... pinched it between thumb and forefinger.

This is what all the mobility and strength training is for. Not bowling a 70mph screamer. Working out what time it is without waking your boyfriend.

Boyfriend.

A wide smile appeared.

She slowly drew in her arm, gripping the watch, then dangling it in front of her face.

09:50 ?!

Blimey. Breakfast finishes at ten. Oh crap.

Hang on. What about Room Service? That would hit the cutoff time and give us time to get decent.

She glanced across at Matt.

Sorry, darling. Girl's gotta eat. Peak physical specimen and all that.

She stroked his wrist. A noise emerged from his throat. She eased his hand up onto her breast.

'Mmm,' he growled.

'Morning, darling. It's me. Brooke.'

His eyes snapped open. Then his eyebrows tightened into a vee, and he pinched her nipple. 'Not funny.'

'Ow.' She patted his hand. 'Actually, it's hilarious. And proves that Tweedie, and I, and you, made the correct decision.'

His expression softened. 'You only had to ask, Edie. The day after, the week after, a month after. I'd be an idiot not to take you back.'

She unwrapped their bodies and lay facing him. 'All the same, it's tough. That's why I didn't ask... before.' She trailed fingers over his chest. 'I didn't appreciate what a load it was on any boyfriend of mine. I thought they, you, could take whatever came along. That you would *get* it, me, my life.'

He stroked her cheek. 'I do now.'

'But even *I* struggle at times. You saw that. Supporting me, dating me, putting up with me, *loving* me, is tough. Not only because of what I do. You have the added complication that I'm me.'

'It's not a regular job, that's for sure.'

She put her nose to his. 'You did so well last time. Almost nailed it. We both did. Now, we'll be stronger. Right?'

He kissed her. 'Definitely. And I don't blame you. Even the greats of the game go through bad times, lose their form, have mental struggles, emotional dark patches. That's not a weakness. That's humanity. You're a person, Eden Palmer. Not a superhero.'

'Apart from that cartoon. The one Adam drew.'

'Yeah. Seam Girl. We'll have to see if he'll do one for Brooke. She'll be the only person in the squad without one.'

'I'll drop Ellie a text. Tweedie's birthday in a couple of weeks. That'll be a nice surprise.'

He pressed close. 'You're good at surprises. The shower ones are my new favourite.'

She eased him away. 'Steady on, Romeo. It's nearly ten o'clock, and a downside of not being a superhero is that I have to eat. We have five minutes to order Room Service.' She stroked his pecs. 'And the rest of the day to work off the calories.'

Matt didn't expect that "working off the calories" meant going to the hotel gym. Still, he could have spent an hour sorting recycling bins or manicuring Eden's lawn, and it wouldn't have mattered so long as she was there. He'd spent six months with barely a word passing between them, which was five months and twenty-nine days too long.

After a gentle workout followed by a lazy half-hour in the hotel pool, they had a light lunch in the restaurant, then retired to the room.

He considered coaxing her back into bed, but that didn't fit their relationship. With Brooke, the night might have been more one-dimensional—but he'd never know, and had no desire to. It was inconceivable that she could be more perfect than Eden. Choosing Brooke would always have been a second best. Not a rebound, more a distraction, a way to cut off the shackles of loss and longing.

He'd rather have Brooke as a friend. After all, she might be Eden's Matron of Honour...

'What're you thinking about?' Eden asked.

He jolted from the dreamscape. 'Nothing.'

'It made you smile.'

'Being with you *always* makes me smile.'

She poked his ribs. 'Sneak.'

'Okay. I take it back. It's like sticking pins in my eyes. Hot pins.'

'That's more like it.'

'You're impossible, Edie.'

She cupped both hands under her chin, like a movie starlet. 'Thank you,' she trilled.

'What were *you* thinking about?'

'Honestly?'

'Was it Profit and Loss accounting, or Business Rate Relief?'

She poked out her tongue. 'No. Cricket.'

'The next match?'

She fell serious. 'Yeah.'

'I thought this was coming.' He slid a hand into hers. 'You don't have to make amends, baby. You don't have to win the match single-handedly. I know it's the Stars. I know it's a rematch. It's a Final. It's silverware. I know it's really, *really* important. But it's also just a game. A team game. And there are two other trophies later in the season.' He stroked her cheek. 'Be gentle on yourself. I will love you, with all my heart, as I did before, regardless of how you do, with the ball, with the bat, or as a team.'

'Thank you,' she whispered.

'You're amazing. And you don't have to prove that to *anyone*.'

She nodded sagely, then an eyebrow lifted. 'Unless the England selectors are there, of course.'

He put his face close to hers. 'Oh, in that case, try not to be shit.'

Eden worked hard to stay off her phone and give Matt her undivided attention, but the inevitable WhatsApp from her housemate arrived late in the afternoon.

Holding her breath, Eden opened the message. Brooke's note was simply a question mark. Letting the tension from her frame, Eden replied with a smiley emoji. Brooke sent back an x.

It appeared that things between them were fine.

In the evening, she and Matt luxuriated in an early three-course dinner at the hotel, then headed home.

Eden let herself back into the house.

Brooke appeared in the hallway. 'Well?' she asked impishly. 'Spill the tea.'

'All good, Tweed. All good. Perfect, in fact.' She pulled the girl into an embrace. 'Thank you.'

'What are friends for?'

Eden took Brooke's hands and fixed her in a direct look. Inside, her pulse raced. This was the acid test of their relationship.

'Matt and I are back together. If you want... details... wait til I've had a couple of cocktails.' She grinned, then fell serious. 'But this is important. You need to be honest. More than at any time in our lives. Are we really okay?'

'Yes, Ede. We're okay. We're more than okay. I've spent the last six months,' Brooke smirked. 'though maybe not *every* day, wondering if you were better, wishing you were. Now I *know* you are.'

'I am. I have back everything I want. The game, him, and us.'

In the morning, they headed to the Aurora Stadium for training. This was followed by a detailed briefing session from coach Susie and the analysts, dissecting the Central Stars and setting out tactics for the following day's County Cup Final.

There were plenty of lessons learned from the recent loss, but the squad knew they'd have to be on their A-game to beat the best side in the country.

Eden didn't need reminding about the stakes. She had her own demons to quash. Equally, she needed to follow Matt's advice and not blow it up into something overwhelming.

Nevertheless, that evening, she and Brooke settled down on the sofa, put her laptop on the coffee table, and spent two hours discussing the strengths and weaknesses of the other club.

Then she climbed into a bed that was too empty and fell asleep dreaming about it being occupied every night.

48th Over

Matt wasn't walking on air. He wasn't that naïve. He'd been on cloud nine in the first few days after hooking up with Eden two years ago, sensing he'd found the perfect woman. She was strong inside and out, beautiful, funny, cheeky, driven... the list went on.

Eden was still all those things, but now he knew there would be bumps in the road. He'd lost some youthful innocence, gained a lesson from life's travails. His girlfriend hadn't suddenly become immune to pressure, mistakes or quarrels. Neither had he. They had grown wiser, though. While the breakup and aftermath were a deep low, the last two days had shown it was a mistake. They had lost the battle but won the war.

Still, there were more battles ahead. One was tomorrow.

He arrived at the stadium at seven in the morning, ready to prepare the pitch and the wicket for the game.

Alan and Eggs were in the hut, brewing up. The lad seemed subdued, so when the teas were made, Matt walked with him to the ride-on mower.

There was small talk about Matt's time away—he kept details to a minimum, but Eggs didn't pry. A few short weeks had put five years of maturity on the lad. Previously, he would have asked what Eden was like in bed—an easy topic, because Matt already had months of that heady experience. Now, he looked forward to years more.

They discussed tasks for the day, Ray's return—he was due back that morning—and Eggs' decision to drop the moniker so that people took him more seriously.

Of course, for every silver lining, there is a cloud...

Ben leant against the hover cover. 'So... the thing is, I bought Geraldine a gift, like you said, to celebrate our one month and... well, she said it was sweet and everything, but was I getting the wrong idea.' His shoulders fell. 'Turns out it was a middle-age rebound thing on her side and just a bit of fun. So we talked about it, all civil and that, and... that's it, really. We broke up.'

Matt patted Ben's shoulder. 'I'm sorry, mate.'

'I know you reckoned I was an idiot, but I suppose it was a big ask for something serious to develop. Anyway, no hard feelings between me and her, plus she didn't sue me for dropping her vibrators. Actually, she gave me four stars on Google.' He shrugged, then a glimpse of the cheeky Eggs appeared. 'For the van move and that, not for the shagging.' He grinned.

'I suppose that's a result,' was all Matt found to say.

'She never liked cricket anyway.'

Matt's brow arched. 'Do *you*?'

Ben gestured towards the pavilion, where a few players mingled. 'It's pretty exciting, as it goes. Thought it was all serious white jumpers and days of bugger all happening. But you can't take your eye off it.'

'Not if you want to avoid a ball in the face.'

'You should have been here last time, when the boss got ill. Brooke was great. She can run, I tell you. And took this awesome catch.' He looked Matt straight. 'And I'm glad the three of you straightened stuff out. I don't like an atmos.' He drained his tea. 'So you and Eden are an item again?'

'Very much.'

Ben patted Matt's shoulder. 'Good on you. Anyway, we should crack on.'

Mid-morning, Ray arrived and was welcomed back by the entire crew. After a chat and a brew, he walked Matt to the wicket to check on progress. Matt and Eggs had brushed, raked and cut the strip. Now it was time to mark the creases.

The previous week, Ray had selected the pitch for the Cup Final. It was number 4 on the square, apparently Eden's favourite—not for sentimental reasons, but because it yielded her best bowling figures. There was no discernible science behind it, but Matt—and especially Eden, as a mathematician—recognised that statistically there would always be one pitch which gave the most favourable results.

Hopefully this would be a psychological help, not a hindrance, to her the following day.

He began carefully chalking the lines.

'How was the conference?' Ray asked with poorly disguised nonchalance.

Matt hadn't provided any details of the event, the date, the unexpected substitution, or the result. Had Eden? Should he play it cool?

'It was good, thanks.'

'Anything notable happen?' Ray held his gaze.

'Are you fishing, boss? Or playing innocent?'

The man shrugged faintly. 'Edie said she popped up to see you, her excuse for not coming to visit the old man. I may not be an accountant, but I'm alright at putting two and two together.'

'So... fishing *and* playing innocent.'

'Give me a break, son. I nearly died,' Ray joked.

'How long are you going to play that card?'

'Til people tell me to cut it out.'

'Right. Well, as far as you putting two and two together, Eden and I were busy putting one and one back together. To make two. Or one, depending on your view of relationships.'

Ray gripped Matt's arm. 'It's the result we all wanted, right?'

'I think so, boss, yeah.' In fact, Matt had been damn sure he wanted Eden back, was pretty convinced that Ray wanted the reunion, and hoped Eden felt the same.

'State of mind is a big factor in performance. So you taking her back should be good in a lot of ways.'

'Eleven players on the team, Ray. Let's not pin all our hopes on just one, eh?'

'I'm not. But let's give her a good Garden, son. And cross our fingers that my daughter, your girl, can walk off smiling.'

49th Over

'Got everything?' Eden asked.

Brooke tapped her kit bag and lifted her med bag. 'One and one.'

'Let's go and win some silverware.'

They'd played rock-paper-scissors for the honour of driving to the ground—a relic of youthful days—and Brooke had lost.

'How're you doing?' she asked as they drove.

Eden reflected. 'I'm good. Really good, actually. But feel free to keep telling me to chill the fuck out.'

'A couple of early wickets and we'll *all* chill out.'

Eden laughed. 'Yeah.'

Silence fell for a minute. Eden's thoughts drifted to the game ahead.

Luckily, Brooke prevented any nerves from building. 'Ede?'

'Hmm?'

'I went to watch Sophie play. That girl from outreach.'

Eden remembered the redheaded youngster with Type 1 diabetes. 'Oh? And?'

'She has great pace for her age. Said she wants to play for England one day.' Brooke glanced across. 'She's a fighter, that one. And her dad's very supportive.'

'They can be amazing, dads.' Eden grinned. 'When not being a royal pain in the arse.'

Brooke nodded. 'Yeah. So... I'm going to mentor Sophie. Girls like her are the future.'

Glowing with pride, Eden gripped her friend's hand. 'That's amazing, babe.'

They eased through the Aurora Stadium's gates.

Let's do this.

Three hours later, as the warmup drew to a close, Eden allowed herself the luxury of revelling in the atmosphere. She took a long, slow look around the stands, picking out a few familiar faces. Outside the groundsman's hut sat two *very* familiar ones. The elder she'd known for twenty-seven years. The younger she hoped to know—and be with—for decades to come.

She resolved to do them proud, then scratched that and focussed on doing herself proud.

As she walked back to the pavilion, ready to change out of training gear into game kit, a few youngsters thronged around the steps, offering scoresheets, shirts or bats to the players as they passed. Eden stopped to sign dozens and smile for selfies.

Halfway up the flight stood Lily and Toby.

'Go well, coach,' the girl said.

'Thanks, Lily. Are you... *going* well?'

Lily self-consciously glanced at Toby. 'We're... negotiating the tough first few overs.'

'Gets easier after that.' Eden winked at the boy, gave Lily a high-five, then moved on.

Towards the top of the steps was someone that, for a second, Eden couldn't place. Then the penny dropped.

'Hi. Nice to see you. But you didn't ask for those free tickets.'

'Maybe next time,' nurse Kathryn said.

Eden crouched down to the young girl. 'Hello, Ruth. It's nice to meet you. Would you like me to sign your bat?'

'Yes, please.'

She talked to Kathryn as she wrote a personal note in black Sharpie. 'Does Ray know you're here?'

'I texted him, yes. Not sure I'm allowed to walk round to his man cave.'

Eden returned the bat, capped the pen, smiled at Ruth, and stood. 'I never heard him call it that. But maybe I should ask one of the staff to escort you round, so you can vet that he's cleared out the unhealthier of his biscuit stash.'

Kathryn beamed. 'I'm sure you and Matt can handle it.'

'We'll try. Anyway, must go. Catch you after the game.'

Eden and the team jogged onto the pitch. The PA boomed, music pumped, and applause rang out. She absorbed that for a few moments, then shut out everything beyond the boundary.

The Scorpions were fielding first, so Danica drew Eden and Brooke into a conversation.

'Which end do you want?' Brooke asked.

Eden was touched. 'Um, I'm usually better from the pavilion end.' She looked at the captain. 'Okay if Harry takes the first over?'

Danica tossed Brooke the ball. 'Cool. What field do you want?'

After a brief confab, the players took their positions, the countdown hit 0, and the umpire dropped her arm.

Eden, fielding at Long On, clenched a supportive fist as her bestie ran in to deliver her first ball.

Matt's attention moved between Eden, Brooke, and Ben. The lad was immersed in Brooke's bowling, showing enthusiasm and support. Perhaps the interest was no longer merely objectification...

As Eden took the ball for the second over of the match, Matt pushed positive thoughts in her direction. It didn't work. If Brooke conceding 7 runs off her 6 balls was disappointing, Eden giving away 10 was worse.

Come on, baby. That's just a few looseners. You've got this.

Things marginally improved in the next two overs, with Brooke taking one wicket, an iffy LBW decision.

Matt got a bad feeling, which became worse as the minutes ticked past. The Scorpions' three spin bowlers were unable to make headway—possibly because the pitch didn't suit them. Yet, with the squad depleted by the absence of England players, the coach had been reluctant to select pace bowler Jade, who was having a poor season. She'd put her faith in Eden and Brooke, but neither was doing themselves justice.

Ray sauntered over, mug in hand. 'What d'you reckon?'

'I think, on a different day, Eden could have had one already. And the game's not done.'

Ray checked the scoreboard. The Stars were 92 for 1 after 12 overs.

'We'll need to bat well, son. They have better pace than us, and it's a pace wicket. Or Edie needs to start pulling rabbits out of her hat.'

Eden ran her finger along the ball's stitching.

Brooke leant in, shielding her words from the non-striker. 'Get her to play across the line.'

Eden recalled their detailed analysis of the batters. 'Yeah.'

She walked back to her mark, checked the field, and ran in. The Stars' opener tried to flick the ball off her legs, but Eden had beaten her for pace. The ball smacked into the batter's knee roll.

Eden collected her body up out of the follow through, pivoted and threw her arms up.

'Howzaaat!' she exclaimed in unison with wicketkeeper Izzy.

The umpire's finger rose into the air.

Eden punched the sky with both fists. The crowd erupted. Brooke pelted over, lifted Eden off the ground and squeezed tight.

When the mêlée of teammates broke up, she conferred with Danica and Brooke as the Stars' fourth batter came to the wicket. They adjusted the field settings, Eden returned to her mark, selected the delivery to aim for, and ran in.

The batter wafted at the off-pace ball, eliciting an Ooh from the crowd.

Eden puffed out a frustrated breath, toyed with the bracelet, and walked to the start of her run-up, wiping the ball on her trouser leg. Brooke jogged over.

'Hmm?' Eden asked.

'She doesn't like it into her body.'

'Got it.'

Eden surveyed the field, then beckoned to Gemma at Short Fine Leg, bringing her in by a few yards. Then she checked the batter's position, lasered her focus, and set off.

The ball, short and fast, arrowed into the batter's midriff. Surprised, she fended it off with a raised bat, clipping the ball up over her left shoulder...

... and looping into Gemma's hands.

'Come on!' Eden yelled.

Matt stood and applauded, shameless support for his girlfriend. Her dander was up. Positivity buzzed around the Scorpions.

'That was no accident, right?' Ben asked.

'Nope. She knows *exactly* what she's doing. Hold on to your hat, mate. There's going to be fireworks.'

Two deliveries later, Eden bagged another. At the end of the over, she'd taken three wickets for no runs. The Stars' score was looking less healthy.

In the next over, Brooke outfoxed the new batter with her first ball. LBW. Then she bowled four in a row, all landing on the same sixpence, and the batter couldn't score. Then, with the final delivery, she placed it perfectly for an easy cut shot, which the batter gratefully took on, desperate to score *something* from the over.

Brooke and Danica, however, had stationed Freya perfectly at Point, and she took a great diving catch.

Matt leapt in the air. For the first time, he had an insight into why Brooke had been drafted in to play alongside Eden. Their history, their understanding, their talent, were a perfect team.

50th Over

At the beginning of Eden's next over, the last of the four she was permitted, she again conferred with her friend. The Scorpions were in a great position, the opposition under pressure, with both batters yet to score. The batter on strike was the girl who'd shared the winning last-wicket partnership with Brooke the previous year. The day that Eden bowled the worst six balls of her career. Slow balls.

Still, let's try this.

She opened with a slow ball, which the batter slapped for 4.

That's it. Well done. Now have this.

The yorker sliced between bat and pad, uprooting Off stump.

Eden leapt in the air. 'Yes!'

Amidst the high-fives and hugs from teammates, she spied Matt and Dad on their feet, applauding. Her heart overflowed.

The batter trudged off.

After the celebrations had died down, Eden returned to her mark and glanced at the scoreboard. She swallowed hard, wishing she hadn't looked. She fingered the individual beads of her bracelet.

It's a team game. You don't have to win it single-handedly.

The incoming batter was a left-hander, and Eden's next three deliveries were off line, all going for runs.

She stood at her mark, toying with the ball that would be her last delivery of the match. Altering her line might bring an LBW, but the percentages were elsewhere. If she tweaked her length, and the batter again hit Leg side...

She ran in.

The ball landed with Eden's last reserves of pace behind it, the mistimed bat flayed, and the ball went vertically upwards.

'Mine!' called wicketkeeper Izzy.

Eden stopped dead, breath held.

The ball dropped out of the sky into Izzy's wide gloves. The crowd erupted.

Shit. I've done it.

Brooke nearly knocked Eden off her feet. They jumped up and down together, squealing.

This. This is why. Nirvana. Why give this up?

As the celebratory music faded, the announcer said, "Eden Palmer finishes with figures of five for twenty-seven."

Discombobulated and bursting with pride, she paced aimlessly until a hush descended for Brooke's fourth over, the last of the match.

Eden glanced at the scoreboard. HARRIS 3-21.

If you get 5-26, Tweedie, I'll never speak to you again.

Only kidding. You go for it, babe.

Matt couldn't sit any longer. He was standing, limbs jittery.

Ben leant in. 'Fifer. Wow.'

Matt's eyes widened. 'You *know* what that is?'

'Yeah. I looked it up. Five wickets. Pretty cool, huh?'

'Too right. Eden gets the match ball.'

'Unless Brooke gets five too.'

Matt laughed. 'Never happen. And it would be too cruel. They can't cut the ball in half.'

Two minutes later, the smile had vanished. Brooke had taken her fourth wicket. Matt pinched himself.

Come on, Tweedie. Don't get competitive. Let Eden have the glory.

The Stars' last batter walked out. Matt knew this player—a tail-ender with a death-or-glory attitude. He watched as the field was fine-tuned. Danica was marshalling her chess pieces. If the batter hit one or more of the last three deliveries for a 6, the Stars' score would look much healthier.

Eden jogged to Deep Mid-wicket, which was close to the groundskeeper's hut. Her face showed a mix of joy and bewilderment. Matt cupped his fingers into a heart shape. Eden put a fist to her chest.

Brooke's next delivery was clattered for 6. Matt glanced at the scoreboard. Two more balls to go. Eden was beckoned five yards to her left.

Brooke ran in, blonde ponytail swinging. The batter stepped forward, connected with the ball, and hoiked it high towards the Mid-wicket boundary. Would it clear the rope? Would it clear Eden?

Matt's hands came to his head as Eden back-pedalled, tracking the ball's arc as it dropped out of the sky. Her boots were a yard inside the rope.

She stuck her right hand up, plucking the ball out of the air as she leant backwards, Matrix-style, toppling, stumbling, gripping tightly.

Shit!

Knowing she was going to step backwards over the rope, she had to let go of the ball. If she took it across the boundary, it would be a 6 and the catch wouldn't count.

Planting her feet one, two, just inside the rope, she tossed the ball aloft, lurched backwards across the rope, regained her balance, lunged forwards and caught the ball with both hands, thundering to the turf, rolling, clinging on for dear life.

She came to her knees, found the ball still in her grasp, and raised it high. Breathless, disbelieving, her face cracked into a grin.

Besieged by Scorpions, she was helped up and smothered in hugs.

'You fucking beauty, Ede!' Brooke squealed.

As her teammates hustled away to make the most of the short innings' break, Eden emerged from a daze.

Matt and Ben sidled past on their way to the wicket. She raised a palm, and Matt slapped it. Brooke, her arm around Eden's shoulder, also put up a hand.

Ben gave her a tap. 'Nice work. Five each. Should've had a tenner on that.'

'Thanks,' Brooke replied. 'But we're only halfway done.'

Eden came to a stop. 'That was your fifth? Of course!'

Brooke gave her a hug. 'Couldn't have done it without you.' She pointed at the big screen, which was replaying Eden's acrobatic catch that ended the Stars' innings.

Warmth spread through her insides.

You don't get that from accountancy, Mum.

Ten minutes later, Eden took a space on the bench and watched Fi and Kat walk out to open the batting.

The endorphin rush of her performance was quickly halted as Fi was bowled out for a duck. Two overs later, Kat followed.

By the match's halfway mark, Eden was getting a sinking feeling. All that effort for nothing. Proof that she couldn't win the game single-handedly—or even in partnership with Brooke.

Chasing 162, the Scorpions were stuttering at 133 for 7 when Brooke, padded up and ready to go, plopped onto the bench beside her.

She shot a wry smile. 'At least we have our fifers.'

'Never over til it's over, Tweed. Feel free to hit someone for seventeen again.'

Brooke patted Eden's leg. 'I'll see what I can do.'

Five minutes later, the neighbouring bench erupted in applause. Eden's shoulders fell. Brooke offered a gloved fist. Eden bumped. Brooke strode out. Eden went to the changing room, pulled on her pads, and trotted back out. The scoreboard read 144-8.

Then it read 144-9.

With shaking hands, she pulled on her gloves, glimpsing the bracelet as it disappeared under her sleeve. She blew out a breath, shook nerves from her frame, and walked out to the middle.

Brooke met her with a fist bump. 'Putting the band back together, Ede.'

'Seems like it.'

'No rush. Take it easy.'

'Will do.'

Eden went to the crease, turned a full circle, memorising the field positions, took guard, gripped the bat, and told herself she only had to get through one ball before Brooke took strike.

Ray came to stand beside Matt. 'What d'you reckon?'

'Can I get a shot of whisky, boss?'

Ray laughed. 'Tonight, I suggest. Win or lose. I'll have one too. Open the birthday bottle. Don't tell her, though. But I'm drinking to what she already did today, whatever happens in the next ten minutes.'

'She's nothing to lose. You can't blame two tail-enders for not winning a game.'

'True.'

He watched as Eden—her tongue poking out in a familiar, adorable fashion—took guard. She defended the ball for no run, then conversed with Brooke as the Stars' bowler readied herself. One thing in their favour was that the opposition, sensing blood, had used up their best pace attack. The Scorpions, needing 19 off 12 balls, still had a fighting chance. If Eden and Brooke held their nerve.

The first ball to Brooke was defended for no run.

The second she swiped into a vacant area, setting off like a hare. Tapping her bat in at the other end, she turned for the second run. The fielder scooped up the ball.

'No!' Eden's bark carried across the pitch.

Brooke retreated, holding up a glove in apology.

Eden's heart rate eased.

Christ, Tweedie, what is it with you and risky 2s? Don't you trust me?

She took guard. Tap, tap.

Focus. Breathe.

She picked the delivery early and clattered it, albeit awkwardly, past Cover. The boundary fielder dived in vain and the ball bobbled over the rope.

Phew. No duck for me.

Brooke walked up. 'Nice.'

'I'll take the rest in Byes. But, yeah.'

'Sorry about the 2.'

'S'okay.'

'Lot of slower balls, so watch for the changeup.'

'Will do.'

Fist bump. Back to the crease. Tap tap.

Eden left the next ball alone, and it was called a Wide.

One less run to get.

She padded the following delivery away to vacant Mid-wicket, took a single, and rested on her bat.

Don't look at the scoreboard.

The next ball, to Brooke, was Leg side, so she flicked it deftly down to Long Leg.

Come on, Tweed.

The final, seventh ball—arguably a bonus—couldn't be worked away. A missed opportunity.

The speakers boomed. "With one over remaining, the Scorpions need ten runs for victory."

Applause of encouragement circled the stands.

Eden pulled off her helmet, wiped sweat from her brow, and refastened her gloves. At the other end, Brooke nodded sagely. This familiar gesture spoke volumes. If Eden lacked belief—it was playing on her mind—Brooke didn't. Of course, Eden's easy, maybe cowardly, option was to steal a single and put the burden on her teammate.

But sometimes you have to stand up and be counted. And, in her favour, the bowler was a spinner—who'd struggled to conjure much spin from this pitch. She was beatable.

Cool head. Deep breath.

The first ball was an attempted yorker, which she *juuust* kept out.

She grimaced. At the other end, Brooke motioned for calm. Yet Eden's heart raced.

She took a few seconds, refastening her gloves, tamping down the grass, asking the umpire for middle stump. Delaying, trying to get into the bowler's mind.

10 off 5. What would Tweedie do? She'd attack.

Fuck it.

She took guard. Tap, tap.

As the next delivery came down, Eden advanced down the wicket and smacked the ball through Mid-On to the boundary. The Scorpions' bench cheered as one.

Brooke sauntered over, grinning. 'Class.'

Eden reviewed the field. 'What do you reckon?'

'One, two, four, whatever. Just stay with me, Ede. But I think she'll try the arm ball.'

'Okay.' The bowler had taken two wickets that way in the previous Final.

Eden positioned herself on the batting crease, swallowing down nerves. Watching the ball like a hawk, she dealt with the tricky floating delivery, despite gasps from the Stars' keeper and bowler.

6 required off 4. The next ball needed to go for runs. The pressure was already monumental. No point in leaving it until the last gasp.

Eden watched the fielders move. The captain was trying to cut off ones and twos, strangle easy runs, turn the screw. Away to Eden's left, a familiar figure stood with hands on his head. His voice echoed in her head.

"Don't play for anyone else. Play for yourself."

And the team, darling. And the team.

Tap, tap.

Focus. Breathe. Watch the ball.

The delivery was coming in short, a drag down. Eden took one step, two steps down the strip.

Connect, or you're stumped.

Crack.

Vibration shot up her arms. The ball lifted. Higher, further. Over the Mid-On fielder. Over the Long-On fielder.

Over the rope.

Joy exploded in her veins. She dropped the bat and crumbled to the turf. A wailing banshee collapsed on top of her.

'You bloody beauty, Ede!'

Chaos erupted on all sides. Tears leaked across her cheeks. In her peripheral vision, flames leapt into the air.

"The Scorpions win by one wicket."

Brooke helped her up, then took her in a long embrace. 'Looks like it's one match ball each.'

Eden took off her helmet and wiped her eyes. 'This is... nuts.'

Brooke grinned. 'Nah. It's just cricket.'

Super Over

Matt pulled Eden closer under the covers.

'I still can't believe it,' she said.

'Which part?'

'Dad and Kathryn,' she chuckled.

He eased back and shot her a query. 'No way.'

'I could be wrong. It does happen.'

'Not on a cricket pitch, based on today's evidence.'

'Aw, that's sweet.' She kissed him. 'Not sure I can believe it either, actually.'

'That you won the Cup? Never in doubt.'

'Not even you, probably not even Dad, have that level of unquestioning belief in my ability to put my big girl pants on when it counts.'

He clutched his chest. 'I'm hurt.'

She poked him. 'You're not funny. Anyway, the Dad situation is me wanting him to get back on the horse, romantically. Not that

I'd wish the old sod on anyone, but he seemed pretty keen on you and me getting back together, so I should return the favour.'

'Actually, I had a crazy theory that Ben wants to give Brooke a shot.'

Eden's eyebrows arched. 'Brave lad.'

'I think brave Brooke, too.'

She fluttered a hand. 'Not our place to meddle. If Tweed is happy, with or without someone, that's what matters.'

'Amen. She's a force of nature at times.'

'Yeah. I told her so. So pleased she wants to make a difference to young people with the condition. Whether or not they want to get into sport.'

He touched his nose to hers. 'Don't forget what you went through, baby. And where you got to today. With the ball, in the field, with the bat.'

She stroked his cheek. 'It *was* a team game, my love. Don't build me up too high. That's as bad as being at rock bottom. I just... I'm happy to have made amends. In a lot of ways.'

The following morning, Eden arrived back home. The otherworldliness of it all had largely faded, and as she dug the match ball from her kit bag and placed it on the shelf, things became very real.

'Yours counts double.' Brooke was at the doorway, dressed in a robe.

'How?'

'Five wickets *and* the winning runs.'

She shook her head. 'Neither of those would have happened without you, Tweedie.'

Brooke grinned. 'I know *that*. How was your night?'

She spied the bags under her friend's eyes. 'Fewer cocktails than yours.'

'But more sex.'

'I don't know. Is Ben upstairs?'

Brooke laughed. 'No.'

'I reckon he wants to be.'

'I reckon too.'

'Playing hard to get?'

Brooke shrugged. 'Things happen when it's right.' She coughed. 'Did Loz speak to you yet?'

That had been the cherry on the icing on the cake—for Booke, at least—a call from the England head coach, Laura Hamilton. A new Development XI was being put together. A first chance for Eden's bestie to pull on an England shirt. Shame that Eden would miss out again this year. Still, life *was* pretty damn fine.

Eden bit her lip. 'No. But unlikely they'll take us both.'

'All the same—'

'It's fine. It *should* be you, Tweed. All day long. And don't you *dare* feel guilty. I'll cheer the loudest.'

Brooke beamed. 'Because if I'm off with England, you're nailed on for a squad spot here?'

Eden swiped at her. 'Snake.'

'I would love if we both got the call-up, Ede. But, yeah, it's a long shot.'

Eden thumbed over her shoulder at the match ball. 'Like us hogging the scorecard yesterday.'

Brooke winked. 'Never in doubt. And Ray was there to see it.'

'It'll take more than a bit of heart surgery to keep him away from the Garden.'

'Or me.' She pulled at her hair. 'My contract is only one year but... if they want me, I'll stay.'

Eden embraced her. 'We're very lucky.'

'Thanks. But... I'll find another house. You did say this was temporary.'

'Really? I'm that hard to live with?'

Brooke laughed. 'No. But you and Matt need space. Together. I'll be out before the wedding night. Promise.'

'You're the best.' Eden plopped onto the sofa. 'Now—'

Her mobile rang. Tutting, she hastily yanked it from her pocket.

The caller's name made her eyes light up. With a shaking finger, she pressed the green icon.

'Eden Palmer,' she said in her best telephone voice.

'Morning, Eden. This is Laura. How're you doing?'

THE END

The Scorpions squad

Season 2

NAME	NICKNAME	AGE	ROLE
Ellie Waites	"Ells"	32	Top order batter
Bryony Taylor	"Bry"	23	Top order batter
Fiona Plummer	"Fi"	25	Top order batter
Katherine Davidson	"Kat"	30	Batter
Freya Baker	"Bakes"	34	Batter
Phoebe Butcher	"Butch"	24	Batter
Danica Pritchard (C)	"Dani"	31	Batter, spin bowler
Gemma Enstone	"Gemstone"	29	Batter, seam bowler
Jade Black	"Jet"	25	Seam bowler
Rose Jones	"Rojo"	23	Seam bowler
Eden Palmer	"Ede"	27	Seam bowler
Brooke Harris	"Harry"	28	Seam bowler
Naira Rodrigues	"Roddy"	22	Leg spin bowler
Abi Miller	"Mills"	19	Leg spin bowler
Sarah Hawksley	"Hawks"	25	Off spin bowler
Izzy MacGregor	"Mac"	27	Wicket Keeper
Georgia Cole	"George"	21	Wicket Keeper

Fielding Positions

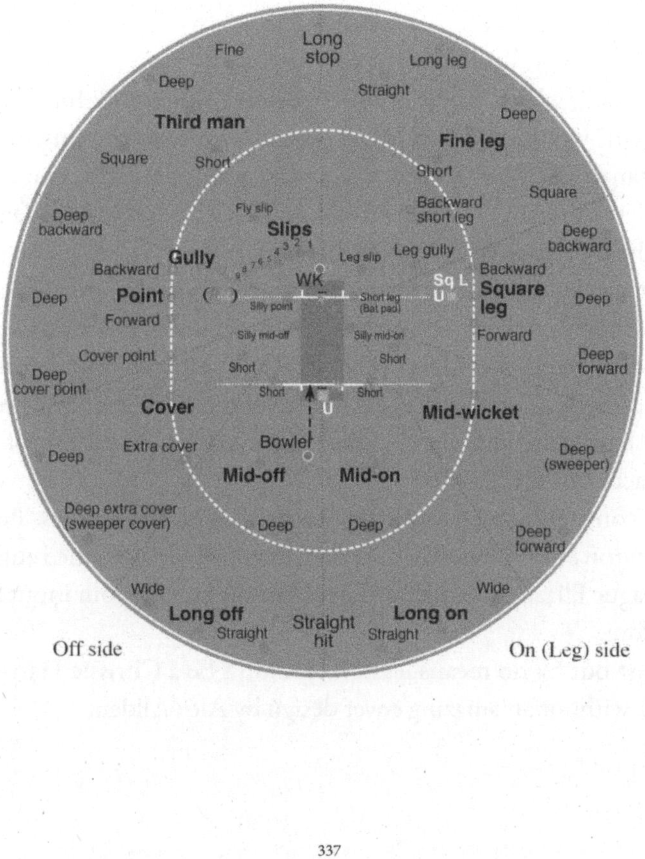

Acknowledgements

This book, which builds on the research groundwork for Wicket Maiden, would not have been possible without the unstinting assistance of a Tier 1 women's county team. Sometimes, it's the smallest things, like a few words with Mary Taylor and her family that help shape vital aspects of the story.

I'm indebted to Sophie Singer for her insight into life as a professional cricketer with Type 1 diabetes, and to Danielle Devlin for additional information. Thanks also to Max, a groundsman at Guildford Cricket Club. I also have to namecheck young cricketer Lilly Rogers, who was something of an inspiration for one of the characters in the book.

It continues to be a pleasure to work with my editors, Becca Errington & Ellie Hawkes. A special mention for my valued author colleague Elizabeth Holland. Thanks to all three for your input and wisdom.

Last but by no means least, it wouldn't be a Chrissie Harrison book without an amazing cover design by Alex Allden.

About the Author

Writing romcoms is my happy place. After working in other genres for many years, I couldn't resist the pull towards comedy and romance. I have a soft spot for stories with strong women, nice guys, and a touch of the bittersweet. I like the connection between my protagonists to be more than physical – a bond that helps solve their problems. Often I shine a light on mental health issues, especially neurodiversity, which is close to my heart. Fundamentally, I try to write the books I like to read – those with wit, heart and intelligence.

Away from the writing desk, I enjoy great scenery, a relaxing train ride, delicious coffee and cake, and catching up with friends and fellow authors.

Chrissie Harrison is a pen name.

Find me on Instagram @AuthorChrissieHarrison or in other places via Linktree

Also by the Author

The Cathedral City Comedies – a rom-com series

"Floored"
"Appy Ever After"
"Before We Wrap" – 15 October 2026

She Can Play – a women's cricket rom-com trilogy

"Wicket Maiden"
"Seams Like Love"
Book 3 – April 2027

The Touchline trilogy – a sports rom-com series

"Match Daze"
Book 2 – 2027 TBC
Book 3 – TBC

Also from the Publisher

Here's a selection of books from Valericain Press.

Whether your reading taste includes sci-fi, romance, comedy, or something quirkier, there may be a story here for you.

Romantic Comedy

Historical Romance

Quirky romantic comedy / cosy mystery

Post-apocalyptic

Space opera

Absurd humour

Dating humour